MARY WAGNER

Carolina Blue

ISBN: 1501044214
ISBN 13: 9781501044212

chapter 1

WILLOW MOONE AND her faithful dog Wolfe sat on the ridge of Blackheart Mountain admiring fall and all its splendor of brilliant red, gold and orange colors of leaves from the beech, sourwood, yellow birch, mountain maple, dogwood and many more trees that consume the Appalachian Mountains. The bright, blue and cloudless Carolina sky that touched the horizon along the mountainside brought out even more of the radiant colors of the leaves.

The layer of old clothing Willow is wearing keeps the brisk fall air from causing her old bones to become rigid. The pair of old trousers from a neighbor's discarded bag of clothes that she has on under her dress, keeps her legs pretty warm on this chilly day. The red bandana under her old torn and tattered Stetson hat keeps her head warm. Her hands and legs ache and throb, but she never lets that pain take over her mind or her body. The struggles she has endured throughout her life as a Cherokee Indian living in the tough mountain environment just feeds her spirit to never give in to adversity. Willow is a fighter.

The voices of *Roy Acuff* and the *Smokey Mountain Boys* can be heard on the radio coming from one of the neighbor's homes below in the holler singing the "Wabash Cannonball", and Willow sings along with them.

While singing along with Roy and the boys, Willow follows the trail of smoke as it dances out of the chimneys on this brisk morning. In her seventy years of living on Blackheart Mountain, this is Willow's favorite season.

"I've been on this old mountain a long time Wolfe. My days here are near numbered." Willow gave Wolfe a big hug. "If it weren't for you boy and Miss Sady and her mama and daddy, the Good Lord would have taken me a long time ago. I guess He just doesn't want this old bag of bones yet or maybe He has a mighty big job for me to do before He calls me Home."

Willow hesitated before she spoke to Wolfe again and inhaled the fresh smell of pine that enveloped her sense of smell that day.

"Before I do leave this mountain, I just want to see this awful war end and see our boys come home, 'specially Sady's boy, Eddie. Just wish they would let me go to Germany, I'd get rid of that crazy, no 'count Hitler feller. No sir-re. By the time I got finished with him, the buzzards won't even want to taste his hide. That man is goin' straight to Hell Wolfe. Satan is goin' to put him in charge of throwin' empty jars of water on a fire that ain't ever goin' to burn out. That devil of a man is goin' to be toastin' marshmallows off his own burin' carcass!"

Willow started to laugh, but her laughter was halted by an all too familiar sound she had sadly heard many times before.

The sound is an earsplitting shrill of a woman screaming coming from a run-down home in the holler across from Harmony Creek. As Willow and Wolfe descended down Blackheart Mountain and crossed the bridge at Harmony Creek, she knew exactly where the horrifying screams were coming from. She knew exactly who the faces behind the voices were.

Willow and Wolf made it to a small clearing on the other side of Harmony Creek. Willow stopped and put a dab of snuff under her bottom lip while she listened to the argument coming from the home of Roby and Eva Prestel. Roby Prestel is a big abusive drunken bully. His wife Eva is like a small delicate violet. She is the target of her abusive husband, along with their fourteen year old son Dewey and their eighteen year old run-a-way daughter Becky.

Roby, in a drunken stupor, was shouting at his wife Eva. "Eva, where's my other bottle? Don't you ever hide my booze woman! I'm gonna' give you about two seconds to find it, bitch. Then I'm gonna' beat you from this holler to the next!"

Eva frightened and knowing what is coming next, pleads with Roby. "Roby, I ain't hid your bottle. You drank it all last night. There ain't no more!"

Roby clutched Eva by the hair, hit her in the face, then threw her on the floor and raised his foot to kick her, but thankfully he missed Eva's body.

Eva screamed. "Please Roby, don't. You're hurtin' me real bad. Please stop! I can't breathe!"

Roby laughed and looked down at Eva. "Hurt you, you lazy bitch. I'm gonna' show you what a hurtin' feels like. My booze is my booze woman. Ain't nobody fools with Roby Prestel's bottle!"

Roby walked over to the kitchen drawer and got out a knife and glanced down at Eva on the floor.

Just then their son, Dewey, came through the back door, threw down a load of firewood that he had gathered, and confronted his father and knocked the knife out of his hand.

"Pa, listen to me! Leave Ma alone! You're hurtin' her. I'm the one that hid your moonshine. It's out in the barn."

Roby turned to Dewey with a look that could kill. "Why would you do that boy? You know what you are? You're a son of a bitch ... that bitch lyin' on the floor."

"The drinkin' makes you sick Pa, you know it does."

"Sick, sick! I'll tell you what makes me sick – you, your mama and that whore of a daughter I got!"

Eva looked up at Roby with disgust. "Stop callin' Becky a whore! She's not a whore. She's your baby girl."

Roby bent over and grabbed Eva's face and said, "ain't you had 'nough Eva? You want more?" Then he looked at Dewey and said, "what about him Eva? Ain't nobody in my family crippled up like this boy. You was probably foolin' 'round while I was login' at the saw mill. Dewey don't even favor me, even a little!"

"Roby how can you say that. I never done no such thing! You're just hurtin' Dewey with those words, not me. I told you that doctor in Boone said Dewey's bone in his left leg didn't develop the right way."

"Yeah, and what did you do for that doctor to tell you that far-fetched story?"

"Roby, it's the truth. We can go see that doctor together and he'll tell you the same thing he told me."

"I ain't goin' no place with you woman." Roby just got madder at Eva and stepped toward her to grab her throat.

Dewey stepped in front of Roby to stop him from hurting his mother. He tried to help his mother get off of the floor. "Ma, please be quiet, because he's goin' to hurt you some more!"

Eva got up slowly while holding her arm. "I'm ok Dewey. Just hurry and go get his bottle. Hurry!"

Roby grabbed Dewey by the neck. "You ain't back here in five minutes gimp, don't come back 'cause you ain't gonna' have no Mama. You ain't gonna' have to limp anymore 'cause I'll break your good leg and they'll both be even! You understand gimp!"

Dewey looked up at his father. "Yes sir, I do understand. I'll be right back with your bottle Pa. Please leave Ma alone!"

Dewey ran out the front door to the barn.

Roby walked to the front screen door and gazed out and noticed Willow standing in the clearing about fifty feet away. She was clutching a Bowie knife on her side that belonged to her father.

After seeing Willow standing in the clearing, Roby got his rifle and walked out onto the porch to confront Willow. "Who you starin' at you one-eyed, wrinkled up red-skinned piece of river garbage? I ought to come over there and knock your other eye out, and hang your red Injun ass on that oak tree over yonder."

Willow spit her snuff on the ground and pulled out her knife.

Roby laughed. "What ya' goin' to do with that? You gonna' cut my bullets in half while I'm shootin' at you?"

Willow spit again and said, "don't let this patch on my eye fool you. I can see better with one eye than you can with both of yours. If you hurt that woman and boy of yours again, you won't be needin' that rifle anymore."

"And just what do you intend to about it? That's my woman and my boy and I'll tend to them whatever way I feel like."

Willow looked at Roby and was silent for a few seconds. "What I mean Roby is you ain't gonna' have no arms or hands left to cock that rifle of yours. I'll cut those suckers off! You won't be beatin' up on Eva or Dewey anymore."

Roby knew not to second guess Willow Moone. As much of a bully that he was, Roby still had doubts about what Willow could really do to him if she wanted to. There were several stories about Willow, some true, some not so true, that folk spread around the Mountain from years back. These same stories and a few new ones are still being spread in the Mountain. Roby had no idea what Willow and Wolfe were capable of doing to him.

Willow just stared at Roby while Wolfe growled. Roby finally put his gun down to his side. By this time Dewey had his bottle of moonshine and was watching this odd stand-off between his father and Willow. He realized that he just witnessed the first person from Harmony Creek that his father couldn't bully. Willow was the first person to ever stand up to his brute of a father that Dewey had ever observed.

Roby, with eyes full of hate, grabbed the bottle of moonshine from Dewey, gave Willow a piercing look and said, "you're one lucky Injun today, Willow. Got my bottle. I'm a happy man now."

As Roby cautiously turned his back on Willow and walked to the barn to drink, he hollered, "next time you step on my property, you're gonna' be one dead Injun!"

Willow laughed. "You think so Roby! Next time you won't even see or hear me!"

Roby full of rage turned and cocked his gun. There was no Willow or Wolfe in sight. They vanished that quickly.

Roby bellowed loudly, "next time, next time, you one-eyed old piece of vermin - you're dead next time! Nobody treats Roby Prestel with dis-respect, nobody! I'll do you in the same way your daddy was years ago!"

Dewey heard what his father shouted to Willow and did wonder what he meant about her father being *done in*, but there was no way he was going to ask his father. He was more concerned over his mother and ran in to see how hurt she was. While his father was in the barn getting drunk, Dewey knew he had an important question to ask his mother and went back in the house.

Dewey tried to help his mother with her scratches and bruises from the beating she just got from Roby.

"Dewey, can you get me that bag of iron clay I hid behind the stove. Willow brought it to me the last time Roby did this to me. She showed me how to make mineral powder into a paste to put on my wounds. She called it a poultice."

"It's a good thing Pa didn't know she was here. He would have killed both of you."

"Just hurry Dewey before he comes back. Heat it in that pot on the stove into a paste. Hate to ask you to do this, but I fell on my arm and it hurts."

Dewey heated the iron clay into a powder paste and helped his mother put it on her injuries and the arm she fell on.

"Ma, why do you let him do this to you? He's goin' to kill you one day. I hate him! I wish he was dead. Why don't we leave him and get gone from here?"

"Son, where we gonna' go? Most folks 'round here are scared of him. He'll just come lookin' for us. We'll always be runnin' from him!"

"Why can't we stay with Willow? She ain't afraid of Pa. Or, why can't we stay with Miss Sady. I bet Miss Sady ain't afraid of Pa either."

"Dewey, Willow lives way up in the mountain in the woods with a real Wolfe that she calls 'Wolfe'. I know she ain't afraid of nothin'. Sady is tough. She's been through a lot. Plus, Dewey, she's got her hands full taken care of Grace and raisin' 'backer (tobacco) on her farm."

"Did you forget Ma, Grace is your grandbaby too? Don't you miss her? She's part of Becky. I don't think it's fair that we never get to see her. I know she's part of Eddie too, but he's not here."

"Well who else ain't here Dewey? You forget Becky ran away over a year ago and left her baby. Even animals care for their young better than Becky cared for Grace. Eddie didn't leave Grace. He's off fightin' a war over in Germany or he would be here taken care of her. You want that baby around a drunken man that don't care what he says or how he hurts us? Well, I don't. She is better off with Sady."

"The real reason Grace ain't here ain't because Pa gets drunk and beats on us."

"What in the world are you talkin' about boy? You're not makin' any sense."

"You know what I'm talkin' about. You just don't want Pa to do the same things to Grace he did to Becky."

"I still don't know what you're talkin 'about son. He beat Becky as much as he beats you. No, I don't want that little girl beat on."

"Ma, Becky could take the beatins'. So can I. That's not what I'm talkin' about and you know that."

"Dewey, why don't you tell me what you're talkin' about since I don't understand what it is you're tryin' to tell me?"

"I'm talkin' about the dirty things he did to Becky since she was a little girl. Ma, we slept in the same room up until her and Eddie ran off and got married. Maybe you can put it out of your mind, but I can't."

"Stop your dirty talkin' right now. I don't want to hear no more."

"I watched Pa come into our room most every night. I saw him get in bed with her and I listened to her cry. It made me sick to my stomach. I knew if I said anything to him, he would probably beat me to death. I would lie still for hours hopin' he would just leave or just die! After a while, I put pillows under my covers to make it look like I was in bed sleepin' and crawled under my bed and slept there at night, because I couldn't stand to hear Becky cry. There was another man beside Pa that would come in at night sometimes. He would just watch what Pa was doin'. He didn't talk. He just would breathe real heavy. All I could see was these black and white snakeskin boots. I can still remember that one snake head was missin' off the other boot. I found that snakehead on the floor next to Becky's bed, and I carry it around with me to this day. I'm hopin' one day I'll see a man with those same boots on."

"If Roby was doin' these sinful things to Becky, why didn't she tell me? And there weren't any other men in my house after I went to bed."

"Ma, you knew what he was doin'. Didn't you wonder where he was at night? Becky didn't have to tell you. I know you could hear her cry. So many nights I prayed that you would come in with the shotgun and kill him. Why didn't you? You knew what was goin' on and you didn't do nothin', nothin' 'cause you were afraid of him. And that other man Pa brought into the bedroom, someday I'm goin' to find out who he was and kill him! You're the reason Becky ran away!"

Furious, Eva slapped Dewey in the face. "Get out! Get out! I love Becky. I would have given my life to save her. Get out!"

"Well you still have your life Ma, and Becky's life was ruined by that drunkin' man you make me call Pa!"

Dewey hurriedly walked outside and slammed the backdoor.

Eva ran to the back door and hollered to Dewey, "Son, forgive me. Please don't leave me. I'm sorry. Please forgive me!"

Dewey turned for a second to look at his mother. He hated to leave her with that brutal man he called Pa, but he couldn't take any more of the abuse.

He crossed the small bridge over Harmony Creek and started to climb Blackheart Mountain.

Dewey made his mind up to leave and never look back. His mother was on his mind and the beatings she would eventually be getting from his father. He couldn't force his mother to leave. He couldn't even get her to admit to the sexual abuse Roby forced on Becky. No, in Dewey's mind, today was the last time his father would ever verbally abuse him or ever put his hands on him again.

Dewey had a hard time climbing Blackheart Mountain. The briars would wrap around his legs and the thorns would cut into his clothes and scratch his hands when he would try to pull them off. He knew that Willow lived on the top of the mountain, but he wasn't exactly sure where she lived. As far as Dewey knew, no one had ever seen Willow's place or climbed to the top of Blackheart Mountain.

chapter 2

DEWEY SAT DOWN to rest in the middle of a bunch of briars, and was thinking out loud, "how in the world does Willow climb this mountain bein' old like she is?"

No sooner then Dewey ended his sentence, he heard a **whoosh** sound over his head. The next thing he saw was a big knife standing straight up at the bottom of his foot about a half inch from his shoe. He was so startled, that he rolled into a gully that was beside him. He looked up and saw Willow standing there holding her knife with a big snake hanging off of it without its head. Wolfe, of course was standing beside her trying to jump up and bite the snake. The body of the snake was still moving.

"You know what this is boy? It's a copperhead. One strike and you're a goner'. What in tarnation are you doin' up here? How In the world you gonna' run from one of those big black mama bears? You got to run boy, not limp, 'cause you're goin' to be supper for her and her babies!"

"I was tryin' to find you Willow, and I can run as fast as anybody else in Harmony."

"Well, you almost made today your last day on this good earth boy. These woods ain't no school playground. There are snakes, bears, bobcats and all kind of creatures ready to pounce on you up here."

"Thank you Willow for savin' my life. I'm runin' Willow. I can't live in that house anymore with him. I hate him. I hate what he did to Becky. I hate the beatins'. I hate what comes out of his mouth – the names he calls us. I just hate ..." Dewey put his head down and cried.

"Hate, son, that's an awful deadly word to use boy. That's a word full of poison. God doesn't want us to use that word, 'specially when it comes to somebody's pa. The devil got to your pa and put evil in his head. Your pa ain't like you and me Dewey. We're strong. We won't let the devil have power over us. Roby just gave up and took on the devil's evil ways. If that man don't change his ways and ask for forgiveness, he's goin' straight to Hell and burn for eternity."

"I don't care Willow. I hate him and will always hate him. I wish he would die today."

"You come on up to my house with me Dewey. I'm goin' to make you a nice cup of blackberry tea with a little bit of honey I stole from a big ole' beehive behind my house. Picked the blackberries this past summer, and they are really nice and fresh. Come on now. Get yourself up and follow me and Wolfe. I know where all the varmints are around this mountain so ain't no animals gonna' attack you. Let's go boy!"

Dewey followed Willow the rest of the way up Blackheart Mountain until they finally came to a little clearing in the woods. He was surprised how spry and fast Willow could climb the mountain.

Finally, the top of Blackheart Mountain came into view, and surrounded by the biggest buckeye tree that Dewey had ever seen and mountain laurel stood Willow's little house.

"Come on in son. Don't have much to look at, but you sit here at the table and I'll get our tea ready."

"Willow, you have a nice place. It's far away from people and so quiet up here."

"Has its down side too Dewey. I kinda' get a little lonely bein' up here all by myself."

Willow poured them both tea and they sat and talked a while.

"Willow, can I ask you a question?"

"Sure can boy, go ahead, ask."

"When Pa told you he would **do you in** like your daddy was, what did he mean?"

"Dewey, come over here and look out the winder. You see that big ole' buckeye tree with that cross nailed to it?"

"Yeah, I do. What's the cross for Willow?"

"Years ago my pa was the head of the Cherokee Council in this part of the woods. Back then people 'round these parts didn't like Injuns. You could see the hate in their eyes when we would go into Harmony for our supplies. People in town hated my kin as much as they hated the colored folk, maybe even a little worse. The only people 'round here that treated the Cherokee and colored people like human beins' was Sady's ma and pa. They respected the Cherokee families 'round these parts and treated my family and the other tribe members with dignity."

"One evening before dusk, two white men broke into this house and took my father. One was just a young boy about fifteen, and the other man maybe in his late twenties, early thirties. I was only 'bout five years old or so. Me and Ma were pickin' blackberries at the time. We heard my pa holler *"adisgalodi", "adisgalodi"*.

"What does that mean Willow?"

"Hide, it means hide. He was shoutin' the word so me and Ma would just . . . hide. He knew these men didn't know the Cherokee language."

Willow hung her head down told the rest of the story.

"Me and Ma hid behind that big Mountain Ash over yonder. Ma had to hold her hands over my mouth and eyes, but I could still see what was goin' on 'cause her hands were so tiny they just couldn't cover my eyes. There was nothin' we could do. They had guns and knives and we couldn't get to the house to get our rifle."

"Willow, what did they do to your pa?"

"Somethin' you don't ever want to see boy. The older man beat him over and over." Willow had to stop to wipe a tear from her eye. "Then he took a big knife and scalped my pa. Pa screamed for God to take him. Then the older man made the young boy help lift my pa up. The older man put a rope around his neck and hung him from that branch where the cross is nailed. After that Ma was never the same. She lost her mind and died in an insane 'sylumn down in Lenoir. Miss Sady's ma and pa took me in until I was old 'nough to come back up here to the mountain and my home."

"Did you know who the men were?"

Willow did know who the men were but she didn't want to say anything to Dewey.

"No, I didn't, son. After what happened, I looked at the face of every white man that crossed my path. After all these years I had to put that terrible day aside before it drove me crazy like it did my ma."

"I'm so sorry Willow. Those men remind me of my pa. Willow, that's kinda' why I came up here to find you. I can't go back home. I just can't. Willow, can I stay with you a while. I'll do whatever kind of jobs you give me to do. I don't eat a whole lot and ..."

"Dewey, what about your ma? If you ain't there to help her when your pa starts beatin' on her, he's gonna' kill her. Your ma needs you."

"She don't need me none Willow. I begged her to run away with me and she won't. I told her we could stay with you or Miss Sady 'cause neither one of ya' are afraid of my pa. She still wouldn't come. My ma said my pa takes after his father. He was mean to Granny just like Pa is mean to her and me. Nobody knows what happened to Grandpa. He just took off one day and nobody's seen him since. Did you know him Willow?"

"I did know him Dewey. He was meaner than a rattlesnake. Best thing ever happened to your granny was when he took off and left."

Willow reached up and touched the patch on her eye. "Yeah, best thing ever happened to everybody in these parts is when Silas Prestel left Harmony and Blackheart Mountain for good."

"Ya' never know Willow, he might just come back."

"Come back boy. He'd be close to one hundred years old or older! I'm pretty sure he ain't comin' back to these mountains ever again."

"How come you're so sure Willow?"

"Tell you what son. You best go back down to the holler 'cause it's gettin' dark. Your ma is probably worried about you. I'll sneak on by tomorrow while your pa is layin' up drunk in the barn and try to talk some sense into your ma. You be lookin' for me now."

"She ain't goin' to listen to you Willow. I know she ain't"

"Son, don't you worry none, I got ways of convincin' people what's best for 'em. If she says yes, you and her can move in here with me. That devil for a father won't bother you or your ma anymore."

"Ok Willow, I'll go back, but I know she ain't goin' to say yes."

"You just leave that worry up to me, son. Wolfe, you show Dewey the way out of here down to Harmony Creek. You take care Dewey."

"Thanks for everything Willow. Come on Wolfe, let's go."

Dewey had no plans to go back home. He just couldn't take the abuse from his father anymore. When he got down to the dirt road beside Harmony Creek, he told Wolfe to go back home and he did. It was getting dark and Dewey knew Willow was right about bears and other critters that lived on Blackheart Mountain. He was a little scared, but he was determined that he wasn't going back home.

Dewey had to try one more time to convince someone whom he knew cared about him to let him stay with her, which would really be his last chance – Miss Sady.

chapter 3

IT WAS DARK and getting late when Sady finally came into the house from
the barn. She and Mr. Tibbits had been hanging tobacco all day. She
was so tired. She was also grateful Mrs. Tibbits kept Grace overnight
since Mr. Tibbits was coming back the next day to help Sady hang more
tobacco from the rafters in the barn.

Sady knew how lucky she was to have Henry and Lena Tibbits helping her on her small farm. Their son Thomas and Sady's son Eddie were
friends and enlisted in the Army together. It was unusual in Harmony
Creek to see many colored folk, but Sady felt she was blessed to have
them for her friends. They were good hard-working people that she
could count on to help her whenever she needed them.

Sady felt so good after taking her bath and getting that old
tobacco dust off of her. She put her night gown on and sat in front of
the mirror to brush her long hair. As she stared into the mirror after
letting her hair down, she noticed several more strands of gray hair
showing through her beautiful long dark brown locks. She noticed a
few more wrinkles in her skin as she put cream on her face, probably
from the months of the hot summer sun shining on her skin while she
worked in the garden and tobacco field. Sady always had a tint of an
olive complexion. She wished so many times she had her mother's fair
skin, but she figured she took after her father's side of the family; they
weren't as fair as her mother's side of the family. Sady just accepted the
gray hair and wrinkles as something that happens when a person turns
forty-two years old.

After Sady put the lamp out, she noticed a light on in her barn.
She thought that maybe she left a lantern lit. Sady took her rifle and

another lantern and headed for the barn. Everybody in the holler knew Sady had the best tobacco around. She actually thought maybe some-one was trying to steal the tobacco that she and Mr. Tibbits worked for days cutting and hanging. No sir, she figured if there was a thief in the barn, she was going to surprise him.

Sady cautiously opened the barn door. The barn door creaked, and the light that she saw shining in the barn quickly went out.

Sady cocked her rifle. "Who is in here? Either speak up or I'm goin' to shoot you so full of buckshot that the only use you're gonna' be is to be used for a waterin' can. So speak up!"

"Miss Sady, Miss Sady, please don't shoot. It's Dewey, Dewey Prestel, Eva's son."

"If it is you Dewey, come out here and let me see your face."

Dewey slowly stuck his head out from one of the empty cow stalls. "I'm sorry Miss Sady for scarin' you. I wanted to knock on your door, but it gettin' dark and all, I thought I'd wait til' mornin' so not to scare you."

"Well come on in the house Dewey. It's gettin' cold out here. Where's your coat boy? You ought to know better livin' in these moun-tains all your life, that this time of year it gets right cold."

"I didn't get a chance to take my coat when I left home Miss Sady."

Sady and Dewey went into the house and Sady took him into the parlor.

"Dewey sit down. I'm going to get us some hot tea and you're goin' to tell me why you're hidin' in my barn."

While Sady was in the kitchen getting the tea ready, Dewey couldn't help looking at her family pictures scattered throughout the parlor. There were pictures of his niece Grace, his sister, Becky with Eddie, and of course Sady's family. The warmth from the fireplace and contentment Dewey felt being in Sady's home actually made him doze off.

"Hey sleepy head, wake up. We got a lot to talk about before I let you fall asleep. Now tell me what's goin' on Dewey."

"Miss Sady, my pa is gonna' kill my ma. It's gonna' happen. She won't leave. I gotta' get out of there 'cause I'm gonna' kill him. I know I am. I hate him. I hate him."

Tears started to run down Dewey's face. Sady held his hand and tried to comfort him.

"Hate and kill Dewey . . . they're two nasty, powerful words. You know you don't mean it."

"Yes, I do. I mean every word of it. He beats Ma, and beats her, then he starts hittin' on me. I know Becky must have told you what he did to her. Why won't my ma leave, why?"

"I wish I could answer that question Dewey, but I can't. She has her own reasons. I can't imagine bein' beat by a man every day or bein' scared of a man I married. Me bein' me — I would have left him a long time ago 'specially if he beat on my children. I know what he did to Becky and it caused problems in her mind and in her marriage to Eddie. I just don't know. God gave me a good man and your ma got an evil man. But God took my good man and a son along with him and left the evil man live. God has got his reasons why he does what he does and we ain't supposed to question those reasons. I had to be a stronger person because I lost my husband and son. I wish I had an answer for you, but I just don't."

"Miss Sady, can I please stay here with you and Grace? I can help take care of her and help you and Mr. Tibbits hang your 'backer in the barn. Please Miss Sady. I can sleep in the barn. I just can't go back there now. Please!"

"Tell you what Dewey. I do need help, and Grace needs to get acquainted with her uncle. You can help in the evenins' after school and after your homework is done, or on the weekends."

"But Miss Sady, I quit school last year. The other kids made fun of me because I limp and don't have nice clothes. Miss Sady, I can't go back."

"Mr., you will go back to school. I will have a talk with the teacher you get and you will have nicer clothes and you won't have to be ashamed anymore. I saved all of Eddie's clothes that he wore years ago. Some of them are like new. We'll go to church tomorrow. I know your ma goes. I'm goin' to have a talk with her and your pa."

"Thank you, thank you Miss Sady. I'm gonna' be the best worker you ever had. You won't be sorry."

"We'll talk about this tomorrow. Let's get some sleep. And you ain't sleepin' in the barn. You go on upstairs and I'll show you Eddie's room. There are twin beds in his room, one for you and one for him when he comes home from this war."

Mary Wagner

"Miss Sady, I heard the town folk talkin', and they said the war might be over pretty soon. Maybe Eddie will be comin' home before you know it."

"I hope so Dewey. That sounds real good to me. I hope so."

chapter 4

HARMONY CREEK FIRST Baptist Church is one of two Christian churches in the town of Harmony. Its parishioners are white folk. The second church is Harmony Church of God which is also Baptist, but the people who worship there are the colored folk of Harmony. One church is on one end of town, and the other church is at the other end of town. There was no question about segregation in the 1940's; it was very prevalent in the small town of Harmony.

There were very few American Indians left in Harmony at this time. Even though Willow is Cherokee and a Christian, she didn't attend church as much as she would have liked to. She understood that she was judged by what she wore, where she lived, her race, and the fact that she was poor and not being able to contribute to the collection didn't help. Willow usually sat outside of church on Sundays with Wolfe, but she happened to see Sady, Grace and Dewey go into church and she wanted to sit with them this Sunday.

"You stay Wolfe, and wait for me. If these nice church people let me stay, I'll probably be 'bout an hour," Willow said as she walked up the steps and into church.

As Willow walked through the church doors and walked down the aisle, she could hear whispering coming from some of the parishioners and knew that she was being talked about. There was even some light laughter and she noticed a few children holding their noses and looking at her as she advanced further into church.

Willow didn't want to embarrass Sady, so she turned around to walk back out of church.

Sady turned for a second and noticed Willow walking out of church. Sady called to Willow, "Willow, come up here and sit with me and Dewey. Come on, there is plenty of room."

Willow felt so proud when Sady called to her, particularly after all the hateful looks from the church members. She put her head up high and strolled down the aisle with a bit of a bounce in her step – a bounce full of pride, then sat down in the pew with Sady, Grace and Dewey.

Of course the looks and sneers never stopped, but Willow didn't care now. To her Sady was more important than anyone in that church. Most of the people were 'pretenders' as far as Willow was concerned. Willow knew just who the 'pretenders' were, but her Cherokee upbringing would never allow her to point these people out and throw into their faces what secrets she knew about their families. Yes, she could embarrass a lot of these good God-fearing people, but she was above that. Willow's philosophy is, "judge me from what you see outside; He will judge me from what He sees inside."

Sady put her arm around Willow and said, "It's about time I saw you walk through those doors. I come every Sunday. You stop by the house and come with me the next time. It's too far for you to walk, and you're comin' home with me today for Sunday supper."

"But Sady, you don't have to . . ."

"Have to what Willow? You're like one of the family. You were always there for Mama and Daddy. I'm here for you. Now don't start fussin', and bring Wolfe. I have a special treat for him."

"Ok Sady, I'm not one to argue, 'specially in church."

Just then the church organ player, Miss Bea Allen, played the hymn "The Old Rugged Cross" and the congregation joined in singing.

After singing the hymn, Reverend Daniel Marshal stood at the podium to offer up prayers.

"Before we begin with the Gospel readings today, I would like for everyone to bow their heads in prayer. Dear Heavenly Father, we ask you to please look after and protect our boys that are fightin' in this war. Please end this war and bring our boys home in our community that are fightin' for our freedom in Europe and Japan. We pray for Eddie Milsap, Sady's son, Lester and Treva Hicks' son, Tony, Chester Sellers' son, Pete, and all the sons of all parents in America. God please bring our boys home to their families. Please help President Truman bring an end to this war, and God, get these boys home by Christmas. Thank you Dear Lord. Amen. Shall we all turn to page 142 for . ."

Sady started to clear her throat, and the sound is loud enough to interrupt Reverend Marshal.

"Sady, is there somethin' you want to add to our prayer today?" Reverend Marshal asked.

"Reverend, let us not forget Thomas Tibbits, Henry and Lena's boy," Sady said loud enough for those in the back of the church to hear.

Reverend Marshal gave Sady a questionable stare for a second then said, "of course, Sady. Even though the colored church down the road is more than likely prayin' for their own, we can also remember Thomas in our prayers."

Sady looked up at the Reverend and said, "thank you Reverend, he's my Eddie's best friend."

Some of the people looked at one another, shaking their heads or whispering. It didn't bother Sady. The Tibbits' family went way back and lived in the community for as long as she could remember. The older Tibbits, who are now deceased, were always there to help Sady's parents. Of course, Sady's parents are also deceased, but the Tibbits' family were always a part of their life. Henry and Lena were there for her now and she cherished their friendship.

While Reverend Marshal was giving his sermon, Dewey looked around and noticed his mother sitting in the back row.

When their eyes met, Dewey felt the suffering inside that his mother was going through since he left home. He could tell from the look in her eyes that she was sorry for the argument they had and that she really missed him.

Reverend Marshal's sermon wasn't very long this Sunday. As a matter of fact, he made the sermon extra short so that he and Miss Bea Allen and a couple of the younger girls could go down to the river and have a picnic. The Reverend and Miss Allen were somewhat engaged but had no plans in the near future to be married. Reverend Marshal was too involved with activities involving the younger children and teenagers to be in a permanent relationship at this time.

Mary Wagner

This gave Eva and Dewey a chance to talk before Roby came to pick Eva up from church.

Eva waited for Sady and Dewey at the bottom of the church steps. She had to clear things up with Dewey.

Sady didn't want to embarrass either one of them and sent Dewey over to privately talk to Eva.

Eva looked up at Dewey with tears in her eyes. "Son, are you doin' ok? I was worried sick when you didn't come home. I miss you Dewey."

"Ma, what do you want me to say? I can't live in that house with him anymore. I hate him. Don't tell me you don't feel the same way. I can't take his insults and beatins' no more. I'm goin' to wind up killin' him if I stay. He ain't ever goin' to change. I don't understand why you don't leave, and it ain't because you love him."

"You're right about everything Dewey. The worst thing he did was what he did to Becky. I turned my head because I was afraid of him. I had you and Becky and no place to go. I prayed every day son that I would find him dead in the barn after one of his drinkin' spells. I hate him as much as you do, but my life was over a long time ago. Look at me boy! I can't fight him no more."

"You don't have to fight him Ma. Come with me to Miss Sady's house. He won't bother you there."

Dewey turned to Sady. "Miss Sady, can you come over here for a minute?"

"Sure will Dewey."

"Hi Eva. Dewey is goin' to stay at my place for a while to help with the 'backer. Is that ok with you? I can really use his help."

"I appreciate you lettin' Dewey stay with you. I'm sure he told you about Roby."

"Yes he did. I'm also offerin' you a chance to come and stay with us. You will be around your Grandbaby, Grace. You won't have to worry about Roby anymore. I won't put up with his ways and you know that Eva."

"I appreciate your offer Sady, but Roby is fit to be tied now because Dewey left. I don't want to bring any trouble into your home. Sady can I hold Grace for a minute?"

"Of course you can Eva. Grace is your granddaughter too. You come over whenever you want and hold her all day."

"If I could get away Sady, you know I would. It's hard to sneak out with Roby home now. Oh no, here he comes now Sady! You take Grace back."

"What are you scared of Eva? You hold Grace. I'm goin' to have a talk with Roby anyway."

"Sady, I don't think that's such a good idea. You don't understand how mean he can ..."

"Eva, stop. I can take care of myself and I'm not afraid of Roby."

Roby pulled up in his beat-up, dirty Ford truck. He climbed out of the truck. For once he's not drunk but you can see the meanness in his eyes and the hostile way he walked over to Eva, Sady and Dewey. Willow is standing across from Sady holding Wolfe. Most of the people in the church yard have already left the church grounds.

Roby headed straight over to Dewey, yanked his shirt by the collar and said, "boy, you're comin' home. Go get in the truck. I'll take care of you later."

"Pa, no, I'm not comin' back home. I'm stayin' with Miss Sady. I'm helpin' her with her 'backer."

Roby threw Dewey to the ground. "The hell with you boy. I ain't puttin' up with your disrespectin' way of talkin' to me. You little ..."

Just then Wolfe ran over and seized Roby's pant leg and pulled at the leg with his teeth.

Roby pointed to Willow and said, "get over here you crazy ole' one-eyed Injun bitch and get this devil dog off of me before I cut his throat!"

"You lay one finger on my Wolfe and your sorry carcass won't see another light of day!" Willow shouted to Roby.

As Willow pulled Wolfe off of Roby, Sady, infuriated, walked over to Roby. "You're one disgustin' excuse for a man. Maybe you can bully and hit a little woman and a son half your size, but if I was a man right now, you would be pullin' your head out of your backside! You need a real man to put you in your place! If my Jack was alive he'd put you right where you belong!"

Everyone just looked amazed at Sady. She never backed down. How proud Willow was to watch Sady stand up to Roby the way she did.

Sady and Roby stood face to face. Sady wouldn't budge. You could just about fit a baseball bat between them, that's how close they stood together.

Mary Wagner

Roby, in his perverted demeaning way said, "ya' still missin' Jack, Sady? A pretty woman like you shouldn't be alone. No wonder you want my boy around."

Sady smacked Roby in the face. "I don't expect anything nice comin' out of your mouth."

Roby laughed. "I didn't know you liked 'em young Sady. You know he can't give you what I can. Your man has been gone a long time. A good-lookin' woman like you needs a real man like me to satisfy her."

Sady asked Roby to come a little closer. She whispered in his ear. "You're right Roby. I need a real man like you. You know what I would do with a real man like you? The first thing I would do is get me a big ole' butcher knife and cut your manhood off. Won't have to worry 'bout you doin' dirty things to little girls anymore."

Roby jumped back away from Sady. His face was so red and he was so mad that Sady was waiting for the steam to come out of his ears. "You're just another bitch that needs to be put back in her place. Your old man couldn't do it. Maybe I'll get the chance to do it for him."

"My Jack respected me and his children. My place was right beside him, not behind him. You could never be a quarter of the man he was! Any man that beats on a woman and a crippled boy and molests his own daughter ain't no man."

Roby, with a crude smirk on his face, looked over at Grace in Eva's arms. "Since you brought up my Becky, Sady, how's my Grandbaby Grace. Her grandpa would sure love to hold her."

Sady had daggers in her eyes while looking at Roby. "You know what you're gonna' hold Roby, what I told you I was cutin' off of you. And Roby, that's really gonna' hurt."

"Think you're so tough Sady? Maybe one day we'll see how tough you are. Eva come on; get in the truck – NOW!"

Eva handed Grace back to Sady and whispered to her. "Sady, thank you so much for takin' care of Dewey and lettin' him stay with you."

"Well now don't you forget. You get a chance, you leave Roby and you come and stay with me!"

"I won't forget Sady, I won't forget."

"Eva, get in the truck now!"

Dewey walked over to Sady. "Miss Sady, I appreciate you standin' up for me and my ma. I just hope he don't take it out on her because I won't go home with him."

"Dewey, your mother is a grown-up woman. She has to make her own mind up about this situation with your father. I can't make her leave him. She has to do it on her own."

"I guess, Miss Sady, I'm just scared for her."

"Dewey, I am too. I am too. We just have to pray that he doesn't hurt her. Now, come on Willow and Wolfe. We're goin' home and have a nice Sunday dinner. I think we deserve one after what just happened. Let's go home."

chapter 5

SEVERAL WEEKS PASSED after the confrontational meeting between Roby and Sady in the churchyard. October flew by and Thanksgiving was right around the corner and soon to be celebrated. Thanksgiving was an unforgettable memory to Sady, but one she would like to forget. It would be five years that Sady's husband, Jack, and her older son, Donny, were killed in a horrible wreck just a few miles from home. It was the week before Thanksgiving on a snowy night. Jack and Donny were coming home with little Eddie in the back of the truck. The three of them were hunting for deer and a nice big turkey to cook for Thanksgiving Day. Eddie, at the time, was fifteen years old and wanted to sit in the back of the truck with the big buck that his big brother Donny shot. Eddie shot the turkey and was so proud that he wanted to keep an eye on those two prized possessions. Eddie was curled up and covered with the hide off a big black bear Jack killed a few years back. He was nice and warm.

As Jack's truck climbed the steep grade up Blackheart Mountain, Eddie noticed a truck following them. The truck turned its lights off. That was really a dangerous thing to do on those sharp mountain curves. Before Jack's truck entered the rapid downhill grade, and around the narrow bend in the mountain, the other truck disappeared.

Right before entering Jack and Sady's road to go home, the same truck, with lights blaring, sped out from a side road and rammed Jack's truck and sent it rolling down the mountainside. The truck sped away. Sady was told that Jack and Donny were killed instantly. Eddie was still alive, but barely.

Mr. Henry Tibbits just happened to see Jack's lights still shining at the bottom of the ravine. He was coming home from working on a farm as a hired hand at Dyson Sand and Gravel Yard. He climbed down the side of the mountain and down the ravine. There, Mr. Tibbits found Jack and Donny. Father and son were both dead. Luckily, Mr. Tibbits heard moaning coming from under the bed of the truck. There was a slight opening, enough that he could crawl under. He found Eddie and pulled him out from under the truck. Mr. Tibbits tried to console Eddie, who was badly hurt and going into shock. He wrapped Eddie in a blanket he had in the truck and drove as fast as he could to Sady's house for help. Mr. Tibbits always said he could never forget the terror on Sady's face when he carried Eddie into the house.

Sady just fell to the floor and was inconsolable. She felt her life had ended. Mr. Tibbits telephoned Sheriff Guy Hardin in the town of Harmony, but couldn't reach him right away. After finally getting a hold of him, Sheriff Hardin came out with the rescue squad to pull Jack's truck out of the ravine and up the mountain. It was too late for Jack and Donny, but Eddie's life was saved. Eddie was taken into Boone to the hospital after another rescue squad picked him up from Sady's. At least Sady had Eddie. Eddie had a head concussion and several broken bones. He never could remember what happened that night after they were hit.

Thanksgiving had always been a sad time of the year for Sady to face because of that terrible day in November. Jack and Sady were childhood sweethearts. They married young and the love they had for each other never faltered; it just grew with the birth of their two sons. Now with Eddie being away fighting a war she just couldn't understand, Thanksgiving was a holiday she would rather not celebrate. The memories of what happened the night of the accident are too hard for Sady to bear.

The only bright star in Sady's life now was Grace. She wasn't about to show Grace how sad she really felt. Sady was determined to celebrate Thanksgiving with her closest friends, the Tibbits, Willow, and Dewey. It would be a blessed Thanksgiving if Eddie was to come home and Eva would leave Roby and come and stay at Sady's house.

The tobacco was curing in the barn and turning a beautiful color of brown. Sady always raised the best tobacco crop in Harmony. Her tobacco was sweet, with a light flavor that the buyers favored whenever she took her crop to the warehouse in Boone to be auctioned off.

That day Sady, Dewey and Mr. Tibbits were in the barn surveying the tobacco leaves to make sure they were getting enough of air for curing. The stalks would be ready to be stripped and graded of their leaves within the next three weeks, preferably before Christmas. Mrs. Lena Tibbits took Grace home with her so Sady could work on her tobacco crop.

Sady turned to Mr. Tibbits and Dewey. "I want you both to know I appreciate everything you have done for me. I wouldn't be able to get this 'baker in town on time and sold if I didn't have you all helpin' me."

Mr. Tibbits said, "Sady, weren't nothin'. All you and your mom and dad did for me and my family all these years. I can't ever repay you."

"Henry, you and Lena have always been there in my time of need. You saved my Eddie's life Henry. If you wouldn't have been there, I wouldn't have had any family left."

"It weren't just me Sady. I can't take all the credit. The Good Lord had a hand in it. He led me to that mountainside that night. I wish I could have gotten there right after it first happened. Maybe I could have saved Jack and Donny. I know you worry about Eddie not rememberin' what happened that night, but maybe it is for the best."

"You're probably right Henry. But I'd love to know who the coward was that hit Jack's truck then drove off and left them there to die."

"Someday Sady, if the Almighty wants you to know, you will."

Dewey looked at Sady a little puzzled. Miss Sady, does this mean I gotta' go home after we sell the 'backer?"

"No sir Dewey. I need you around here permanently. I got a lot of chores for you to do. Don't go worrin' about that."

Dewey felt relieved that he would be staying on and had this big smile from ear to ear.

Sady heard the sound of a car speeding up the dirt driveway while kicking up dust in its path. Sady briskly walked out to see who in the world would be driving like a crazy person. Something inside her told her to take her rifle with her. Sady told Henry and Dewey to stay in the barn and finish inspecting the tobacco leaves.

The car came to a stop. Sady looked at the driver and had no idea who he was. Just then the passenger door opened and Becky Prestel got out of the car. Sady noticed how thin and pale she looked. She was hardly recognizable. She sure didn't look like the pretty young girl her son Eddie married almost two years ago.

"What's the matter Sady? You look like you've seen a ghost. Yeah, it's me, Becky. I stopped by to see Ma and she told me you were takin' care of Grace. Can I see my baby?"

"Why yeah, you do look like a ghost. You took off over a year ago. No letters, no phone call, nothin'. And Grace ain't here right now. Who's that guy in the car?"

"You sure are nosy Sady. All I asked was to see my little girl. She is mine you know, not yours."

"No, Becky. Grace became mine when you took off and left her. You just can't ride through with whoever you got in that there car and upset Grace then ride back where you came from. And you look terrible. Are you sick?"

Just then the boyfriend got out of the car and slammed the door. He was quite a large guy and intimidating, but he didn't scare Sady.

"Look here lady, just go get the kid. It belongs to her not you. And my name ain't *whoever*, it's Leroy, Leroy Crager."

"Let you and me, Leroy, get somethin' straight. You ain't nobody as far as I'm concerned and you're standin' on my property. My granddaughter ain't a "*IT*". And I'm gonna' give you ten seconds to get back in that car while I talk to Becky. One, two, three, four, five, six . . ."

"You better get back in Leroy. She's crazy enough to shoot you."

"I'll get back in the car Grandma, but it ain't over between you and me."

"Son, you're threatin' me, and I'm the one holdin' the rifle. You don't think that's a little weird big fella'?"

"Why you old bitch. I ought to . . ."

"That's enough Leroy. Just get in the car and shut your mouth while I talk to Sady!"

"Just tell me where she is Sady. All I want to do is hold her for a few minutes."

"I just don't trust you Becky. You left Eddie and your baby for no good reason. If you were goin' to stay around these parts for a while without your Leroy, I would consider you comin' over and bein' part of her life again."

"Well that ain't ever goin' to happen Sady. Eddie joined the Army and I didn't like bein' alone."

"Alone, alone. You had a beautiful daughter. You were never alone."

"You're just mad because I left your precious Eddie. Get over it Sady, because he might not ever be comin' home. And the law is on my side as far as Grace is concerned."

"Eddie will be comin' home and law or no law is goin' to make me give you Grace! Get off my property, NOW, and I don't ever want to see you or Mr. Muscles around here again."

"I'll go, but you'll be hearin' from me again. You can bet on that!"

Just then Dewey and Mr. Tibbits came out of the barn to see who was arguing with Sady.

Dewey ran up to Becky to hug her, but she pushed him away.

"Becky, I knew you would be back. Did you come back to stay?"

"Are you kidin'? I wouldn't come back to these mountains if somebody bought the whole community of Harmony and gave it to me."

"But Becky, Ma really misses you and needs you."

"I bet she does. Too bad. Where was she when I needed her? She knew what was goin' on and didn't do nothin' about it. It's over. I'm finished with this place."

Becky turned around and started to get in the car.

Dewey held her arm. "Please Becky. Please, at least go talk to Ma."

"Let go Dewey, don't touch me. I saw Ma today and he is still there. I'll never go back. Now move out of the way."

Becky looked at Sady and sarcastically said, "I'm comin back tomorrow Sady. Grace better be here."

"Don't waste your gas. Just go back where you came from. I'll never let you see her again as long as you hang with people the likes of him!"

Becky laughed loudly as her and Leroy drove off.

Sady, Mr. Tibbits and Dewey headed back to the barn to work on the tobacco.

Dewey said, "Miss Sady, what's the matter with her? I don't understand. That guy, Leroy, looks like a bad person for her to be with. He's scary."

"Dewey, just like your ma, Becky needs help and needs to make her own mind up. She knows right from wrong and that guy Leroy is just WRONG. She has to come to that decision on her own."

"Mr. Tibbits, do you think Lena would mind keepin' Grace tonight and watchin' Grace tomorrow? I don't trust Becky. Maybe she could go into Boone tomorrow and pick up a few things for me. After, maybe she can stop and spend some time with her sister. I'll pick Grace up after we finish here tomorrow. Can you ask her for me?"

"Sady, one thing that woman likes to do is go shoppin' even if she ain't got no money and she thinks the world of Grace."

They both laughed.

"Henry, why don' you go on home now, get yourself a good nights' sleep and come back early tomorrow. You all worked so hard today. Thank you both."

"Fine with me Sady. I'll talk to the Mrs. about what you said. Sady, please don't go worrin' about Becky and what she said. Everything is gonna' be ok. Night everybody."

Sady looked at Dewey with a worried look on her face. "Dewey, come on in, I'll get supper started. Tomorrow will be here before we know it."

chapter 6

SADY, STILL SHAKEN and upset about Becky insisting to see Grace, tried to put that thought in the back of her mind. Her tobacco crop and getting the tobacco cured, stripped and graded was something she really had to keep her mind on. This was her only income she could depend on for the whole year. After all, Lena Tibbits was going to watch Grace today. Maybe Becky and that disgusting guy she was with would just go back where they came from and leave her and Grace alone.

The town of Boone is about twenty-five miles from Harmony Creek. Mrs. Tibbits went shopping for Sady the next day. Boone is a small town, surrounded by mountains on both sides. It is such a beautiful town that it is like a picture ready to be taken.

As Mrs. Tibbits pushed Grace's stroller down King Street picking up a few items that Sady requested, she noticed a car slowly following her. The car was almost alongside of her and Grace. Lena walked a little faster to get away from the car.

Becky and Leroy were inside the car. "Leroy, STOP! STOP!" Becky hollered.

"Shut up Becky, you're going to draw attention to us. Sit down! You just had a fix. You want a cop to stop us so we can get locked up?"

Becky started punching Leroy. "I said stop you stupid jackass! It's Grace, my baby. Pull over – now!"

"Watch yourself. If you get picked up, I'm out of here. You're on your own Becky."

Becky jumped out of the car and ran up behind Mrs. Tibbits while trying to compose herself so Lena didn't realize she had just shot up some heroin.

"Mrs. Tibbits, Mrs. Tibbits! Please stop. It's Becky, Becky Prestel, Grace's Mama!"

"Becky, what a surprise! What are you doin' in Boone? It's been a long time since you have been home."

"I'm here visitin' my folks. I ran into Miss Sady and she said you were goin' to be in Boone shoppin' today, and I'd probably get a chance to see Grace."

Lena knew that was a lie. Henry told her what transpired the day before. She knew Sady didn't want Becky anywhere around Grace.

Becky couldn't keep her eyes off of Grace. She tried to be inconspicuous while motioning to Leroy to pull the car closer to her and Mrs. Tibbits.

Lena took Grace out of the stroller and held her. She knew Becky may be up to no good.

"Mrs. Tibbits, can I hold her, please, just for a minute? Please don't deny me this precious time with my baby girl."

Lena noticed that Becky was swaying back and forth and didn't look focused or normal in any way. "I don't know. I' rather clear this with Sady."

"Aw, come on, Mrs. Tibbits, only one incy minute is all I'm askin'."

"No, No. Sorry Becky I need to tell . . . . Ow! My head. Becky, give her back!"

In less than a minute, Becky knocked Mrs. Tibbits to the ground, grabbed Grace, jumped in Leroy's car and they took off out of town.

Mrs. Tibbits started screaming for help.

Two people came to the aid of Mrs. Tibbits and helped carry her to the Sheriff's office.

The Sheriff's deputy took down all the information and wrapped Lena's head with gauze from a first aid kit in the office.

Sheriff Guy Hardin, who is in charge of the Sheriff's office in Harmony, happened to be sitting in that day for the vacationing Sheriff of Boone. He questioned Mrs. Tibbits then drove her back to Sady's house where her husband, Henry, was helping Sady with the tobacco. Mrs. Tibbits was too shaken up to make the drive and had a terrible headache from being pushed to the pavement by Becky. Sady was in store for some really bad news.

chapter 7

SADY, HENRY TIBBITS and Dewey were finishing up in the barn and on their way up to the house so that Sady could prepare lunch for her and the guys. As they walked from the barn to the house Sady noticed the Sheriff's car coming down her driveway. "What in the world is he doin' here?" she said out loud to Henry and Dewey. "Dewey stay here and finish up. Henry and me will go see what's goin' on."

Sheriff Hardin stopped the car and he and Lena Tibbits got out to give Sady the bad news.

Sady's worst fear confronted her. There was no Grace with Lena.

Henry walked over to console his wife Lena. He could see that she was sobbing and incoherent.

Sady ran over to Lena. "Lena, where's Grace? What happened to your face and head? Dear God, don't tell me my Grace is gone. Lena, what happened?"

Lena looked up at Sady. "She took her, she took her. I'm so sorry, so sorry Sady."

"Who took her Lena? Who?"

Sady looked at Sheriff Hardin. "What's she talkin' about Guy? Tell me, tell me now!"

Sheriff Hardin saw how upset Sady was and tried to calm her down. "Calm down Sady, calm down."

"You calm down! Don't you tell me to calm down! Now what happened and where is my Grace? You tell me now Guy, right now!"

Sheriff Hardin explained the incident. "Becky saw Mrs. Tibbits walking down King Street. She approached Mrs. Tibbits. She asked to

Mary Wagner

hold Grace. Mrs. Tibbits refused. Becky knocked her down, took Grace and fled in a car with a male driving."

Lena looked at Sady while still hysterically crying. "Sady, please forgive me, please forgive me. I held Grace so tight, I wasn't about to let Becky even touch her. She punched me in the head, knocked me down, and then she took her. I'm so sorry!"

"Lena, you did what I asked you to. You did nothin' wrong. I don't blame you. I had a feelin' when she left here yesterday she was up to somethin'. I should have kept Grace with me until I knew Becky was gone." Sady then looked at the Sheriff. "So why aren't you out chasin' after her? Why are you still standin' here Guy? Go find my baby!"

Sheriff Hardin said, "You saw them yesterday Sady, what kind of car was it? Mrs. Tibbits can't remember anything. Just describe the car and the driver to me. Just stop bein' so excited and calm down!"

"You're tellin' me not to get excited. Are you crazy Guy? Becky didn't steal my best egg-layin' hen; she took my life, my granddaughter. You and your deputies should be out tryin' to find them now. The license plate had Maryland on it. The car was an old early 1930 Plymouth like my Daddy used to own with a big dent on the passenger's side and it smoked from my driveway to the road. Is that enough? Now get out there and get my Grace back!"

"You don't tell me how to do my job Sady, let's get that straight. And if the car was smokin', there ain't no way it's goin' to make it to Maryland. So CALM DOWN for the last time and let me do my job!"

"This reminds me of almost five years ago Guy, remember. It took you forty-five minutes before anybody could get a hold of you to help my husband and my two boys. Maybe if you had gotten there earlier, they may have lived. You're doin' the same thing all over again!"

"So now you're accusin' me because your husband and boy were killed. I always thought you held that over my head. The coroner from Lenoir said they probably were killed instantly Sady. I wish you would stop tryin' to blame me!"

"I'm not blamin' you Guy and I don't want to talk about what happened then. I want to know what you're plannin' on doin' now to try and get my Grace back. Prove me wrong this time Guy. Bring my granddaughter back. You've got all the information you need. Just do

36

your job! If you ain't gonna' do nothin' about it, I'll load my truck up now and go after them."

"You ain't takin' the law into your own hands Sady. Right now my hands are kind of tied anyway."

"What in the world are you talkin' about Guy?"

"It's Sheriff Hardin Sady. How about a little respect? And what I'm tryin' to tell you is that Becky is Grace's legal parent. Where are your papers sayin' you are her legal guardian?"

"You forget Guy, I mean Sheriff HARDIN, my son is the other legal parent. Right now Grace is with Becky. Becky looked bad yesterday. She looked sick. I don't know what she is on, but she doesn't have her right mind. And that guy she is with, that Leroy Crager, he's mean and nasty and I'm afraid what he might do to Grace."

"Sady, Eddie ain't here right now, is he? And Becky and that fella ..."

"Don't get so smart Guy, Eddie is off fightin' a war so that you can have the freedom to stand here and talk down to me and waste time when you and your deputies could be out lookin' for Grace."

"You got it wrong. I got the highest respect for our boys fightin' this war. But that don't change what the law requires you to have. It's Friday and it's too late to go down to the courthouse to get any paperwork. You go Monday mornin', get the papers and I'll proceed to get on with this case and try to find Grace. My hands are tied 'till I see the paperwork."

Just then Dewey interrupted the conversation between Sady and Sheriff Hardin.

Dewey said, "Sheriff Hardin, Miss Sady is right. Becky didn't look good yesterday. She acted crazy. Somethin' is wrong with her and I have a feelin' that guy she's with, Leroy, has somethin' to do with it. Miss Sady, I'll be back before dark."

"Dewey, where are you goin'?"

"Maybe Ma knows somethin'. I'm gonna' try to find out."

"Son, if your ma found out somethin', get Sady to give me a call."

"I will Sheriff."

Sady said, "you be careful Dewey. You get back here before dark. It's cold and those dark clouds tell me snow is comin' on in. I don't want you catchin' cold and gettin' sick. Be careful."

Sheriff Hardin said, "Sady, you get those papers and I'll alert the authorities in Maryland to be on the lookout for that Plymouth. Right now Becky has the right to have Grace. She's the only parent here right now. Sady, I know how you must be hurtin', but my hands are tied right now. You do what you gotta' do next week and I'm sure everything will be ok."

"Well I want to ask you somethin'. Why can't you go after them because of the assault on Lena? She was hit in the head and knocked down. That's every reason in the world to go after them. I bet if Lena was a white woman or your wife got hit and knocked down, you would probably have them in jail by now."

"Now you know me better than that Sady. I ain't prejudice. That ain't no way to talk. I think highly of Henry and Lena."

"Then that's every reason in the world to get that car of yours out on the road and go lookin' for them."

"You never could hold your tongue back Sady. I don't answer to you. I told you what you have to do. When you got those papers, bring them to my office. That's all I got to say."

"You're wrong Guy. You do answer to me and all the other folks in town that voted for you. Maybe you have been Sheriff a little too long. Lena was assaulted and Grace was kidnapped and you have done nothin'."

"I'm finished here. Mr. and Mrs. Tibbits, would you like to ride back into town and pick up your truck?"

Henry and Lena looked at Sady.

"You two go on now. Lena don't go punishin' yourself over this. I'm the one that never should have let Grace be away from me. While you're in town, you go see Doctor Smith and let him look at your head. You just go home and take care of yourself, you hear?"

"Thank you Sady for bein' so understandin'. I just wish none of this happened. Let's go Henry."

Henry and Lena took Sheriff Hardin up on his offer and rode with him to Boone to pick up their truck.

Sady, exhausted, worried, and mad, walked back into her empty house and shut the door.

chapter 8

DEWEY WAS DETERMINED to find out what information about Becky and Leroy that he could from his mother. He stayed in the woods above the house until dusk and watched his father go into the barn with his bottle of moonshine. Dewey figured he would be in the barn until the bottle was gone and maybe he would even fall asleep. The wind started howling and snowflakes started to fall and cover the ground. It was so cold. He watched his father close the barn door. Dewey ran down to the house and watched through the window as his mother did the dishes. He quietly knocked on the back door.

Eva opened the door and was surprised to see Dewey. "Dewey, get in here, it's so cold son. You don't even have a coat on. Come on in, hurry before he gets back!"

"Ma, did you talk to Becky and that Leroy fella' that was with her? It's important. Did she say where they were goin'? Did she say anything to you ... did ..."

"Son, you're goin' on and on. I don't understand. What's wrong?"

"Ma, I don't have time to waste. Pa might come back any minute. I don't want him to see me here. Did Becky say where she was goin' after she leaves Harmony?"

"I can't remember right off. I know Pa catches you here, he'll beat both of us!"

"Ma, I ain't goin' nowhere until you can remember somethin'. Becky and that guy, they're crazy. No tellin' what they'll do to Grace. They took her Ma. Becky hit Mrs. Tibbits in the head and knocked her down and took Grace. The Sheriff won't help Miss Sady until she can get some kind of legal papers sayin' she is Grace's guardian. Come on

Ma, think. Grace belongs to us as much as she belongs to Miss Sady! I know you don't want nothin' bad to happen to her."

"Sady, Sady, Sady. I'm tired of hearin' about her. Nobody understands what I've had to deal with all these years. Your Pa is a MONSTER!"

"Stop bein' jealous of Miss Sady. She has always been good to us. Instead of leavin' that monster, you let him run me and Becky away. Now you're goin' to lose Grace."

Eva furious over what Dewey said, turned and went back to washing the dishes as if nothing was said.

Dewey, disgusted over his mother's actions, turned to leave and walked out the door.

Eva ran to Dewey and tried to stop him.

"Dewey, your right, son. I'm sorry. You don't know how sorry I am. I can't ever make it up to you and Becky, but I can do the right thing for Grace. He ruined Becky's life and I turned my back and let him do that. I lost her. I don't want to lose you or Grace. Becky sent me a few post cards and a picture of her from Maryland. I hid them from your pa. Maybe there's somethin' in them to tell us where in Maryland they are goin'. I'll be right back. You just keep on the lookout for Pa."

While Eva was looking for the picture and post cards, Roby, unexpectedly, walked into the kitchen and just stared at Dewey. Right at that moment, Eva came running out of her bedroom with the pictures. "Dewey, I know where she is goin', she's goin' . . . Roby!"

Both Dewey and Eva looked at Roby like they had just seen a ghost.

Dewey with fear in his voice and trembling said, "hi Pa. Just came over to get my heavy coat with it snowin' and gettin' colder outside."

Roby still standing to the entrance to the kitchen, drunk, and with his bottle still in his hand said, "you don't want me to believe that lie, do ya' son, cause I don't."

Eva walked over and stood in front of Dewey. "It's true, Roby. You can see it's snowin' outside and when Dewey left, he didn't take none of his clothes."

"Get out of the way woman. Ya' look like you're ready to mess yourself boy. Not so brave now are ya' like you were up at the church. You gonna' back talk me now like ya' did then? Ain't got nothin' to say boy?"

Roby pushed Eva out of the way and grabbed Dewey's arm. "You ain't come over here for no coat boy. See this cigarette son. I'm almost finished smokin' it. I hate to put it out in your eye. My pa put his cigarette out in the eye of a crazy young Injun bitch - -after he got what he wanted, because she spit on him and that really made him mad. We both know who I'm talkin' about, don't we. You gonna' tell me why you're here boy?"

Eva got up and confronted Roby. "You wanna' take it out on somebody, take it out on me. Leave him be!"

Roby turned and looked at Eva with a vicious look in his eyes and then smiled. "Don't you worry none woman, you're next."

Thinking he caught Roby off guard, Dewey kicked Roby in the shin and knocked the cigarette out of his hand which made Roby twice as mad.

"I'm goin' to kill you boy!"

Roby threw Dewey up against the stove. Dewey hits his head and lay motionless on the kitchen floor.

Eva, hysterical and sobbing, ran over to Dewey's limp body and called his name over and over again. "Dewey, Dewey, please get up son. Please get up!"

Eva looked up at Roby and said, "what did you do? I hate you, you bastard!"

Roby, enraged from what Eva just called him, looked at her and said, "what did you just call me, you bitch?"

Roby grabbed Eva by the arm, almost pulling it out of its joint, picked her up and put his hands around her throat. Eva, trying to take his hands from around her throat, backed up to the kitchen sink.

While blood was dripping from the corner of Eva's mouth from Roby punching her, she noticed that he was thoroughly enjoying what he was doing to her. Roby beamed with joy over this harsh beating he was giving Eva.

Eva had been down this road several times, but the beatings were never this violent. She knew this time Roby was going to kill her. She knew this was probably her last day on earth.

Roby put his hands around Eva's throat again and started choking her. While choking her, Roby said, "see these big brown eyes Eva, they're the last things you're gonna' remember." He then laughed in his sarcastic, drunken way.

Just then Roby's big brown eyes showed horror in them. His taunting laugh subsided. His hands slowly left Eva's neck.

Eva was stabbing him with a knife that she managed to put her hand on that was lying in the sink. Eva stabbed Roby in the heart.

While stabbing Roby, Eva stared into his big brown eyes and said, "sorry Roby, you got that all wrong. I think the last thing you're gonna' remember is lookin' into my 'Carolina Blues' you filthy, wicked bastard."

Roby finally fell to the floor. Eva couldn't stop stabbing him. The hate poured out of her heart and into her hand. She stabbed him over and over again until you couldn't make out who was lying on the floor because of the great amount of blood.

Blood was all over Eva. She finally dropped her knife and came to her senses and rushed over to Dewey's limp body. He was still breathing and she knew she had to get help immediately. But in her mind she had to evaluate who she could trust. The only person she could think of was Sady.

Eva managed to pull Dewey into her bedroom and got him in bed.

Eva put on Roby's heavy coat, boots, and her scarf, got a lantern and shut the door behind her. Eva knew she had to get help right away for Dewey. She thought of nothing else, but the dead body on the kitchen floor – her husband, Roby.

chapter 9

THE LIGHT SNOW coming down had already turned into a blizzard. It was so cold; cold and dark. There was no moon this night to light the way for Eva. Roby's truck sat in the driveway with a flat tire. But that didn't matter. Eva never did learn how to drive. Dewey tried to teach her once when Roby was working at the saw mill, but she couldn't get the knack of shifting. No, this cold night the only way Eva was getting help was to walk.

Eva's mind was going around in circles. "Will Sady help me? Can I trust her? What did I do? I killed Roby! I'm goin' to spend the rest of my life in jail! I don't care. All I care about is keepin' Dewey alive. Please God, I know you're mad with me. Just let me get to Sady's house. I'm goin' to have to trust her. Please, I beg you Lord. I done wrong, not Dewey, not my son."

Just then Eva saw the flickering of a light up ahead. With the wind howling, the snow blowing and drifting and the sound of Harmony Creek flowing violently and hitting the boulders, she could only hear the sound of a muffled voice. But then she heard the bark of a dog.

Eva hollered out loud, "Willow, Willow, is that you and Wolfe?"

Just then Wolfe came running to Eva and continued to bark and wag his tail.

"Wolfe, I was never so glad to see you!" Willow saw Eva and ran over to her. Eva was so happy to see Willow. She said, "thank you God."

Willow held the lantern up to Eva's face and saw how swollen and bloody her face was.

"I'm goin' to kill him. Where is he Eva? He ain't got long in this world when I get a hold of him. This is his last night on this Earth! What happened woman?"

"Willow, I killed the son of a bitch!"

Then what are you doin' out here in this awful storm Eva? Let's go back. I'll doctor up your face and we'll drink some of this moonshine I made just for a special occasion like this!"

"I need help Willow. I have to go and get Sady. Dewey is unconscious. Roby threw him into the stove and he hit his head! I've got to get Dewey to the hospital in Boone."

Eva started crying. "Willow, it's all my fault. I should have left long ago. If Dewey dies, I'm goin' to lie down right beside him and die too."

"Stop that nonsense talk. Ain't nobody dyin', 'cept Roby of course. You drink some of this moonshine. It will warm you up. You go ahead and get Sady. I'll tend to Dewey 'till you get back. Now go on before this blizzard gets worse!"

"Thank you so much Willow. I don't know what I would do without you or Sady."

"You just go on and hurry. Don't worry about Dewey."

Eva, cold and scared, trudges on through the snowstorm towards Sady's house.

In the meantime, Sady was worried sick about Dewey. He had left hours ago. She paced back and forth looking out the window and looking up at the clock. She had a terrible feeling in the pit of her stomach that something terrible had happened.

Sady picked her phone up and talked to the operator. "Leanne, this is Sady. Oh, I'm fine and you? Leanne, I know the Prestel's don't have a phone, but do any of the neighbors around there have one? If they do, can you connect me.? Nobody around there has a phone? Ok thanks anyway. Yeah, looks like this first snowstorm is a bad one. Ok, you take care too. Bye."

Sady wasn't waiting anymore. She was going to Eva's house to get Dewey. She put her boots, coat, and scarf and grabbed her shotgun. If Roby did hurt Dewey, she was going to make sure he paid for it.

Sady finally got the frozen truck door open and started the truck. It just made a grinding noise. Sady began to talk to the truck. "Come on, old gal. Not tonight. I promise you, when the 'baker sells, I'm goin' to fix you up and you're gonna' be runnin' like a new truck."

Sady tried to start the truck again. It finally started. "I knew you could do it old gal, and I'm not goin' back on my promise to you either!"

chapter 10

SADY HAD TO take a detour around Blackheart Mountain. The bridge over Harmony Creek was overflowing which took her at least an extra forty-five minutes to an hour to drive the usually short distance to Eva's house. Her truck just couldn't get much traction with the snow turning into ice and freezing as soon as it hit the dirt road. It was surely a mess and not a night for anyone to be out. Sady was scared. One slight slip with her already bald tires and her truck would roll down the steep mountainside. She lost her husband and son on a sharp curve on Blackheart Mountain when they were hit in the rear by a hit-and-run driver. Sady was not going to let this happen to her. She had two important things to do before the good Lord took her. She needed to search for Grace and be there for Eddie when he came home.

The snow was blinding and blowing intensely. Sady could hardly see the road. She then noticed a light in the distance. The closer she got, she could make out a figure of a person wildly waving a lantern. "Dewey," she thought, "I hope it's you."

She finally got closer to the person and rolled the window down and saw that it was Eva.

"Eva get in, hurry, get in. You're lucky you didn't freeze to death. How long have you been walkin' in this blizzard Eva?"

Eva got in the truck and turned her face towards Sady and lowered her scarf from her face. "I guess I been walkin' almost an hour Sady. I was afraid to cross the creek."

Sady got a good look at Eva's face. "Oh my God Eva, what did he do to you and where is Dewey?"

Eva was shivering and incoherently muttering under her breath. "I killed him Sady, I killed him and I'm glad I did. I stabbed him over and over. I couldn't stop. I stopped when I heard him take his last breath, then I stabbed again and again. Sady, I'm a murderer. I'm goin' to be locked up for the rest of my life."

"Eva, snap out of it and tell me what happened. Where's Dewey?"

Sady started driving again in the blowing snow towards Eva's home.

"Dewey asked me if I knew where Becky and that Leroy might be livin'. I told him Becky sent me somethin' and I was lookin' for it. Roby come in drunk and got mad at Dewey and threw him across the floor. He hit his head on the stove and passed out. I got mad and called him a bastard. Roby started punchin' me in the face; then he started chokin' me. I couldn't breathe. I grabbed a knife out of the sink and you know the rest. I came lookin' for you to take me and Dewey to Boone to the hospital. He was really hurt bad Sady. I'm scared. Willow is there with him now. I'm goin' to Hell Sady. I committed murder!"

"If anybody went to Hell today Eva, it's Roby. He's there now. Satan reserved a room for him years ago. I'm sure him and his daddy have rooms that connect, that is, if Silas ever died. As far as murder, get that out of your head. If you didn't have that knife in the sink, you wouldn't be talkin' to me right now. There are a lot of people in this community that Roby did real dirty that would have loved to be the one to put that knife in his heart. So stop sayin' you're a murderer. I don't know how you put up with the beatins' and him mistreatin' you, Dewey and Becky all those years. I would have either left him or put that knife in him years ago. My question is . . . what took you so long?"

"I'm not strong like you Sady. After a while, I just gave up. I couldn't fight him. I had no folks left, no place to go. Everybody in these parts was scared of Roby 'cept you and Jack and even Willow. I couldn't put my burdens on you and your family."

"That's the very thing you should have done. You should have come to me years ago. I would have helped you and your kids. I didn't hear about what he did to Becky until her and Eddie got married and moved in with me. Eddie wanted to kill him then. Thank God he joined the Army. Right now Eva, we got to get Dewey to Boone to the hospital. Dewey has a lot of fight in him. I know he is goin' to be ok. If need be, I'll tell the Sheriff that I walked in while Roby was chokin' you. We'll talk about this later. Here we are Eva. You want to sit in the truck or do you want to go in with me?"

"I have to face what I did Sady. Come on, let's get this over with."

chapter 11

SADY SLOWLY OPENED Eva's front door. She was afraid of what she would be seeing. Sady and Eva walked into the kitchen where Roby's body was lying. To Eva's surprise, there was no body, not even a pool of blood where Roby lay. Willow was nowhere to be found either.

"Sady, somethin' is not right. Roby was lyin' here when I left. Where's Willow?"

"Doesn't matter Eva, we need to tend to Dewey right now. Where is he?"

"He's in my bedroom Sady. I can hear him moanin'!"

They both enter Eva's bedroom to find Dewey semi-conscious with a scarf wrapped around his head and some very smelly stuff under the scarf.

Eva gently walked over to Dewey and kissed his forehead while holding his hand. "Son, Son, can you hear me?"

"Ma, what happened? My head really is hurtin'."

Eva began to cry. Sady said, "he's goin' to be ok Eva."

Just then Willow entered the room. "Of course that boy's goin' to be ok. Why wouldn't he be ok?"

Eva walked over to Willow and hugged her. Willow didn't exactly know what to do. She was not used to anyone hugging her. "What you gushin' all over me for Eva?"

"'Cause when I left here Willow my Dewey didn't look like he was goin' to make it. Now look at him. Thank you so much Willow. I owe you more than I could ever repay you."

"Oh stop it. All I did was rub some Elder oil with six drops of spirits of wine on Dewey's head. Took the swellin' down and helped with the pain. It's one of my daddy's old mountain cures he used on our animals when they got hurt. We still got some more doctorin' to do though. He's in and out of it but he's goin' to be fine."

Eva looked at Willow with a questionable look upon her face. "Willow, that person that was on the kitchen floor, where is he?"

"Well . . . you two come over here, don't want the boy to hear. Did you see that big tater sack outside?" Willow asked.

Sady said, "yeah, Willow, I did notice it when me and Eva walked in. Why?"

"That sack ain't got no taters in it. It's you know who."

Eva looked startled. "Willow, is Roby in that sack?"

"Yes ma'am, he sure is."

Sady just had to ask Willow one more question. "Willow, how did you get him in there?"

"Sady, it weren't the easiest thing I ever done, and it weren't the hardest either. I went out to the barn and got a saw. I had to saw most of his parts to fit in the sack. I lined it with some old plastic I found, cleaned the blood off the floor, and tied the sack up. It's easier to move him that way. There's no blood trail."

Eva grabbed a bucket, threw up in it, and ran outside for some air. Sady went out to see if she was ok and brought her back inside the house.

Eva's face was white. She started to cry again while talking to Willow. "Willow, I was gonna' turn myself in to the Sheriff. Now I'll hang for sure when they see his body like that."

Willow shook her head and said, "now Eva, there ain't no way that Sheriff we got is goin' to believe anything you tell him. Do you really think you would get a fair trial? Probably be all men on the jury, and half of them likely beat their women like Roby did you. Maybe they wouldn't hang you, but you would be in jail the rest of your life. Is that what you want?"

"She's right Eva. But Willow – what do we do now?" Sady asked.

"Well I knowed Roby smoked a lot. You could say he got drunk and burned the barn down. But there wouldn't be any body to be found. The way I figure, the best way to deal with this and get rid of all the blood that I can't wipe up is to tell the Sheriff he got drunk, beat on you and Dewey real bad, then he went to the barn to drink some more. You and Dewey ran to Sady's house to get away from him. Can't say Dewey ran. He is hurt too bad. We'll think of somethin'. You can tell the Sheriff when Roby got back he figured Sady talked you into callin' the Sheriff on him this time. He got scared that he might get locked up, burned the house down, and took off and run away."

"But Willow, I can't let you burn my house down, it's all me and Dewey got."

Sady seemed quite surprised at Eva. "Wait a minute Eva. Don't include Dewey in on this. He is livin' with me now and he is happy. What kind of memories do you and Dewey have here? Beatins', molestin', ain't nothin' but evil been in this house for years. I got a big house. You and Dewey can move in with me. You're gonna' have to concentrate on what tomorrow is going to bring. Don't look back on all the evil he did to you. You can sell this property later and find yourself a little home of your own if you want."

Eva said, "Willow, Sady, what am I gonna' tell Dewey when he starts to remember? His ma killed his father. How is he goin' to live with that? How am I supposed to live with that?"

Sady raised her voice for the first time to Eva. "Stop! Listen to you. I told you if it weren't him bein' killed tonight, it would have been both you and Dewey. Did you think Roby would have a change of heart while he had his hands around your neck squeezin' the life out of you? No! Why can't you see that? Dewey ain't deaf, dumb, and blind. I talked to Dewey. He was just about ready to kill Roby himself if he would have caught him beatin' you again. You know that Eva. Nobody is ever goin' to know what happened here. Would you rather Dewey had killed him. Could you live knowin' your son was either goin' to be hanged or rot in jail the rest of his life for killin' an evil man like Roby?"

"I'm sorry Sady. You're right. I guess I got to live with this the rest of my life," Eva said hanging her head.

Willow added to the conversation. "Did you hear what you just said woman – "the rest of my life." You and Dewey have a chance to have a life to live now. If you didn't put that knife in his heart, you would be lyin' on this floor instead of him."

Eva finally made her mind up and said, "ok ladies, you're both right. Sady, me and Dewey, we won't be no trouble to you. We'll do our part around the farm to earn our keep. I just got to know one thing Willow. What are you gonna' do with that sack of manure outside the door in that tater sack?"

For the first time, they all laughed.

Willow told them her plan. "You two put Dewey in the truck and head for Sady's house. It's about 10:30 now. I got this sled out of your barn Eva. I'll put that tater sack on it and take it up on Blackheart Mountain. There is a big hole about a mile down in the ground. Used to be an old mine, but nobody knows about it 'cept me. I'll toss the tater sack down the hole. That is as close to Hell as I can get him. The Good Lord has to do his part and take him further on down to Hell! Sady, you call the Sheriff when you get home. Tell him Eva wants Roby arrested for beatin' her and Dewey real bad. He won't do nothin' tonight 'cause of this weather. I'll come back down the mountain about 2 or 3 in the mornin' and light this place up like the fourth of July!"

Eva with a questionable look at Willow said, "won't the Sheriff wonder what happened to Roby?"

Willow answered her. "Eva, don't worry about anything. He'll just think Roby ran off. This is the first time you ever wanted the Sheriff to arrest him for beatin' you and Dewey. The Sheriff will think Roby got mad, burned the house down and took off runnin' for the hills. We all just got to stick to the story. You did nothin' wrong. Get that in your head. Roby deserved what happened to him tonight."

Eva said, "I don't want to know any more Willow. You just do what you got to do. Sady, I wanna' get a few things and put them in the truck before we leave."

"Sady, you and Eva better hurry. You don't want to get stuck in this snowstorm. Me and Wolfe are gonna' take care of everything. Don't neither of you fret over this. Satan and all his evil works are gonna' be outta' this house once I light these matches. Eva take that bloody dress off and give me Roby's coat and boots. I'll throw all of them on the fire too. Now you two get Dewey and get gone."

Concerned about Willow, Sady had a few words for her before they left. "Willow, you be careful. Are you sure you don't need me to help pull that sled up the mountain? You come by the house as soon as you can to let me know you're ok. Promise me!"

"Sady, promise I'll be ok. I got a lot to do. This snow storm ain't goin' to let up 'til tomorrow sometime. At least all the footprints and sled tracks will be covered up with snow. Now you three get gone."

Eva hugged Willow again. "Bye Willow. You take care, and I mean it.

Eva and Sady carried Dewey out to the truck. The truck had no problem starting this time.

Sady was worried about Willow, but she knew Willow could take care of herself.

As for Eva; she felt she was having a nightmare and maybe when the sun came up in the morning, that's exactly what it hopefully, would be— a nightmare. But Eva knew it was no nightmare. It was real. She could tell this by her swollen face when she touched it and the ache in the rest of her bruised body.

chapter 12

ON THE WAY to Sady's house the wind shifted and the snow drifted away from the road and more into the mountainside. This made the drive to Sady's a lot less treacherous than it was going to Eva's house.

Sady couldn't help but be worried about Willow. "I wish Willow would have let me help her. She's really gettin' up in age. I worry about her. She's not as tough as she used to be."

"Sady," Eva said, "Willow can handle anything that comes her way. She is still tough. You two, you're kind of alike."

"What do you mean, we're alike?" Sady asked.

"I mean, I admire both of you. You both are not afraid to face horrible people like Roby. You're both headstrong and determined. Wish I had just a little bit of that in me," Eva said.

"Eva, you got more than a little bit of that in you. I ain't ever had somebody tryin' to kill me. You didn't know if he was gonna' knock that knife out of your hand or not. It took courage to pick it up and try to save not only your life, but Dewey's life too. I don't know what I would have done in that situation."

Eva pulled some postcards out of her pocket to show Sady. "Sady, these are some postcards and a picture of Becky that she sent me from Maryland. I was goin' to show them to Dewey so that he could give them to you when Roby walked in."

Sady, excited, stopped the truck to look at the postcards and the picture.

"Eva, all these cards are postmarked Baltimore. Here is a picture of Becky. She is standin' in front of a street sign. I believe it reads East Baltimore Street. Do you think this is where they're goin' Eva?"

"Sady, I don't know. Maybe this is where that Leroy lives. At least it is a start."

Sady put the truck in gear and started driving again.

"Eva, I'm goin' to Maryland. I'm gonna' find Grace if I have to look in every corner in Baltimore. We both need Grace, and when Eddie comes home, I know he's gonna' need her."

"But Sady, you're not used to the city. Those streets are dangerous. You can't go by yourself. Why don't you let me go with you?"

"No, no. Dewey needs you, 'specially now. I wouldn't tell Dewey how Roby died. Just tell Dewey, by the grace of God, you managed to get to my house. He really can't remember anything, and tell him you don't know where Roby went. He'll find out about the fire in a few days when he is fully conscious. Nobody has to know about tonight but you, Willow and me."

"Sady, I have no intention after tonight of ever mentionin' what happened."

"Good. I'm leavin' day after tomorrow, soon as I can get to the bus station. The Sheriff ain't goin' to do nothin' for me. You know that. Grace ain't his grandbaby, she's ours. Do you mind takin' care of the farm 'til I get back? I don't know how long it's goin' to take. I might not be home for Thanksgivin'."

"Do I mind? Sady, after what you're doin' for me and Dewey, if I can't do that little bit for you, then I'm a sorry excuse for a woman and a friend. Don't you worry about anything. Just, if you can, give us a call and let us know if you're ok."

"Thanks Eva. Well we're here. Let's get Dewey in and to bed. I'll make that phone call to the Sheriff."

Sady and Eva carried Dewey in and went upstairs to put him to bed. While Eva stayed upstairs to tend to Dewey, Sady came down to make her phone call to the Sheriff.

Sady dialed Leanne, the telephone switchboard operator. "Leanne, please dial 52 for Sheriff Hardin's office. No, everything is not ok Leanne. I need to get a hold of the Sheriff. I have Eva and Dewey Prestel here stayin' with me. Seems Roby beat them both real bad tonight, almost killed Dewey. If you have to ring him at home, I don't care. Thank you."

Sheriff Hardin picked up the phone at home. "What's the problem now Sady?"

"I don't have a problem Sheriff. Seems like Roby is up to his old tricks again. He beat Eva and Dewey pretty bad this time. I finally talked Eva into havin' Roby arrested. Eva and Dewey just about made it to my house. Eva had to pull Dewey on an old sled because he couldn't walk. He was in and out of consciousness. They are stayin' with me for a while. Eva is afraid Roby will kill them if they go back. You have to help them."

"It's too bad out tonight to go over there to arrest Roby. I'm gonna' have to talk to Eva first anyway. She's the one that has to sign the papers. I'll be over first thing in the mornin' if this snowstorm slows down. He's probably still drunk. I don't think you'll have any problems with him botherin' you tonight. If he does come over, you got your rifle. Do what you have to do. Good night."

"Good night Sheriff."

Eva came down from tending to Dewey and Sady reassured Eva everything would be ok.

"Eva, I told Sheriff Hardin that Roby beat you and Dewey. I told him you had to pull Dewey on an old sled you had because he was in and out of consciousness, and you are stayin' with me. So, you need to remember that. There is an old sled out in my barn in case he wants to see it. I also told him you want to press charges. He'll be here in the mornin'. You need to tell him the same thing that I did. The Sheriff was here the day before when Dewey told him he was goin' to see you; the day Becky took Grace. There is no need for Dewey to talk to him tomorrow. He really doesn't remember anything after he hit his head. The Sheriff can look at him and tell he was hurt bad."

"I hope he doesn't insist on talkin' to him Sady. Dewey might tell him he remembers seein' Willow or even you at my house."

"Well, I hope he doesn't say anything. If he does, we will just have to say he was havin' hallucinations."

"Don't you worry none Sady. I made my mind up to be strong like you about this. You are right. I had no other choice. I did nothin' wrong. If I tell the truth, I'll go to jail. I'm not leavin' Dewey. He needs me and I need him. There's no reason for him to know the in-between's. You, me, Willow and God knows what happened. I'm startin' over tomorrow Sady. You are givin' me and Dewey a new chance to start a new life

Mary Wagner

and that's just what I'm goin' to do. Thank you so much for givin' me a chance to change the rest of my life." Eva hugged Sady.

"Eva, you earned every bit of that right. You gave yourself a chance to start over, not me. That took courage Eva. Now let's go upstairs and get some sleep."

chapter 13

IT WAS ABOUT 4 o'clock in the morning when Sady's phone rang. It was Sheriff Hardin.

"Sady, is Eva there? I need to talk to her right away!"

"I'll go and wake her up Sheriff. What happened? Did you find Roby and arrest him?"

"Sady, I'd rather talk to Eva. No, I didn't find Roby. Seems you were right about him. He must have gotten mad at Eva leavin' and burned the house down early this mornin'. One of the neighbors high up on the ridge called me early, right after he smelled the smoke. I figured the fire started about 3 this mornin'."

"Oh no, Sheriff, why would he do that. I'll go get Eva."

Sady ran upstairs, woke Eva and told her what the Sheriff said. "Don't forget Eva, stick to the story!"

Eva picked up the phone. "Sheriff Hardin, Sady told me what happened. I really want Roby arrested for what he did to me and Dewey and for burnin' my house down. That house is all we had left."

"Don't you worry about that Eva. Once we pick him up and lock him up in jail, he'll never taste another drop of his precious moonshine or put a hand on you and Dewey."

"Thank you Sheriff. Then I don't have to fill out any paperwork?"

"Oh no, not now. Not after he burned your house down. Do you have any idea where he went?"

Eva glanced at Sady and rolled her eyes. "Well Sheriff, he always talked about some kind of cousin he had in Kentucky. Said this cousin could get him a job minin'. Where at in Kentucky, I don't know."

"Well, I don't know anybody of authority in Kentucky. We really don't know what part of Kentucky he went to. I'll just alert authorities here in North Carolina to be on the look out for him. You just be careful. A crazy person like him is bound to do whatever his crazy mind tells him to do. You and Dewey take care now."

"Thank you Sheriff for lettin' me know about the fire. Bye now."

Sady smiled at Eva. "You did real good Eva. What Guy or rather Sheriff Hardin don't know won't hurt us. I really don't care about him."

"Sady today is Sunday. I don't know about you, but I can't go to church today."

"Eva, I'm sure there won't be any service at church this mornin'. The weather is way too bad for anybody to even think about bein' on the road."

"Sady, I don't know if I will ever go to church again even in good weather."

"Eva, I thought we talked about this yesterday. You better start gettin' tough-skinned about what happened. Murderin' ain't right, but that was your only choice and God knows that. Why can't you accept that? God was there with you. That knife was left in that sink for a reason. He didn't want you to die Eva. You have a good heart and God wanted you to survive that night. Evil had to die that night, and it did. Now let's get back to bed and try to get some sleep."

Morning came, and the snow let up quite a bit. Sady was making breakfast when Eva came downstairs.

"Sady, Mr. Tibbits just pulled up in the driveway."

"Eva, I hope everything is alright with him and Lena. Come on in Henry. It's too cold for you to be out in this bad weather. Is everything ok?

"Everything is just fine Sady. Miss Eva, me and Lena heard about the fire. We're real sorry. Lena wanted me to bring some of Thomas' clothes for Dewey and a few things for you. If there is anything we can do for you and Dewey, you just give us a holler."

Eva said, "Thank you so much Henry. Please thank Lena for me. That was such a thoughtful thing to do. You shouldn't have come out in this bad weather."

"Miss Eva, I been out in a lot worse snowstorms then this one."

Sady said, "Henry, I have a favor to ask you."

"Sady, you can ask me for anything. You know that."

"I need someone to take me to the bus station in Boone tomorrow. I made my mind up to go to Baltimore to look for Grace. Would you mind droppin' me off?"

"Of course not. I'll be by tomorrow mornin' to pick you up. But Sady, maybe you shouldn't go there alone. That's a big city that you don't know nothin' about."

"Henry thanks for the concern, but I'll be fine. My daddy taught me how to face danger when I'm confronted by it. But I do have one more favor Henry. Roby beat Dewey pretty bad. He has a head injury. While I'm gone, do you mind takin' care of gradin' the 'baker. I don't know when I'll be back. And in case I am back by Thanksgivin', you and Lena are invited over here for dinner."

"Yes ma'am I surely will take care of the 'baker. I'll look in on Miss Eva and make sure Dewey is healin' up. Don't you worry about anything? And yes-sir-re, we'll be here for Thanksgivin'. It gets kind of lonely just me and Lena on these holidays without our Thomas. Lena can bake some of her special apple and pumpkin pies. You tell Dewey to let me know when he's feelin' better so we can go up on Blackheart Mountain and shoot a big turkey for Thanksgivin'."

Eva said, "Henry I hope Sady will be back for Thanksgivin', but if she's not, you and the Mrs. still come over here for dinner."

"I most certainly will. I'll see you tomorrow mornin' Sady."

"Bye now Henry. Say hello to Lena."

After breakfast, Eva went upstairs. When she came back down she handed Sady some money. "I want you to take this money for your trip. Every time Roby got drunk, I took a few cents here and there. He would have killed me if he caught me. It's about two-hundred dollars. You're goin' to need some money for a hotel or somethin'. Please take it."

"Eva, there ain't no way I'm takin' your money. I'll be fine. You keep that money for you and Dewey's future."

"I know I'm not goin' to convince you to take it. But this money is here any time you need it."

"Eva, I appreciate the offer. But there is one thing you can do for me while I'm gone."

"Anything Sady. Just ask."

Mary Wagner

"Well, I know Willow is hard to get a hold of, but if this weather clears up a little, do you think you could go halfway up Blackheart Mountain and call her name. She has good hearin' and so does Wolfe. I just want to make sure she is ok."

"I sure will do that Sady. I'll even get Mr. Tibbits to climb a little further with me when I go. Don't you worry about that?"

"If you do talk to her, tell her that she is also invited over for Thanksgivin' dinner. And tell her to bring Wolfe."

"I'll do just that Sady."

"Well, Eva, guess I'll go up and pack a few things. Tomorrow will be here before I know it. Maybe, just maybe, I'll be bringin' Grace home soon."

chapter 14

SUNDAY WAS FINALLY over and there was Monday staring Sady in the face. The snow had stopped and the sun peeked out of the clouds. Sady thought to herself, "maybe the sun is tryin' to tell me that today is a new day and to think positive. Maybe there will even be some laughter back on this old farm again. Eva and Dewey have a new start, a new life ahead of them. Maybe my little Grace will be comin' back with me."

Just then Henry Tibbits pulled up in his truck to pick up Sady. "Eva, Mr. Tibbits is here. Now you take care and I hope Dewey starts feelin' better."

Eva ran down the steps and hugged Sady. "Sady please take care of yourself. Please call us and let us know you got there. I owe you so much Sady. I wasn't much of a friend. I was jealous of you, because you were the woman I always wanted to be. I hope you can forgive me for not bein' that friend that I should have been. Just take care."

"Eva, you always were the woman that I am. We just got dealt a different hand in our lives. I got the good guy and you got Roby. You've got a new chance now and I just know you're goin' to be that same woman but surrounded by people who love you and that is what is goin' to make a difference in your life. Take care of yourself and Dewey, and don't forget to check on Willow. Bye Eva."

"Bye Sady and good luck!"

When Sady got to the bus terminal in Boone, she started to get a little nervous. The only bus trip she ever made was to Raleigh with her mother to visit an aunt when she was about eight years old. That trip was about three hours by bus. From Boone to Baltimore would be at least fifteen hours or more with stops along the way or even longer. She really didn't know for sure.

Sady thought a lot during the bus trip. There weren't many people on the bus. When the bus stopped in Petersburg, Virginia, a couple of young soldiers got on the bus from the Army base at Camp Lee. Sady couldn't help but to stare at one soldier. He had only one arm. He could have passed for her Eddie. Tears came to her eyes. Sady overheard him talking to the other soldier. He was discharged from the Army and was on his way home to Philadelphia, Pennsylvania.

There was an empty seat across from the soldier. Sady wanted so much to talk to him, so she got her nerve up and sat in that empty seat.

Sady put her hand out to shake the soldier's hand. "I want to thank you for servin' our country."

The young man smiled at her and said, "thank you ma'am. I'm not used to being thanked."

"I appreciate your sacrifice for me, my family, my friends and this country son," Sady said with tear-filled eyes. "You remind me of my son, Eddie. You didn't run into an Eddie Milsap by any chance did you?"

"Sorry ma'am, the name's not familiar. What infantry is he serving with?"

"I know it by heart. He's servin' with the Eighty-Sixth Infantry Division, Company C, 311 Engineerin' Combat Battalion. They call their division the Black Hawks." Sady uttered every word just like the proud mother she was.

"You sure have got that memorized Mrs. Milsap. I know the last time I heard anything about the troops, I did hear the Black Hawks were headed to the Ardennes."

"Oh my, where is that place. And I don't mean to be ignorant; I didn't even ask your name."

"That's ok Mrs. Milsap. Not many people stop to shake the only hand I got left. They act like they're scared to touch me or they might walk away with one arm. My name is Johnny Mehan. And to answer your question, the Ardennes is a forest in Germany. I think it takes in part of Belgium and France."

"Can I ask what happened to you Johnny?"

"Sure. I lost my arm when the tank I was in turned over during a ground fight with the Germans in Poland. I've been on desk work ever since. Finally got discharged and I'm on my way home. I'm surprising my parents. They don't know I'm coming home."

"That is so wonderful. They'll be so happy. Well I'll get back to my seat; we got a long ride ahead of us. I'll let you get some rest. Nice talkin' to you."

"It was my pleasure Mrs. Milsap. I hope your Eddie comes home soon."

"So do I Johnny. Good Luck."

Sady was so sure that just maybe this soldier may have known her Eddie. She was worried about Eddie. She thought, "what if somethin' terrible happened to Eddie? Could I live with it? No, I couldn't. Eva thinks I'm strong, but I'm not when I know my child is hurt or sufferin'."

Sady finally fell asleep. When she woke up, it was dark. The bus stopped for the third rest break. She got a coke to drink with one of the sandwiches Eva packed for the trip. Her body and mind were both tired. The bus driver told her they wouldn't get to the Baltimore bus terminal until about two in the morning.

When she got back on the bus, Sady couldn't go back to sleep. No, she was too nervous. For the next few hours she just counted the signs on the side of the road. She finally saw a sign that said "Baltimore 60 miles".

Sady just fell off to sleep when she heard the bus driver holler, "Baltimore Bus Terminal. All those getting off here wait next to the bus, and I'll get your luggage out of the baggage compartment."

After Sady got her suitcase, she needed to ask the bus driver a question. "Sir, can you tell me how far Baltimore Street is from here?"

"Your best bet would be to hail a cab down. Ma'am, you do not, and I stress DO NOT belong out here alone. Do you know where you want to go?"

"Well, I'm lookin' for somebody and I don't know exactly where to look. I know they might live on or around Baltimore Street."

"Ma'am, I would get off this street tonight, get a hotel, and look for your person tomorrow."

"I appreciate your help, but I have a picture of the person. Maybe somebody might know this person if I show the picture around."

Mary Wagner

"Lady, you do what you want to do, but I'd advise you to get off this street as soon as you can."

"Thank you sir for your advice. I'll try to get a cab to take me to Baltimore Street."

"Do what you got to do lady. Good Luck"

"Thank you."

Sady was overwhelmed. For it being 2 a.m. in the morning, the streets were pretty crowded. Sady's mind was going in circles. Her body hurt from sitting on the bus all that time. She was tired. She didn't know where to go.

This was the first time in Sady's life she had to admit that she was homesick and scared.

chapter 15

SADY DECIDED TO catch a cab to Baltimore Street just like the bus driver told her to do. It wasn't as easy to catch a cab as she thought it would be.

"Sir, over here, over here," Sady said while wildly waving her hand.

Five cabs passed Sady until one actually stopped.

The cab driver rolled his window down. "Where to lady? Come on, I ain't got all day."

"Sir, can you take me to a place called Baltimore Street or it may be called East Baltimore Street?"

The cab dirver stared at Sady for a few seconds. "Lady, you sure that's where you want to go? You sure don't look like you're from this area."

Sady told the cab driver where she was from. "I'm from North Carolina, a little place called Harmony Creek."

The cab driver shook his head. "Oh brother, get in lady. What's the address on East Baltimore Street?"

"Well sir, I don't rightly know. Can you just drop me off there? I'm lookin' for a girl from home that moved here about a year ago. I thought if I showed her picture to some people they might have seen her." Sady showed the picture of Becky to the cab driver. "Can you look at this please? Have you seen her around?"

"Lady, do you know how many girls like her I pick up and drop off. They all look the same after a while. No, I ain't seen her. Maybe you should go back where you came from. This ain't no place for somebody like you to be walking up and down these streets showing a picture to people."

"Sir, just take me where I asked you to take me."

The cab driver drove for only ten minutes. "Here we are lady. That will be fifty cents."

"Fifty cents. I could have walked if I'd known it was this close."

"I'm not trying to be smart lady, but what do you think the odds of you walking here and still be alive when you got here would be? Lady, just pay me. I had enough of complaints today."

Sady gave the cab driver his fifty cents and exited the cab.

"Oh boy, lady, thanks for the tip!"

Sady looked at the cab driver and said, "I'll give you a tip. Try bein' nicer to your passengers, maybe you'll get a real tip."

Sady couldn't believe her eyes when she looked around. The bright lights along with the neon signs seemed like they just about blinded her. Her eyes just got bigger and bigger as she scanned the street. The "Two O'clock Club", the "Gayety Night Club", so many more of these burlesque shows were up and down both sides of the street. There were tattoo parlors, saloons, and other store fronts that showed nude pictures of women. Sady couldn't believe what she was seeing this early in the morning. There weren't these many people on the streets of Harmony during the day for the whole month.

Sady thought to herself, "don't these people ever sleep? And what in the world is a "peep show"?"

There were people of all ages, shapes, sizes, well-dressed and hardly dressed. There were men dressed like women and women dressed like men. It was as if Sady stepped out of one world and stepped into another one.

Sady caught herself amazed and talking out loud. "What would Reverend Marshal have to say about this place?"

Sady knew she had to come out of this trance she was in and start showing Becky's picture around. Most people thought she was a beggar when she approached them and wouldn't even speak to her. The few that did stop and look just shook their heads without saying anything.

One man approached her and grabbed her arm. "What you got in that suitcase pretty lady, some toys we can play with?"

Sady pulled her arm away and told the guy, "touch me again, I'll kick you so hard down below you're gonna' be kissin' your backside goodnight instead of your wife or whoever you go home to."

"That talk don't bother me any baby. I love it when somebody talks dirty to me." The guy then opened up his coat and had nothing on. He was naked.

Sady just looked at him and said, "you're sick, real sick Mr."

Sady ran across the street to get away from the guy. She noticed a lady walking back and forth and stopping different men that passed her. She was scantily dressed as cold as it was, and had loads of make-up on her face. Sady thought she looked like a clown. She was a prostitute. Sady approached the woman to show her a picture of Becky.

Sady said, "Miss, Miss, can I ask you a question?"

The prostitute ignored her and kept walking. Sady got in front of her face with the picture and said, "I know you can hear me. I just want to know if you have seen this girl around here."

The prostitute turned to her and said, "lady get out of my face. Go find your own corner to stand on."

"Why do I want a corner to stand on? I just want you to look at this picture and let me know if you have seen this young girl around here."

The prostitute's voice got a little louder. "No, I ain't seen that girl. Now get out of here or my man is going to come over here and kick you off this corner or do worse. I'm workin' here lady. Now get out!"

Sady looked at her and said, "why is everybody in this town nasty? I ain't leavin' 'till I find somebody who has seen this girl."

The prostitute's pimp spotted Sady and ran across the street to find out what's going on with his woman. "What's gone on Angel Baby? This lady keepin' you from makin' some money for your Daddy?"

"No baby, she's lookin' for somebody. She's leavin' now, right lady?"

Sady being defiant said, "I'm sorry Angel Baby and Daddy, but I ain't goin' nowhere. I'm stayin' here 'till I find somebody who has seen this girl."

The pimp viciously grabbed Sady, slapped her face, and threw her to the ground. He also took the picture of Becky out of her hand and wouldn't give it back. "Oh lady, yes you are gettin' off of this corner. Now scram! Get out of here and don't come back."

No man, her husband or father, nor any other man in Harmony ever grabbed Sady to hit or push her in any way. She was stunned that this stranger just violated her body that way, because she did absolutely nothing to deserve being thrown down so violently.

The worst thing the pimp did wasn't hitting her or throwing her on the street. The pimp kept the only thing that may help Sady find Grace; he kept the picture of Becky and refused to give it back to her. The picture was all she had that may lead her to her granddaughter. No, she wasn't letting this guy get away with this.

The pimp and prostitute just looked down at her on the street and laughed. This made Sady even madder than she ever was. While lying on the street, Sady reached into her purse and pulled out a little derringer gun that her father gave her years ago.

Sady stood up and confronted the pimp with the gun pointed at him. "You're gonna' give me my picture now Mr. Daddy."

The pimp threw the picture down at her feet. "You're one crazy bitch. If you want to live a little longer, I'll give you some advice. Get off the streets. Angel Baby lets go find another corner. You can have this corner lady. Maybe you can make five cents, 'cause that's all you're worth."

After the pimp and prostitute left, Sady put her gun back in her purse. But it was too late. A policeman came running over to her with his gun pointed at her. "Give me that gun lady. I just saw you pull it on those two people."

"That guy hit me, pushed me down and took a picture from me. That's why I drew my gun. I didn't do nothin'." Sady gave him the gun.

"I hear that all night long. I saw you draw the gun on him. Turn around. You're under arrest lady for carrying a firearm and using it." The policeman handcuffed Sady, read her rights, and put her and her suitcase in the patrol car.

"But sir, I didn't do anything wrong. He hurt me. I didn't use the gun."

"Lady, shut up. I don't want to hear another word out of your mouth. You drew the gun with the intent to use it. Don't argue with me, because you're just going to make things worse for yourself."

The police station was right down the street. It surely wasn't a long ride, but it was for Sady. For the second time in the same day, Sady had to admit to herself that she was scared, and alone.

The police station sure wasn't like the little Sheriff's office in Harmony or even the larger one in Boone. No, it looked huge to Sady. The building took up at least a couple of blocks.

Sady was put in a holding cell until morning. She never felt so vulnerable. She felt like she was the turkey at a turkey shoot that Harmony Creek holds three times a year.

All Sady could think of was, "please God, help me. I don't know anybody here. I want to find Grace and go back home. I'm so frightened Lord."

chapter 16

THE HOLDING CELL was in the middle of the precinct. There were two other women in the cell with Sady. Both women were younger than Sady, but their faces looked at least ten to fifteen years older.

Sady tried to strike up a conversation with the youngest woman. "Hi, my name is Sady. Why were you put in here; you're so young to be in here."

"You sure are nosy Sady. My name is Sandy. Really, I'm called Sweet Sandy on the streets. I'm here because I got caught askin' some guy for directions. That's all. Just sweet and simple."

Sady looked puzzled. "That's not right. You didn't do anything to the guy. You only asked for directions."

The other woman let out a loud laugh. "Honey, are you for real. Do you really think she was askin' a guy for directions? Boy, you ain't from around here. Why are you in here? By the way, my name is Shirley."

"I was askin' these two people if they saw this girl in this picture. The man hit me and threw me on the ground and I pulled my little derringer on him."

"You did what?" Sweet Sandy asked Sady.

"I pulled my gun on him because he took my picture from me. A policeman saw me and arrested me. That's why I'm here."

Shirley just stared at Sady. "You know girl, you got 'balls'. I still think if you get out of the charges against you, you better run like hell back home and stay there. Let me see the picture."

Sady showed Shirley the picture.

"You know Sady; I've seen this girl around. She hangs with a guy that treats her like trash. She prostitutes herself for him to get drugs. Did you know that?"

"No I didn't Shirley. Well they came home last week and stole my Granddaughter Grace and brought her back here. That's why I'm here. Have you seen a little girl with them?"

"Sorry Sady, but no," Shirley said. "Is there any way I can get in touch with you, if I get out of here today? If I see her with the little girl, I can let you know. Where are you stayin' Sady?"

"Right now, I've got no place to stay. But I feel so much better knowin' Becky is still stayin' around here. Maybe when the police talk to me, they will help me find her."

Sweet Sandy really felt sorry for Sady. "Look, these cops aren't going to help you Sady to find your granddaughter. This is my address. You can stay with me if you have no place to go until you're ready to go back home or you find your granddaughter. Take it and keep it. My phone number is on the other side."

These two women were the first people to really befriend Sady. For the first time in those early morning hours, she felt like she had a friend, someone to count on in case she needed help.

"I don't know what to say Sweet Sandy. I really didn't think there were any nice people here in this town. I guess I was wrong. I really want to thank you."

Sweet Sandy said, "I mean it Sady. You need help you call me, anytime, day or night."

Sady managed to fall asleep for about two hours. Seven o'clock came and it was time for the day shift to start work at the police station.

Sady watched the faces of the people as they walked by the holding cell. She felt like a criminal when they focused their eyes on her. She didn't realize that she was being stared at because anyone could tell she didn't belong in that holding cell with those two prostitutes.

Detective Alec Karastaupolis, Detective in Charge of the precinct, actually stopped and looked at the three women, but he didn't say a word and continued on to his office.

Shirley couldn't contain herself. She whistled at Alec. "That's what I call a good-lookin' guy. What do ya' say Sweet Sandy?"

"He sure is a handsome hunk of a man even though he's a detective, but he wasn't lookin' at us." Just then both girls looked at Sady.

"What's wrong?" Sady asked.

"What do you mean what's wrong? Didn't you see how that detective looked at you?" Shirley asked.

Sady said, "he looked at all of us. What's the matter with both of you? He's just a man. He probably thought he would scare us if he stared long enough."

Shirley said, "oh yeah, that's what they call it now – tryin' to scare us." Shirley and Sweet Sandy both laughed.

The policeman that brought Sady in happened to still be at head-quarters working overtime. He knocked on Detective Karastaupolis' door.

"Come on in Sam. What's on the docket today?" Alec said.

"Well sir, I think we got a real loony tune out there in that holding cell."

Alec laughed. "So Sam, what's so different about last night com-pared to all the other nights we filled the cell with loony tunes?"

"Sir, I know you saw the woman in the middle of our regular cus-tomers – Shirley and Sweet Sandy."

Alec smiled. "You're talking about the attractive one in the middle with her hair in a bun, no make-up, boots, pea coat and bobby socks? She sure is a dead give away for a prostitute, Sam."

Alec just shook his head. "What's the matter Sam? It must not have been a busy night for you guys. You must be getting desperate to make quotas for your arrests."

"Don't let her looks fool you Boss. She was fighting with a pimp and pulled this little derringer on him. I brought her in here for her own protection. She had a suitcase with her, so I put it in Lockup. She said she just got off the bus from North Carolina. She's a real wildcat!"

Alec looked at the derringer and shook his head. "If she would have shot him, the gun doesn't look like it has enough force for a bullet to even penetrate a big guy's body. Look how old it is. Go get little Miss North Carolina and bring her in here so we can get to the bottom of this. And Sam - go home. You look tired. Joe will be in soon. I'll get him to follow up on this case and close it out."

"Ok Boss. I'll go get the broad, I mean lady, and bring her in here."

Alec stopped Sam for a minute. "Sam, there are no bullets in the gun. Did you remove them?"

"No sir, I didn't. I searched the lady's coat pockets. There weren't any bullets in her coat either."

Alec said, "that's really interesting. She's going to have an awful lot of explaining to do."

Sam brought Sady in and she reluctantly sat in a chair.

Alec put his hand out to shake Sady's hand, but she wouldn't shake his hand.

Alec picked up Sady's folder and said, "Mrs. Sady Milsap, I'm Detective Alec Karastaupolis of the Baltimore City Police Department. I was told that you were in a confrontation with two people on East Baltimore Street early this morning and pulled a gun on a man. You can't pull a gun on another citizen Mrs. Milsap. That is against the law."

Sady spoke up and said, "yeah, but that was after he slapped me and threw me on the street and wouldn't give me back a picture that I was holdin'. I never would have used the gun. There ain't even any bullets in it if you look. I just wanted to scare him for what he did to me."

Alec slammed Sady's folder down on his desk and glared at her.

"No bullets. That makes things even better. What if he would have pulled a gun on you? And, Mrs. Milsap, criminals in this neighborhood make sure they put their bullets in their guns. This isn't the Wild West and you're not Annie Oakley. If it were the other way around, your body would be on a train tomorrow heading back home to your husband and family. I assume you have family back in North Carolina."

Sady lowered her head and her voice. "My husband and one son died about five years ago in a truck wreck."

"I'm sorry to hear that Mrs. Milsap. You said one son died. Do you have more children?"

"Yes sir I do. I have one son in the Army fightin' in Germany."

"You wouldn't want your only son to bury his mother, would you? He already lost his father and brother. Why are you here anyway Mrs. Milsap?"

"While my son Eddie has been overseas in one battle after another with the Germans, I've been taken care of his little girl, my Granddaughter, Grace. I've had her since she was a baby. Her mother Becky Prestel – the one in this picture, ran off and left Grace. Over a year later, last week to be exact, she came back into town with this guy named Leroy Crager and steals her from Mrs. Tibbits who had been watching her for me. There was a picture of Becky standin' under a street sign that said East Baltimore Street that she sent to her mother, Eva. I thought maybe I could find her if I showed the picture around. I'm sure you know the rest of the story."

"Why was your granddaughter with this Mrs. Tibbits? Why weren't you watching her?"

"I raise 'backer for a livin' and Mrs. Tibbits husband, Henry, and Becky's brother, Dewey were helpin' me hang it in the barn."

"I'm sorry, Mrs. Milsap, but what is 'backer?"

"You know, 'backer — those cigarettes you got on your desk."

Alec finally understood what Sady was talking about. "You mean tobacco I get it now. It has to be hung and cured then graded. I'm not making fun of your speech. It's just a North – South thing."

Sady continued with her story. "That's how I make my livin'. I have a few people helpin' me. Mrs. Lena Tibbits watches Grace for me. That day she went into Boone. Becky saw her, knocked Mrs. Tibbits down, and took Grace and rode off in an old car with that Leroy."

"I'm sorry to hear that Mrs. Milsap, but don't most of the smaller towns in your area have a Sheriff to take care of those type of matters? I'm sure the Sheriff is quite capable of going after this Becky and Leroy and arresting them for assaulting Mrs. Tibbits. That should have taken place right away. Those two people would be locked up by now and you would have your granddaughter back."

"You don't understand. Mrs. Tibbits is colored. If it was the Sheriff's wife that got assaulted, I wouldn't be here right now. Like you said earlier sir, it's a North – South thing."

"You don't have to get smart about it Mrs. Milsap. I get the picture about what happened."

"I'm not tryin' to be smart. All I want is my granddaughter back before somethin' terrible happens to her."

Alec put his hand out. "Let me see the picture you have. I see she's under the East Baltimore Street sign, but that doesn't necessarily mean she lives on that street. If this Becky Prestel is Grace's mother, she has every legal right to have her daughter unless you were given complete custody. Were you?"

"Look, Mr. Kara . . ."

"Karastaupolis."

Sady continued. "You sound just like the Sheriff. No, I don't have any papers. As soon as I get Grace back and go back home, I'll take care of that. Everything happened so fast. Becky ran away and Eddie was away overseas fightin' a war with the Germans. All I know is Becky is on somethin' and one of the ladies in the cell with me told me that she has seen Becky. She also said that the guy that is with her makes her do prostitution for drugs. When I talked to Becky a few days ago, I could tell she was different. She was shakin' all over. I don't know nothin' about takin' drugs, but I could see she was on somethin'. I need to get Grace back before anything bad happens to her. If you don't want to look for her, I am."

"And what do you intend to do when you find her? Like I told you earlier, you can't take the law into your own hands, not here in my jurisdiction."

Alec picked up his phone. "Joe, can you come in here for a minute?"

Joe came into the office. "What do you need Boss?"

Alec said, "Can you go look in the files Joe for a Leroy Crager, and see if he has a record."

"Sure Boss, right away."

Alec looked at Sady. "Mrs. Milsap, tell you what I'm going to do. I'm going to forget about you pulling a gun on that guy. If I find out this Leroy Crager has any violations or warrants out, we'll pick him up. More than likely his girlfriend Becky will be with him. I want you to go back to the bus station tomorrow morning, get back on the bus and go back to wherever you came from. Let me do my job. We will take care of finding your granddaughter. By the way where in North Carolina do you live?"

"Harmony Creek, Harmony Creek is where I live, right outside of Boone. But I came all this way, and I ain't goin' back without my Grace!"

Alec tried to explain what he intended to do to Sady. "If what you're telling me is true, Grace will be taken away from this Becky. I have your telephone number. You will get a call and someone from Child Services will personally bring her to you via bus or train. Do you understand?"

Sady was visibly angry. "No I don't understand Sir. You don't think what I'm tellin' you is the truth? What reason would I have to come all this way and then lie? That little girl is part of my flesh and blood. Do you have any grandbabies?"

"Sorry to say, no, I have no grandchildren. I also know how you are feeling about all of this. I didn't call you a liar. We do our job very well here in Baltimore City. I need you to understand that if this child is in any danger, we will do everything in our power to take her from these people and see that you get her back. We don't need to worry about you running around this city getting into trouble, or worse, being hurt by them or someone else."

Sady gave Alec a stern look and was very abrupt with him. "I would like my gun back please. My daddy gave it to me years ago."

"Mrs. Milsap, you'll get the gun back tomorrow when I meet you at the bus station. I'll bring it personally. Would you like a police car to take you to a hotel close to the bus station? I presume you will be staying at a hotel tonight."

Sady sharply addressed Alec. "Of course I'm goin' to be stayin' at a hotel, and I can walk. I don't need a police car to take me there. Just give me my suitcase please."

Alec picked his phone again. "Joe, please get Mrs. Milsap's suitcase. She is leaving my office now. Then bring in any information you found on that Crager guy."

Sady opened the door to leave Alec's office. "You've got all my information. I'll be expectin' a phone call from you after I get home."

"Mrs. Milsap, please trust me. I won't give up until I find your granddaughter. I promise I will keep in touch with you."

Sady turned to face Alec one more time. "Well, I sure hope you're a man of your word and keep that promise!"

Sady slammed the door and walked out.

chapter 17

JOE CAME BACK into Alec's office with a folder and laid it on his desk.

Joe explained to Alec what he found out about Leroy. "Boss, that guy Leroy Crager is a bad ass. Look at the arrests for possession of heroin, burglary, car theft, one assault after another. He almost killed his last girlfriend a few years ago. Wonder if this new girl knows about it? Boss, did you hear what I said?"

Alec is watching Sady walk away from the police station. He was almost in a trance as he watched her walk down the street.

"Boss."

"I heard you Joe. I was thinking about that little lady. She came all this way by herself to find her granddaughter not knowing anything about Baltimore or for that matter Maryland. I don't think she has ever been out of her little town – Harmony Creek is what she called it. It takes courage to take on something big like this by yourself. I'm really going to try and find her granddaughter. If the little girl is with that creep, no telling what's going to happen to her."

Joe gave Alec a light tap on the back. "And she sure is a looker, Boss!"

"Ok, Joe, time to get back to work. And Joe, I'm leaving in about an hour. I'm going to that bus station just to nose around. She has to go there today to get her ticket to go back home tomorrow. I'll see if anybody made any reservations for Boone, North Carolina for tomorrow morning, then I'm going to ride around the city in case I spot Mrs. Milsap. I have a feeling that she might have other plans. And Joe, you forgot your cigarettes, you left them on my desk."

Mary Wagner

"Ok Boss, thanks, I'm lost without my cigs'. I'll meet up with you later for lunch."

Sady had no idea which way to go once she left the police station. Her head was filled with terrible thoughts about what could be happening to Grace right now. She had no idea where the bus station was, and she definitely had no plans on getting on the bus and going back home like Detective Karastaupolis told her to do. Nobody, but nobody was going to tell her to leave Baltimore, not until she had Grace back in her arms.

Just when Sady felt her lowest that day, she remembered that Sweet Sandy gave her a phone number and address of her apartment. Sady found a phone booth, put a nickel in, and dialed the number.

A man answered. "Hello, hello, who is this?"

Sady almost hung up the phone. "Is Sweet Sandy there?" Sady asked.

"No, she ain't, and who wants to know?"

Sady said, "I'm sorry sir. Would you just tell her Sady called?"

The man replied, "maybe I will and maybe I won't. I never heard her talk about anybody named Sady."

Sady just wanted to end the conversation and hung up the phone.

Sady thought to herself. "Boy he sounded like a nasty person, and she seemed so kind."

There was a bench in between two small trees. Sady was so tired she sat down to rest and think. Before she knew it she was nodding her head and could hardly keep her eyes open. She knew enough to keep her hand wrapped around her suitcase handle and her purse strap around her head and shoulder.

Sady was awakened by tugging on her suitcase. Before she knew it the suitcase was in the hands of two guys running down the street and she was chasing after them. The two men turned down a side street and Sady chased after them. The side street was one way. She was trapped. There was no way out. She tried to run back out but one of the men got behind her.

The second man taunted Sady. "Must be somethin' good in this suitcase lady. You can have it back if you do me and my buddy a favor."

Sady not wanting them to know how fearful she was, put her hand in her pocket and said, "the only favor I'm goin' to do for you and your stupid friend is to just shoot one of ya' and let the other one run before I pull the trigger on him."

82

"Lady, who do you think you're dealin' with, two of the Three Stooges? Take your hand out of your pocket because you ain't got no gun."

Sady knew this was it. All she could think was, "I'll fight 'til I can't fight anymore."

Just then heads turned because of the sound of spinning tires heading towards them. It was Detective Karastaupolis in the car. He jumped out, pulled his gun on the men and told Sady to get in the car. He had seen Sady running after the men, but he was going the opposite way. He made the turn and radioed in for a squad car to meet him on the street where Sady ran down.

The two men were taken away by another squad car. Alec picked up Sady's suitcase and headed towards his car. Sady grabbed her suitcase from Alec and started walking away.

Alec hollered at Sady. "You're welcome."

Sady shouted back. "Ok, thank you. Thank you for doin' your job."

Alec was really mad and got in front of her and stopped her from going any further. "I should lock you up, but I can't lock a person up because they are bull-headed."

Sady said. "Lock me up. Put me in jail, I don't care. I don't care anymore!"

"I told you to get a bus ticket for tomorrow then go to a hotel," Alec said.

Sady looked straight at him and said, "I don't have a lot of money to stay in one of these high-priced hotels, and I'm NOT leavin' town. I told you that."

Alec said, "Just get in the car Mrs. Milsap."

"Fine with me, I don't mind stayin' in jail. At least it will be warm and I'll get somethin' to eat."

"I'm not taking you to jail Mrs. Milsap. I had a feeling you would be wondering the streets of Baltimore, so I made a phone call to a friend before I left to find you. Please, just get in the car."

Sady hesitated for a minute. She felt things just couldn't get any worse. So she got in the car.

Alec said, "I'm going to take you some place safe. So don't fight me on this Mrs. Milsap. You can't wonder around on the streets all day and night. You see what almost happened to you."

"If you would have givin' me my gun back, I could have taken care of that situation in the alley. But no, you wouldn't give it back to me. I can take care of myself. Can't you understand that? I'm wastin' my time by not lookin' every breathin' minute for Becky and Grace. If I find Becky, I'll find Grace."

Alec had enough of Sady and her stubborn streak. "What's the matter with you? Those two men were probably going to rape you then murder you right in the alley. I hope you don't think they just wanted your suitcase and maybe your purse. Hopefully, you're not that gullible. By luck I saw you run into that alley."

"Thank you, Mr. Detective. I see you had your gun. That's what stopped them. All I needed was mine!"

"You know, you have a mind as thick as that building over there. You think you're so tough. Maybe you are back in that little hick town you come from, but here you're just another target for rapists or thieves to prey on. I ought to take you to the morgue. I'll show you some women tougher than you could ever think you could be with their throats slashed," Alec said with anger in his voice.

"I don't come from a little hick town and I don't appreciate you callin' my home place a 'hick town'. And you have no idea how tough I am and what I have been through in my little 'hick town'. So don't go judge me – you don't know me!" Sady said.

Alec put his hand out for Sady to shake hands. "Truce, come on Mrs. Milsap. If we're going to be working together, we're going to have to get along. How about it?"

Alec noticed a slight little smile from Sady. "Ok Mr. Kara . . . Sorry, I just can't pronounce your last name."

Alec smiled back at Sady. "Tell you what, you can call me Alec."

"Sounds good to me Alec. You can call me Sady."

"If it's ok with you Sady, I've made arrangements for you to stay with a very good friend of mine. But it's up to you. I trust this person with my life. And there is no hotel bill to pay. What do you say? This way I don't have to worry about you running around the city and getting into trouble that maybe I can't get you out of."

Sady said, "right now I'm dead tired and I want a place to sleep tonight. If you trust this person with your life, then I have to really trust you that my life will be just as safe. But I do want to pay my own way."

"We will talk about that when we get there," Alec said.

"I'll let you know right now Alec, tomorrow mornin' I'm goin' back out on the street again showin' my picture of Becky to people. You can arrest me if you want. I don't care."

"I'll make a deal with you Sady. You wait for me tomorrow morning. I'll pick you up about 9 o'clock. We'll get some breakfast, and we'll both go out looking for Becky and Grace. Deal?"

Sady delayed her response for a few seconds. "Umm, deal. I guess it would be better if you went along, since you know your way around this city and havin' a badge sure don't hurt none."

"Oh, well thanks for giving me that much credit. That's the smartest move you have made since you got off that bus. I also want to be up front with you Sady. I found out that Leroy Crager is not a very nice person. I've got my team out on the streets showing his picture and talking to their informants and other people on the street. If you don't mind, I'd like to take that picture of Becky and have our photographer make several pictures of her to also show around. That is if you trust me with it."

"I guess I'm just goin' to have to trust you Alec. Sure, take the picture and do what you have to do. I'll take all the help I can get."

chapter 18

ALEC DROVE TO the place that he told Sady that she could stay and be safe. "This is it Sady, we're here."

Sady's eyes are wider than marbles. "Glory be, this is your friend's house? It's beautiful. I've never seen any house this big or this gorgeous."

Alec opened the car door and went around to Sady's door to open it for her.

Sady couldn't help but to think how mannerly Alec was. Jack used to open the door for Sady whenever they went to town or church. Not many men in Harmony Creek treated their wives with any respect. Alec did remind Sady of her Jack in a lot of little ways. Alec was very handsome. Jack was handsome also but more of a rugged handsome. Jack was kind and caring. Alec also had that same quality. He did seem like he cared about Sady and her problem and was willing to help her.

This house is called a rectory Sady. The church that is hooked on to the rectory is called "Our Lady of the Rosary". It's a Catholic Church. The building behind it is a small mission dedicated to helping the homeless and abused women. There are about ten small rooms just for abused women to help them get back on their feet again. The mission is run by the Sisters of the church."

"I wish we had a mission in Harmony Creek for abused women."

"Why Sady, I wouldn't think in a small town that there would be a lot of abused women."

"You've got to be kiddin'. It's just a big well-kept secret. The women are too scared to tell on their men-folk. I have a two good friends, Eva and her son Dewey, livin' with me now. They were abused

Mary Wagner

by Roby, her husband, all of their lives. As a matter of fact he is also Becky's father and he had molested her since she was a child."

"I'm sorry to hear that Sady. Maybe that is half of Becky's problem. Sounds like Becky has a scar on her for life because of that bully of an ass. Sorry, but it's men like this Roby that abuse their wife and children and molest their daughters that don't deserve to walk on this Earth. He has ruined her life. She'll always be drawn to men like him because she feels that she is worthless. She doesn't know how to be respected and treated by a good man. She is going to need a lot of help mentally once we find her and get her away from Leroy Crager."

Sady said, "hopefully, we can find Becky and Grace. It's was just me and Grace in that big old farmhouse of mine. Now, Eva and her son Dewey have moved in temporarily until they can both get back on their feet. If I can make Eva and her son's life a little happier, I don't have a problem with that. Eva is also Grace's grandma."

"What ever happened to the bully, Sady?"

"He just took off one night after he burned their house down. Nobody's seen him since. Good riddens is all I have to say. And if he does come back, he's gettin' arrested if I have to do it," Sady said, knowing all too well what really happened to Roby.

"Sady, I told you before, let the law handle everything."

"I know, I know, I'll try to do that but things are done different in a small town compared to a big city like Baltimore. Alec, I'm supposed to call Eva and let her know where I am stayin' and that I'm ok. Do you think your friend would mind me usin' his telephone? I know it's long distance and I will pay him for that."

"He surely wouldn't mind. But Sady, when I pick you up tomorrow morning, we can head over to the precinct and you can go in my office and use my phone, that is, if it is ok with you"

"Thank you. I know her and my friend Willow will be worried, because they haven't heard from me."

"Well Sady, are you ready to go in and meet my friend?"

"Sure, I'm a little nervous though. This is the first time that I've ever stayed with somebody I don't even know."

"You'll do fine." Alec knocked on the door.

The door opened. Standing there is a tall good-looking guy with reddish-blond hair, dressed in black.

88

"Alec, good to see you."

"Sady, I'd like you to meet Father Joe O'Shesky. This is the old friend I told you about."

"This must be Mrs. Milsap. Can I call you Sady? Welcome to "Our Lady of the Rosary"."

"Thank you, and you can call me Sady. Do I call you Father Joe or Mr. O'Shesky?"

"Sady, you can call me Father Joe. This guy here usually calls me whatever he wants to. But me and God just ignore him."

"Father Joe, come on now. You're going to give Sady a wrong opinion of me. When you put that collar on, you got all my respect, most of it anyway," Alec said while snickering a little.

Father Joe got this big grin on his face and smiled. "We both know Alec that you've got a lot of work yet to do in that category."

Alec said, "he's kidding Sady, this guy knows how much respect I have for him."

"Both of you come on in and sit down. Is this Sady's suitcase? I'll take it over to the mission and get Sister Theresa to take you to your room Sady. Just wait here. Don't you move around too much Alec, the ceiling on this old rectory might fall on our heads. This church isn't used to being blessed with your presence."

Alec laughed a little. "Ok Joe, you got your point across. Watch yourself or I'll tell Sady just how bad you were growing up in Canton."

"I'll be right back Sady. Now don't you believe a word he says about me while I'm gone."

"Don't worry Joe. I'm sure Sady isn't interested in what two wild boys did decades ago. Go get Sister Theresa before she takes her nap."

Sady's eyes scanned the rectory and got bigger as she looked at the beautiful artwork on the walls.

"Alec, they are all so beautiful!"

"They sure are Sady," Alec said, while never taking his eyes off of Sady as she gazed at the artwork. There was something about her beside her stubbornness that he noticed the more he was around her. Alec knew that Sady was unlike any woman that he ever associated with. She was compassionate, said exactly what she thought – but was respectful in what she said, and was not going to be pushed around.

Sady could also stand on her own two feet, and to top off the icing on the cake – she was a "good looking" woman.

Sady noticed Alec was staring at her. "Alec, is somethin' wrong? Did I embarrass you in front of Father Joe?"

"Oh no Sady. Don't even think that way. I just noticed this is the first time I've seen you a little more relaxed than usual."

Just then Father Joe entered the rectory with Sister Theresa.

"Sister Theresa, you remember my old friend Alec Karastaupolis?"

"Of course I do. How can I forget a name like that Father Joe?"

Sister Theresa smiled at Alec and Sady. "This young lady must be Sady Milsap." Sister Theresa shook Sady's hand. "So good to meet you Sady. You're going to like it here. Come with me and I'll show you to your room, then we'll get you some lunch."

Sady turned to Alec. "Alec, will I be seein' you tomorrow?"

"Of course you will Sady. Tomorrow we start our detective work and you also have to call your friend Eva to let her know where you will be staying. I'll pick you up at nine tomorrow morning and we'll have some breakfast before we start showing the pictures to people. How does that sound?"

"That's what I want to hear. I'll be ready," Sady said.

Just then Alec put his hand out to shake Sady's hand as a good-will gesture. The handshake was a little bit longer than normal.

Sady had to pull her hand away from Alec's hand. "See you then, tomorrow mornin' Alec. Thank you again Father Joe for lettin' me stay here. I hope I can repay you in some way."

"You can repay me by finding your granddaughter Sady. And if you feel up to it, Sister Theresa takes care of the food pantry and you can help her fill the grocery bags for the hungry that come into the mission and maybe help serve the hungry and homeless in the evenings."

"I would love to do that. You can count on me Father Joe. Bye Alec, Father Joe."

"I'll be by at nine Sady. See you tomorrow," Alec said.

Father Joe stared at Alec for a second and Alec noticed him staring. "Ok, ok, why the look. Go ahead say it. I know you've got something to say Joe."

"Alec, she seems like a very, very nice lady. Isn't it time you started to think about starting over again. I know how Julia hurt you. But not all women are like her."

"Listen to you. You're married to the church. You have no idea how it feels to give your life and heart to a person and have that person that you love so much betray you. You have no idea!"

Father Joe could tell Alec was getting a little mad at him and tried to smooth things over. "Alec, you're right. You're one hundred percent right. I don't know what it is like to be betrayed by a woman that I love. I gave my life, my heart, and my soul to Jesus Christ years ago when I was ordained as a Priest – you were there. I chose that life, but I'm happy with it. I don't see any happiness in your life Alec, and I want to see you happy again. You have to forgive Julia, and then forgive yourself. Look how many times Jesus was betrayed, but he forgave even up to his last seconds on the cross. He asked the Father to forgive them for they know not ..."

Alec said, "look, don't preach to me, ok? You're not in my shoes. Remember Joe, Sicily. I've still got shrapnel in my leg and side and scars from being burnt throughout my body. My loving wife, Julia, couldn't stand to look at me anymore. To her I wasn't the man she married. But I found out that was an excuse. She was seeing other guys the day my unit was sent to Italy. Should I forgive that fat ass dictator Mussolini and thank him for my scarred body, or should I kick myself in the behind for enlisting at the old age of 41? I was going to help save the world. I came home knowing things would be different between Julia and myself, but found out that I had a whore for a wife. No, I'm not ready for any kind of relationship. So don't even go there. I'm sorry I cursed, but you know me and what to expect."

"Ok, ok, Alec, I'm sorry. Truce buddy? I'll never ask you that question again." Father Joe put his hand out for Alec to shake.

Alec shook Father Joe's hand. "You're my best friend Joe. I can't stay mad at you. I know you are concerned about me, but don't be. I can take care of myself."

Father Joe hugged Alec. "I hope we're good Alec."

Alec said, "don't ever worry about that Joe, I mean Father Joe. We're good."

chapter 19

THE NEXT DAY sure did look a lot brighter for Sady. Sady had a nice rest-ful night and was energetic and ready to start searching for Becky and Grace. She even looked forward to seeing Alec that morning. She really hadn't been out to eat breakfast, since her and Jack used to eat at a restaurant called Aunt Barbara's Diner after church every Sunday. No restaurant in Harmony Creek or the town of Boone could compare with Aunt Barbara's cooking. Sady just never went back after Jack and Donny were killed in that horrific truck wreck. No, it brought back too many memories. Sady walked around to the front of the church to wait for Alec.

Sady couldn't get over the amount of cars, buses and streetcars racing by her. She thought, "my goodness, if I see ten cars in one day in Harmony Creek on the road that is a lot." She backed up as much as she could to the church steps afraid that someone would swerve her way. Just then Alec pulled up to the curb. Sady went to open the passenger door and Alec suddenly jumped out of the driver's side, ran around to the passenger side and opened the door for Sady.

"Alec, for goodness sake, you could have gotten hit by a car. I can open my door!"

"No problem Sady. After all these years of living in the city, I know exactly when to duck and when to run. If I have to stop being a gentle-man and quit opening the car door for a woman because I panic over traffic, then I better hide in my apartment and never come out."

After they both got into the car, Sady looked at Alec. "Alec, I appreciate everything you did for me yesterday, and I know I wasn't very nice at times. I often think if I wouldn't have been taken to the police station, I never would have met you and had this chance to find Grace. Thank you so much."

"I feel the same way Sady. I'm not glad Grace got taken, but I am glad it brought you here to Baltimore. Now what do you say we go get some breakfast?"

"Sounds good to me."

"There's this little restaurant on Light Street. The boys and I eat there quite a bit when we're working a hot case. It's called "The White Coffee Pot". They're fast and they have good food, and the coffee is the best I have ever tasted. And what makes it even a better restaurant is that it is open all day and all night."

"Sounds right good to me Alec. I am pretty hungry."

"That's what I like, a woman with an appetite."

Sady said, "you don't have to worry 'bout me none. I'm not shy when it's time to eat."

"Let's get going then. We've got a lot of territory to cover today," Alec said.

While they were on their way to the restaurant, Sady commented on some of the homes and sites along the way.

"Alec, all of these houses are stuck together. I've never seen so many houses on one street. The brick fronts are beautiful. And look at the steps, they are all the same – all painted white and all so clean. There must be hundreds and hundreds."

"Sady, these houses that are stuck together are called row houses. You'll probably never find a dirty set of steps. The bus brought you in the run-down part of the city. And I'm not saying you won't run into another part of the city just like the part you came into. But I have to say, most of the people here in Baltimore City are hardworking people and take pride in their homes. I'm sure your little town has its bad areas too."

"Alec, my little town is so small, if you go to yawn; you're goin' to miss most of it. Yeah, we do have some really poor folk back in some of the hollers. Some keep their places clean and some people are just lazy and their places look like junk yards."

"Well, here we are Sady. Stay right there, I'll get the door."

Again, Sady liked the attention Alec gave her. At times she felt a little younger than her forty-two years. And it was Alec that made her feel this way. Sady put that feeling right in the back of her mind, because it made her feel guilty. She didn't want to betray her memories of Jack.

The restaurant was pretty crowded. After waiting for a few minutes for a table, the head waitress found Alec and Sady a nice table in the corner of the restaurant. Sady sat down, and the attractive waitress gave Alec a big hug. "Alec, it's so good to see you again. We were wondering what happened to you. And who is this pretty little lady you got here?"

"Loretta, this is Mrs. Sady Milsap. We're working on a case together. I haven't been here Loretta, because we're short-handed down at the precinct and I've been working a lot of overtime."

"Sorry about you having to work so hard Alec; but nice to meet you Mrs. Milsap."

Sady put her hand out to shake Loretta's hand. "Nice to meet you ma'am. You can call me Sady."

"Hon, you sure ain't from around here. Where are you from Sady?"

"I'm from a little town called Harmony Creek. It's right outside of Boone, North Carolina."

"Sorry, hon, never heard of it. Here are your menus and I'll be right back with your coffees. You do want some coffee?"

"Now Loretta, you know how I love my coffee. How about you Sady? I really don't even know if you like coffee; I'm sorry."

"Oh, no, no. I love coffee, 'specially in the mornin'."

"I'll be right back to take your orders."

Sady said, "she sure is a right pretty lady."

"You're a right pretty lady yourself, Sady," Alec said.

Sady had not heard anyone tell her that she was pretty for years. Her face got red and she really didn't know how to answer Alec's comment. She put her head down.

Alec put his hand under Sady's chin and lifted her head up. "I can see you're not used to being told you're a pretty lady Sady. I didn't mean to embarrass you."

Sady looked into Alec's eyes. "It has been a long time since anyone told me I was pretty. Thanks."

"Sady, you are an attractive woman and you have got a big heart to go with it. I know this, because in my line of work, I have to be a pretty good judge of character. And here comes our coffees."

Loretta put both coffee cups down on the table. "Are you ready to order?"

Alec said, "we sure are Loretta. What would you like to have Sady?"

Sady said, "that "Workin' Man's Breakfast" sounds good to me – two eggs scrambled, two sausages, two pieces of bacon and two biscuits. How 'bout you Alec?"

Alec looked up at Loretta. "Loretta, make that two, and keep the coffee coming."

"Be ready in about ten minutes. Here's a whole pot of coffee. Need more, just holler."

Sady said, "thank you ma'am."

"Sady, please call me Loretta. Ma'am isn't something I'm used to being called in my line of work."

"Loretta, can I ask you somethin'?" Sady said.

"Sure, ask away, hon."

Sady pulled out an older picture of Becky and Grace.

"Loretta, have you ever seen this girl or this little baby around here?"

"Sorry Sady. Wish I could say yes, but no, I haven't seen either one of them."

"Loretta, if you do see either one of these people, please call me at the precinct. I think you still have my number," Alec said.

"I sure will Alec. I'm going to put your orders in now. Be back in a little."

Sady asked, "Alec, I know it's none of my business, but is Loretta a girlfriend of yours?"

"Sady, I've known Loretta for years. And yes, we did date, but that was a long time ago. We're kind of two different personalities that just didn't click. How about you? I bet there are a couple of guys in Harmony Creek that got their heart broken over you."

"No, no, no. I had one man in my life, Jack. He's gone. My life is my son Eddie, and my Granddaughter, Grace. And I take exception to what you said about breakin' somebody's heart. I would never do that!"

"Just joking Sady. Don't get upset. I've only known you for two days and I know you wouldn't play those games of the heart. Here comes our breakfast. Just in time too!"

chapter 20

On the way to the police station, Sady couldn't help but notice how beautiful and huge Baltimore City really looked. Of course Alec pointed out all the establishments that he thought would be of interest to her. Alec took a few detours just to show her these sites; the Baltimore Basilica – the very first, Roman Catholic Cathedral in America, the Tower Building, Federal Hill, Emory Street – the birthplace of Babe Ruth, the Royal Theatre where Cab Calloway, Billie Holiday, Louie Armstrong and many other famous jazz singers and musicians played.

Alec thought Sady looked so cute. Her eyeballs got bigger and bigger as she took in all the sites. At times her mouth just stayed open because she was so astonished at some of the places. The Basilica was one of the most beautiful places Sady had ever seen. "Alec, now is when I sure do wish I had a camera. Tellin' somebody about how beautiful this buildin' is ain't enough. They have to see it."

Alec rode past Baltimore City Hall. "Sady this is where our Mayor, Theodore McKeldin conducts all the business for the city. Most of our bigger court cases are tried here."

"Oh my gosh! We have this little courthouse in Boone for big cases, and a wee-little jail cell in Harmony Creek where our Sheriff, Sheriff Hardin is in charge. Once in a while he might have to lock up somebody that had a little too much moonshine to drink."

"Boy! That sounds like my kind of town. No criminals, no violence, no murders – and no job! Living here does pay my bills," Alec said.

Sady said, "now hold on a minute! If you farm and put your heart and soul into it every day, you can also pay your bills. My mama and daddy farmed and their folks before them. We always had plenty to eat, a roof over our heads and respect for each other. You didn't have to go out and rob a bank, or kill or hurt somebody for a thrill. Most people in my town were raised with morals and believe in God. There are a few that should be spendin' the rest of their lives in Hell and ..."

"Ok, ok. If I want a sermon I can go to Our Lady of the Rosary and let my good friend Father O'Shesky preach to me. Here we are. Let's go in so you can make your phone call home."

Alec took Sady into his office so that she could make her phone call. He walked out so she could have some privacy.

"Eva, it's Sady. Just want you to know I'm ok. Yes, everything is fine. Did you get to see Willow? She's ok, thank God. How about Dewey. How is his head? Oh, that's good news too. Eva, I might not be home for Thanksgivin'. I know, I know. I'm goin' to miss everyone too. There is this detective fella' here named Alec. He is lettin' me ride with him to show Becky's picture and Leroy's picture to people to see if they might know where they are. No, don't worry about me. Just make sure you have a nice Thanksgivin' and don't forget to ask Willow and the Tibbits for dinner. I'll let you know when I'm comin' home. Take care Eva. Bye."

When Alec came back into the office, he noticed Sady wiping a tear from her eye. "Is everything good at home Sady?"

"Home; it's not home until I have my Grace back Alec. She had her first Thanksgivin' last year. Turkey, 'taters, cornbread stuffin', beans from my garden. I won't be home this year, neither will she."

"Alec took Sady's hand and held it. "Sady, you can't give up. Think about next Thanksgiving. Grace will be there and I bet Eddie will be home too. From what I'm hearing the war might be ending soon. Just have a little faith. I have a feeling that things are going to turn around."

For the first time Sady felt a tenderness not only in Alec's hand, but also in his words that he spoke to her. He started to show an emotional side of him that he probably kept hidden that most people didn't see. Alec only allowed people to see the hard-nosed detective side of him. Sady had to admit to herself that she really liked the softer side of his personality.

"Here is that picture of Becky that you gave me. The photographer did a pretty good job. I gave a few to my guys that are working on this case to show to their contacts on the streets. Sady, let's get out on those streets and start showing these pictures of Crager and Becky. Somebody out there had to have seen them."

Sady and Alec canvassed a good part of the city. They really showed the pictures more in the "not too nice parts of the city" where Alec thought someone may have seen Leroy or Becky.

"How are you holding up Sady? I bet your feet are killing you. I'm used to this. If you want to go back to the mission, I'll take you. I can finish this myself."

"Are you kiddin'? Farm work is early mornin' 'til late evenin'. I'm on my feet all day. Climbin' rafters in the barn and hangin' 'baker sure don't make your feet feel like you're walkin' on a cloud. I just can't believe nobody has seen either one of them."

"Sady, you have to understand the code of the streets. Some of these people may have seen them; but they are not going to be labeled a "snitch" and maybe get beat up or even murdered for talking to a detective. What scares them even more than being murdered is not getting their heroin or other drugs that they have to take every day. They are addicted and can't live without their "fix"."

"Alec, I don't care what kind of snitchin' they do or don't do. I'll do whatever it takes to get somebody to tell me where they are!"

"It's getting late Sady. Around 5:30 it is going to be dark. We'll go one more place then I'm taking you back to the mission. There is a place called Lexington Market where a lot of people do their shopping. Inside the market, there is a sandwich shop called "Pollock Johnny's". They serve the best Polish sausages and hot dogs around. How about it? You hungry? I know I am. After we eat, we can ask people if they have seen Becky or Leroy. What do you say partner?"

"As long as you promise me you will take me out again to look for them. I'd go by myself, but I don't know my way around the city yet."

"Sady, I can't make a promise because I have no idea who is going to rob a bank, commit murder, or destroy somebody's property tomorrow. I can go on and on but I think you get the idea. I'm trying to do the best I can to find your Grace. I have at least two other detectives investigating their whereabouts."

"I know you're doin' everything you possibly can to find Grace. It doesn't help to have a crazy grandma on your back all the time. I know

Mary Wagner

you and your guys are doin' their best to find them. I don't want you to think I don't appreciate the help you have given me so far."

"I know you appreciate it Sady. Things are going to turn around. I know they will."

As soon as Alec and Sady drove over to Lexington Market, they ate at "Pollock Johnny's" and wasted no time showing the pictures of Leroy and Becky to the vendors.

Alec questioned at least five vendors. Not one of them had ever seen Leroy or Becky. Sady, however got lucky. There were two vendors who remembered Leroy and Becky. One vendor sold cake goods. She told Sady that Becky stole a bag of cookies and a large cake. By the time the vendor came from around the counter, Becky was gone. The second vendor sold pizzas. Leroy ran off with two boxes of pizza while Becky drew the attention to her so that Leroy could get away. Since then neither vendor had seen neither one of them.

"Looks like we're getting closer to finding them Sady. I'll have a few of my men mingle with the rest of the customers tomorrow and ask questions. I have a really good feeling they'll be back here again. They got away once. Usually I find those kind always come back again to test the waters. They will probably just try another vendor at the opposite end of the market. You're so sad looking Sady. Wish I could make tomorrow a better day for you."

"I'm sad Alec because no one said that a little girl was with either one of them. Alec, where is she? This is actually makin' me sick. What did they do with her?"

Sady's eyes teared up. Alec put his arm around her to comfort her. "Sady, I'm not going to give up until she is in your arms again. Did you hear what I just said? I'll never stop looking for her. Please have some trust in me. I know we haven't known each other that long, but I have the best of the best of my men out on the streets Sady. I promise we will find her. Just trust me Sady."

"I do trust you and your men Alec, I don't trust them."

"Sady, I'm one person you can trust. Can you wait here for a few minutes? I need to call the precinct to see if the guys have heard anything or need me to come in today."

As Sady waited for Alec, she watched all the little children, especially the little girls Grace's age, hold their parents hand while they

100

walked through the market. Her heart was so empty and was filled with such sadness. She looked up and said," please Dear Lord, send my Grace back to me."

"Were you talking to me Sady?" Alec said.

"No, Alec. I was just thinkin' out loud."

"I'm needed down at the station Sady. I'll take you back to the mission. Don't worry, I'll keep in touch. We will get her back Sady!"

Alec drove Sady back to the mission. With her heart in her hand, Sady walked to her room and waited for another morning and a new day to look for Grace.

chapter 21

IT WAS WEDNESDAY of the following week and Sady didn't hear from or see Alec for the past five days. Sady even missed not seeing Alec, but, of course, that was something she would never admit to anyone. Sister Theresa, nevertheless, kept Sady pretty busy packing food boxes for the poor for Thanksgiving. Being busy helped Sady not be so homesick. Thanksgiving was the next day and there still was no Grace to be found.

Sady's mind traveled back to her mountain home. She could imagine seeing the smoke travel out of the chimney while the turkey cooked in her oven. The smell of the turkey, stuffing, corn bread and Mrs. Tibbits' sweet potato and pumpkin pie not only brought her mind and senses back to her home and her friends and family, but made her oblivious to the conversation that Sister Theresa was trying to have with her.

"Sady, Sady, are you ok?"

"Sorry Sister Theresa, I was just thinkin' about home, and how I would surely love to be there with Grace and my friends tomorrow."

Sister Theresa put her arm around Sady. "I know Sady how hard it must be on you, but I have this feeling inside my heart that Alec is going to find your Grace and you two will be home and in the arms of family and friends before you know it. I bet you'll have Grace back way before Christmas. You have to have faith dear. Please don't lose the faith you have in the Lord, Sady. He's not going to let anything happen to that little girl."

"Sister Theresa, I have been a good Christian woman all my life. But after I lost my husband and son, and now with Grace missin', I find myself questionin' God. I know that is wrong, and I have even told my friends back home that it is wrong to question God when somethin' terrible happens in their lives. I find myself askin' God, why? Why me? Isn't one great loss enough? I struggle in my mind not to question Him, but then I get mad at God, and I know that I shouldn't. Then I feel guilty and I feel like somethin' worse is going to happen because He is mad at me!"

Sister Theresa snickered a little at what Sady said. "Sady, Sady, Sady, don't ever think He is mad at you for having those feelings. He understands grief, pain, and the loss of someone that you love. Don't forget, His Son Jesus Christ walked this earth as a human. His blood was the same color as yours. He understands our fears, our anger, and our love for one another. Everybody says, "you're not supposed to question him". I personally don't believe that. I believe he wants us to question him. That's the mystery Sady. When we question him, we let him know we believe in him. We are here for a short time Sady. You are here for a purpose, His purpose, and one day He will show you exactly why you are here Sady. He will touch your heart and you will have your questions answered."

"Thank you Sister Theresa. You know, you made me feel a lot better than I did before our conversation."

"Well that's good to know. Some of the stores in town donated some clothes, coats, shoes, and other personal items. They are in the back in a large box. Would you mind sorting them into piles so we can also give them away?"

"I surely will Sister Theresa."

Sady started pulling the articles out of the box and pulled a coat out that she just couldn't take her eyes off of. The coat had so many beautiful bright fall colors in it. Sady thought, "I know Willow would love this coat."

Sady went back out front to talk to Sister Theresa. "Sister Theresa, how much do you want for this coat?"

"My goodness Sady, everything here is free for the poor. Sady, if you want that coat, it's yours. But I have to say, it is very flashy and bold. Are you sure you want it? There are other coats in the box that aren't so flashy that you might like."

"Oh no, it's not for me. It is for a friend of mine. She also doesn't have very much and really could use a nice coat."

"In that case, the coat is yours. I hope it keeps your friend warm this winter."

"Thank you so much Sister Theresa. She is going to love this coat!"

"Well I know one thing for sure Sady. You will be able to see her coming from a distance."

They both laughed and Sady went back into the room to sort the articles.

After about an hour of sorting, Sady heard a familiar voice – a voice she missed for several days, Alec's voice. "Sister Theresa, is Sady around, I would like to talk to her for a few minutes."

"She sure is Alec. She is in the back sorting some of the clothes we're giving away tomorrow. Just go straight back, you can't miss her."

"Thanks, Sister Theresa."

Alec walked into the back room where Sady was sorting the clothing. Their eyes both meet at the same time. Sady just had to get in the first word. "Well stranger, where have you been? Didn't take long to forget about me and Grace, did it?"

"Now Sady, calm down. It's been hectic down at the headquarters. This is a big city. I didn't forget about you. We are shorthanded and I had to pitch in and help the other guys. I even walked a beat the other night. We've had at least five robberies, six muggings and two people murdered. That doesn't even include all the normal petty crimes that go on every day, twenty-four hours a day."

"I'm sorry Alec. I know you have to work all cases, not just mine. You could have just stopped in for a minute just to say hello. By any chance, did you find out any information on Becky, Leroy or maybe where Grace might be?"

"As a matter of fact Sady, we were able to trace Leroy and Becky to the motel where they were staying. As soon as we got there, everything was gone. You could tell they just had left. I've got a lot of ears out on the streets. We're getting closer to finding them. It's just a matter of a few days now."

"That sure makes me feel a lot better Alec. Please thank your men for me."

"Believe me Sady; they all know how appreciative you are of them. I did come over here for a reason though. I know I'm not Eva, Willow, or Dewey and the Tibbits you talk about, but I'd like to cook you a

Mary Wagner

Thanksgiving dinner tomorrow, at my apartment, if that is ok with you. I feel bad that you won't be home with your family this year, and I am not a bad cook."

"Alec, I don't think I should. I appreciate you askin', but it just don't seem right – me bein' in your place and all – you know - alone."

"Sady, it's just dinner, then I'll take you right back to the mission. But if you feel that way, I'm fine with it. Sady, you should know by now that you can trust me. Did I ever give you the impression I would take advantage of you?"

"Oh, no, never! Alec, please don't be mad. You're the only one beside Sister Theresa that I can trust. I'm supposed to help out here tomorrow anyway. Sister Theresa and I are serving turkey and all the trimmins' tomorrow for the homeless. Why don't you stop by and have your meal with us? You can even volunteer and help us. How about it?"

"I will if you promise me that you will let me take you to this little place near the Baltimore harbor after we eat. It's a place I think you'll like."

"Ok, it's a deal. We start servin' at two o'clock."

"I'll be here tomorrow two o'clock sharp. You're still going to miss my cooking."

"Alec, I'm sure you're a very good cook. I'm the one who wouldn't be very good company to be around now. I'm already homesick and worried about Grace. Please forgive the way I feel but I really do look forward to seein' you tomorrow."

"I understand Sady. See you tomorrow then."

Sady watched as Alec walked away. She thought to herself, "what is wrong with you? He is a nice man and is interested in you. Men like him don't come into your life every day. But what would Jack say? I can't hurt Jack like that. No, I can't hurt him! Why am I even thinkin' about a man this way? It's so wrong Sady!"

chapter 22

THANKSGIVING MORNING FINALLY arrived. Sady got very little sleep. It had almost been two weeks and not a trace of Grace or Becky or even Leroy could be found. Sady was fearful for Grace and homesick for her farm. She was worried about Willow, Eva, and Dewey. She thought about her son, Eddie. Why hadn't she heard from him? If the soldier on the bus was right, Eddie's unit was heading into a big battle in France or Belgium, she couldn't remember. All Sady could think of was," please God, please keep my Eddie safe and get him home to me and Grace!"

Everything just clouded her mind that morning. Her mind was going in circles. These thoughts went around and around and wouldn't stop. She felt like her insides were going to burst if something good didn't happen soon. She felt the same way five years ago on Thanksgiving Day. Instead of having a joyful dinner, with family and friends, she was at Harmony Funeral Home staring in disbelief at her husband and son as they lay in their coffins. She could still see their faces and remember every last detail of both of them from their hair to any wrinkle in the cloth in the casket. She would go from the funeral home to the hospital to see Eddie. Sady couldn't stand to be in her room anymore. She ran outside into the cold and sat on a bench in the garden facing a statue of the Blessed Virgin.

The tears just flowed as she sat there. She stared at the statue of Mary through her tears. She started to talk loudly to the statue. "I know who you are. You lost a son too. I lost one, and now, maybe another son. You know what I'm gone through. You know how I feel inside. I know you can hear me in Heaven. Please, from one mother to another mother, please help me find Grace and watch over and protect my Eddie and bring him home soon! If you can't do that, please ask God to take me now, right now, because I can't live like this anymore!"

Sady put her head down and cried uncontrollably. When she lifted her head and looked at the statue, she saw something unusual on the Blessed Virgin's face – a tear in her right eye. Sady put her hand up to see if it was raining. She thought, "could it be a raindrop?" It was a cold day, but a brisk wind was blowing, the sun was shining, and there was no rain in sight.

Sady got up and walked over to the statue. The teardrop fell to the Blessed Virgin's chin and was gone. Sady touched the statue's face where the teardrop was. It was still wet. Sady looked up to the sky and said, "I guess you're tryin' to tell me that you know how I feel and the Good Lord doesn't want this old girl right now, because I'm still standin' here. I guess that means I'm still needed down here. From one mother to another, thank you for listenin' to my prayers."

Sister Theresa heard almost the whole conversation that Sady had with the Blessed Virgin. She was on her way to mass that morning and stood back while Sady talked to the statue. She didn't want to embarrass Sady by letting her know she saw her crying. She knew Sady took pride in being a no-nonsense type of person. "Sady, are you ok?"

"Sister Theresa, I didn't know you were there. I guess you think I'm crazy sittin' here cryin' and talkin' to a statue."

"You weren't talking to the statue Sady. I saw you look up. The statue just reminds us that Mary is His mother and if we need to talk to her, she is always in Heaven and willing to listen to us."

"Sister Theresa, I thought I saw a tear in the statue's eye. I touched her face and it was wet."

"Sady, all I can say is that God works in mysterious ways. He is not ready to walk this earth for us humans to see or to be able to touch him again. He did that once through his son. So He does the next best thing. He lets us know somehow, in some way, that He hears our prayers. Sady, I know you are going through a lot right now, but you have to have faith in Him and believe that something good will come out of all the heaviness on your shoulders that you are carrying around along with this sadness in your heart."

"Thank you Sister Theresa. I do believe I got an answer today from Him. Like you said, I just have to have a little more faith. Where are you goin'?"

"I'm going to Thanksgiving mass before I start getting the mission ready for all the meals we will be serving today. Come on in with me. We do a lot of standing and kneeling and the mass is mostly in all Latin, but you are welcome to come."

"Thank you, but I think I'll mosey on over to the mission and try to get things ready for you. See you there. Oh, I forgot to tell you. Alec said he would be comin' over to help. I hope he really meant what he said because we need the help."

"Sady, I've known Alec a long time. He is a man of his word. See you in about an hour."

There were several volunteers already in the mission preparing the various dishes of stuffing, mashed potatoes, sweet potatoes, corn, all kinds of beans, salad, much more and many desserts. The turkeys were being carved by three of the men who worked in the local grocery store. They did a beautiful job of carving the meat, but then, again, they did this for a living. Sady was really impressed.

Sady's main job was to set all of the tables with plastic cutlery, plates, bowls, and cups and to serve the people when the doors opened to the public. This kept her mind off of her problems for a little while anyway. A few days before, Sady even made little cardboard turkeys as centerpieces for each table and pasted little paper turkeys on the plain white napkins. She felt a little closer to home being involved in so many projects for Thanksgiving.

It was one thirty and almost serving time. There was no Alec. Sady thought to herself, "maybe he got mad because I wouldn't go to his place for dinner. Too bad, he'll have to get glad." Sady knew in her heart she really looked forward to seeing him again. "What if I don't see him again? He's the only one I can depend on to help me find Grace." But there was another reason Sady wanted to see Alec again, but she wouldn't even admit that reason to herself.

Just before serving time, Alec walked into the mission. Sady's heart jumped a little when she saw him. Not admitting to herself that she was really happy to see him, she shrugged it off by telling him, "it's about time. We were goin' to have to grab one of the people in line to take your place to serve!"

Alec just stared at her. "Happy Thanksgiving to you too Sady. I just came off of a twelve- hour shift and rushed over here. I changed my shift just so I could help out today. Thank you, for your concern."

"I'm sorry Alec. I've got a lot on my mind today. Just put this apron on and stand behind the serving table. The doors are goin' to open any minute."

"Aye, aye, captain. If that was an apology from you, I'll take it."

Sady just looked up at Alec again and said, "sorry," then she smiled at him.

Alec smiled back. "I can't stay mad at you Sady. Friends?" They both shook hands, laughed a little, and started serving food to the people.

Sady noticed how hungry some of the families and people who came in alone were. Some of the people even looked sick, and the clothes they had on were torn or ragged. Their coats would never get them through a rough cold and snowy winter. She was glad the donation table was almost piled to the ceiling with clothes, shoes and many, many coats. Sady thought about her life. Even though her family was poor, there was always plenty to eat, and an ample supply of clothes her mother made to keep them warm. A few of the people brought tears to her eyes.

Alec caught her a few times turning to wipe her eyes. Alec turned to her and said, "Sady, you're doing a good thing. If it weren't for Father Joe, Sister Theresa and these volunteers, most of these people would go through the day with very little, if anything, to eat. We're almost finished here. How about sitting over by the window and eating our dinner?"

"Sure, Alec. Everything looks so delicious. I can't wait to eat!"

"Sady, don't forget what you promised me."

"I didn't forget Alec. I'm lookin' forward to gettin' a chance to see the harbor."

Right after eating their dinner, Alec looked at Sady and said, "let's get rid of these aprons and get going. It will be dark soon and you won't get to see anything."

Sady made sure the clean-up committee was there before she left. She and Alec said their goodbyes to Sister Theresa and left.

Sady looked forward to seeing the Baltimore Harbor, and who knows, in the back of her mind she thought she may spot Becky or Leroy. She had to keep the faith like Sister Theresa told her to. She wasn't giving up.

chapter 23

ON THE WAY to the harbor, Alec surprised Sady and took her back to his office to let her call home. Eva cooked a big dinner for everyone. Dewey and Mr. Tibbits went to the top of Blackheart Mountain and shot the biggest turkey Eva had ever seen. Mrs. Tibbits made her sweet potato and pumpkin pies. Of course Willow and Wolfe joined in the festivities. Willow brought her homemade blackberry jam for the biscuits. Sady got to talk to everyone. Alec could see the sudden change in her face and disposition. This was exactly what Sady needed.

"Thank you, thank you so much Alec. You don't know how happy you made me. I miss everybody so much!"

"Sady, I can see from the big grin on your face how happy you are. You never know, maybe one day I'll get to meet your friends. From what you have told me about Willow, she sounds like a tough old bird."

"She's not just tough Alec; she's got this big ole' heart. She helped my mama and daddy way before I was born and she has been there for me since I was a baby until now. I don't know what I would have done without her all these years."

"You're a lucky lady, Sady, to have all these awesome friends in your life."

Sady looked into Alec's eyes and said, "yes, I am, Alec, yes I am. Now let's go to the harbor."

"Yes, my lady. We're on our way!"

On the way to the harbor, Alec rode down several different streets. He was always on the lookout for Becky or Leroy. As he was passing by the Hippodrome Theatre on North Eutaw Street, he got up the nerve to finally ask Sady for a date – that is – only as friends.

"Sady, do you like the movies?"

"Is that what that beautiful buildin' is, a movie house?"

"Yes, it is. If you're here next week ... but of course, I hope we get Grace back way before next week, would you like to go to the movies with me? John Wayne's movie "Tall in the Saddle" is playing. How about it?"

Sady did notice the nervousness in Alec's voice as he asked her to go with him. She thought that was so odd, because all she ever noticed was Alec's super-confidence in everything he said or did.

Sady said, "I haven't been to the movies for years. We don't have one in Harmony. Boone has a movie theatre, but it is still a long way to go just to see a movie. Yeah! I would like to go with you. Sure, why not?"

Alec was elated. "Good, it's a date then. I mean not a date- date, but just two friends getting together. You know what I mean."

"Sure I do Alec. You're my first real friend here in Baltimore."

When Alec and Sady got to the harbor, they sat on the bench by the water while Alec described some of the sites to her. The moon was out and it was so bright and full. The evening was picture perfect for Sady's first look at the harbor.

"You know what's funny Alec? I look up and see that beautiful moon and I think of home."

"Hey, wait a minute. I didn't intend to make you homesick Sady."

"No, no. I mean if I was home in Harmony, I would be lookin' up and see the same moon; only North Carolina is a far piece from here."

Alec moved a little closer to Sady. He picked her hand up and held it. Sady didn't push him away. She actually enjoyed holding his hand. His hand was strong, and the grasp he had on her hand made her feel safe. She liked that feeling. It was a feeling she had not experienced since way before Jack's death. Yes, Jack was a good man. But holding hands wasn't anything he would ever do in public. Sady always thought he was funny that way when it came to showing her any type of affection, and never in front of people. It made her not lean on Jack so much. It made her more of an independent person, but with Alec, Sady liked being shown such adorable affection.

"Alec, can I ask you a question?"

"Sure, hopefully, I can answer it," Alec said.

"Have you always been a detective? Do you really like what you do? Aren't you afraid of somebody hurtin' you or maybe even killin' you. What do your parents think and ..."

"Wait a minute, wait a minute. You said *a* question."

"I know, I know but ..."

Alec cut Sady off. "I used to be a defense attorney for years. I got tired of defending people who I knew were guilty. It kept me up at nights. I joined the police force and worked my way up to detective and, yes, I love what I do. If I can help someone, or prevent someone from being hurt or killed, that makes me happy. Of course, I don't want to be killed on the job or off the job, but after what I saw in Sicily at the beginning of this war, I can deal with any problem here."

Sady interrupted him. "War, you were in this war? What happened?"

Alec walked over to the edge of the harbor and picked up a big rock and brought it back to the bench and sat down.

"I joined the Army Sady. Even though men my age were being drafted, I didn't take any chances. I wanted to stop Hitler, Mussolini, and the Japanese. I was sent to Sicily to fight against Mussolini in the Italian Campaign. I drove a tank. We went through a small village that we just ran Mussolini's men out of. We thought we were safe. I jumped out of the tank to help one of our men who got hit by a sniper and within a few seconds had a grenade thrown close to me by one of the enemy hiding out in one of the houses. I was taken to a nearby hospital. My leg was full of shrapnel. I had third degree burns throughout my body except for my face. Sady, I was a mess, physically and mentally. Most of my platoon was killed. I was in the hospital for a few months, sent back to the states and was told I was to receive a purple heart. I told them to keep that damn ribbon unless everyone in the platoon that survived or the families of those that died got one. I never heard any more from headquarters."

Alec opened his shirt to show Sady only part of the scars that were on his body.

"Does it disgust you Sady?"

"Why would you say that? I never would have known if you hadn't just told me or shown me, and no, it doesn't disgust me."

"Why? I did have a wife at the time. She claimed it disgusted her and I wasn't the man I was before I went into the army. But I found out later, that as soon as I shipped overseas, she started running around with other men. My leg and body was just an excuse."

"Alec, I'm really sorry. What she did was wrong. All I can say is I'm sorry."

"Well, to get to your final question about my parents. They came over here from Greece when I was very small. They opened up a bakery in Canton and we lived over top of it. That's how I met Father Joe. He lived on the Polish side of the street and we lived on the Greek/Italian side of the street. We went to the same school together. I grew up going to Catholic Church and school because my mother was Italian. Later on my father got so homesick he went back to Greece. We never heard from him again. My mother died, I think, from a broken heart several years ago. Now you have it all – the story of Alec Karaustapolis' life."

"Alec, did you ever have any children?"

"You don't give up, do you? No, that was another problem between my wife and me. I wanted children and she didn't. Now you know a good deal about my life, Sady. You know, I have never told anyone this much about me. I am surprised I told you."

"That's because you know that what you told me won't go any further then this bench."

"You're right. It's my turn now. You said you have a son fighting in Germany and you haven't heard from him."

"I am so worried Alec. He wrote me at least once a month. I haven't heard from him for about three months. I am worried sick. I can't lose another son. I talked to a young boy when I was comin' to Baltimore on the bus. He lost an arm in this war. I told him my son's division number and everything and he said he heard they might be one of the division's bein' sent to fight the Germans in Belgium or France. It's a place in some kind of forest. I can't remember."

"The forest is the Ardennes Forest, which includes part of Belgium, and France, and goes all the way to Luxembourg, Germany. Can you remember your son's Division or anything. I know some people in Washington D.C. Sady. I can look into this if you want me to."

"Want you to. I'd be honored if you did that. Alec, that is a kind thing to do. If you don't mind can you ask about another soldier named

Thomas Tibbits. Eddie and Thomas went over together and I even think they are in the same unit. Eddie is in the Eighty ..."

"Wait just a minute Sady. Let me get a pen and piece of paper. Go ahead."

"The Eighty-Sixth Infantry Division, Company C, 311 Engineerin' Combat Battalion. They are also called the "Black Hawks"."

"I can't promise you a lot, but I am going to Washington at the end of December. I'll call you at home just to find out before I go if you heard anything. How does that sound? You never know; Eddie might be home by Christmas."

"Alec, I could kiss you. Thank you so much. To have Grace and Eddie home for Christmas, I'll never ask God for another thing for the rest of my life."

"Why don't you Sady?"

"Why don't I what Alec?"

"Kiss me."

Sady didn't hesitate. She looked up at Alec, whispered, "thank you," and kissed him.

She didn't want the kiss to end; neither did Alec. Sady had feelings for Alec that she hadn't had for years. These feelings were different though; different from the feelings she had with Jack.

Alec was the one who finally broke up the kiss. "Sady, there's this little place down the street from here that I'd like you to see, that is, if you would like to go. I won't lie, it's a little bar, but a nice bar. What do you say?"

"Why not, sure, let's go. It's gettin' a little cold out here by the water anyway."

chapter 24

SADY COULDN'T HELP but notice how small the bar was that Alec took her to, but there were quite a few people there.

She also noticed the juke box was playing a few tunes she heard on her radio at home.

"Don't tell me Alec that you like hillbilly music. I mean, I love it, but I didn't take you for a lover of hillbilly music."

"Sady, I love all music. I try to come here at least every two weeks if I get a chance. And, yes, I am fond of "country music". You call it hillbilly, I call it country. The lyrics tell stories of people's lives, from falling in love to somebody killing their lover and winding up in jail somewhere out West."

They both laughed at this point. "You're right Alec. A lot of the lyrics hit home and mean somethin'. I just took you for a person who liked a different kind of music."

"You are right about that. I love to hear a good blues song or jazz. Sometimes I even go the Royal Theatre on Pennsylvania Ave. I've heard Ella Fitzgerald, Billie Holiday, Louie Armstrong and Cab Calloway sing. Nobody can sing or play the blues like those four people Sady. Most of the people who go are colored people, but they have no problem finding me a seat when I come in. They know me by now and they how much I appreciate and respect good talent."

"Sorry Alec, but I've never heard of any of those people, but if you say they are good, they must be."

"No doubt about that Sady. Hey, I'll be right back." Alec walks over to the Juke Box, puts a nickel in and walks back to their table.

The music started playing and it was Gene Autry singing "Carolina Moon".

"Sady, can I have the honor of dancing with you?"

"Yes sir, you may. How did you know this was my favorite song Alec?"

"Don't know. Just thought, the girl's from Carolina, so maybe she has heard song this before."

"Good guess, Alec."

They both laughed and got up to dance.

At first, a few short words were exchanged between Sady and Alec when they got up to dance. Alec then pulled Sady closer to him. Her face touched his neck and the smell of his after-shave lotion was so clean and fresh that all she could think of was that she hadn't been that close to a man for years. Alec was a tall but muscular built man, and Sady felt protected as if no harm could ever come to her. She savored this moment. She closed her eyes and for a few short seconds her mind drifted to a happier place, a happier time. Then, as if someone hit her in the head, her eyes opened wide and she pulled away from Alec.

"Sady, what's wrong? Did I do something, say something that I shouldn't have?"

"No, no, Alec, it's not you. It's me. Look at me. I'm dancin' with a very handsome man and enjoyin' myself. I shouldn't be here doin' this. I came to Baltimore for a reason – to find Grace! I should be ashamed of myself."

"Where do you get all this guilt from? I don't understand you. Why can't Sady do something nice for Sady? You're a grown woman Sady with feelings. We all know how much you love Grace. Dancing with me doesn't diminish the love you have for her. This is one little dance. I didn't want to tell you what I am going to tell you, because, I didn't want to raise your hopes up."

"What are you talkin' about Alec?"

"We know where Leroy and Becky are staying, but no one has seen them. We got good information that they did leave and within the next week they will be returning to this little run-down apartment they are staying in. I've got two men watching the apartment on every shift."

"Oh Alec, that's the best news I've heard yet. I'm sorry for pullin' away from you. I don't know what is wrong with me. It's just I really like you and why I feel guilty about it, I don't know. I guess where I come from, most women have one man most of their life and when he is gone, that part of your life is supposed to stop and your life should evolve around your family, even though mine always did. You're not supposed to have another man. If you do, you're betrayin' the husband that passed on. Do you understand that, because sometimes I don't."

"No, I don't. It's a good thing you don't live here, because a pretty woman like you wouldn't be alone very long. Is there a homely and ugly group of women in Harmony that have a set of laws they passed that states that when your husband dies, your life stops and you're not allowed to have any feelings for another man any more or you'll go to Hell?"

"Of course not Alec, but you don't understand. It's just a small, tiny community and that's how things are. You just accept them."

"Accept unhappiness and the right to carry guilt around for the rest of your life? Sorry, I'll never buy that. But what I will buy is a beer. I could use one. I'm sure you don't drink Sady, so what can I get for you?"

"I think I will take a little sip of somethin'. Now what do you suggest?"

"Do you like Coca-Cola Sady?"

"I sure do."

"I'll have the bartender put a little sip of rum in your coke."

"Now that sounds good to me. I put a little bit of rum in my Christmas cakes."

Alec brought back his beer and Sady's Rum and Coke to the table. Alec made a toast. "Here's to finding Grace real soon!"

Sady held her glass up. "Here's to me meetin' you Alec."

"Hold on Sady, you're supposed to sip it, remember?"

"This stuff is really good Alec. It tastes like sweet punch. Can I have another one? For some reason I'm thirsty tonight."

"Ok, but drink it slowly, not like it's the last glass of liquid on earth!"

A few hours passed and it was getting a little late, and Alec could see that Sady was starting to slur her words and kept asking him to order her more "punch". He knew he had to take her back to the mission but didn't want Sister Theresa to see her drunk. Then he thought just maybe Sister Theresa would be asleep and he could sneak her into her room.

But it wasn't five minutes after Sady got into Alec's car, when he heard her say, "Alec, I don't feel good, I'm hot. I've got to take this coat off. I feel sick . . ."

It was too late. Sady threw up all over her dress. Alec felt bad about the whole incident. He wasn't about to take her to the mission like that. He decided to take her to his apartment and try to clean her up before going back to the mission.

Alec carried Sady up the steps to his apartment. Sady was almost passed out and still sick. Alec laid Sady on his bed and gently took her dress off. He washed her dress in his bathtub and hung it up to dry. He went back to his bedroom and wiped her face with a cold rag. Sady turned on her side and he covered her up. While covering her up, he noticed a bright pink mark below her neck close to her left shoulder.

"What in the world is that?" He got closer and noticed that it was a birthmark in the shape of a small heart. "Well I'll be. A birthmark that looks like a little heart. I better let you sleep little lady because tomorrow you're not going to feel so good."

Alec kissed Sady on the forehead, turned the light out, shut the door, and went out on the couch and went to sleep.

The next morning Sady woke up and started to scream. Alec ran in the bedroom. "Sady, you're ok. You're in my apartment. I didn't want to take you back to the mission like you were."

Sady pulled the covers up over her slip. "Where are my clothes Alec? I don't understand. What happened?"

"Let's get something straight first. You threw up all over your dress. I took it off and washed it. Let's put it this way- it stunk really bad. I never touched you."

"I never would have thought you would take advantage of me Alec. Never. You're too much of a gentleman. But is my dress dry? Sister Theresa is goin' to think we spent the night together. I've got to get back before she suspects anything."

"Don't worry about Sister Theresa. I'll explain everything to her. Sady, grow up. You're a woman that doesn't owe anybody any explanation about anything. People are going to believe what they want to believe anyway. You know and I know you did nothing wrong, that is, except get drunk, have a good time and then get sick.

Stop worrying. I did notice that cute little birthmark on your left shoulder though."

"My mother told me it almost covered my whole back, that's how tiny I was when I was born. She said that when she saw that heart, she knew I was special and one day I would be special to someone else."

"That's a really nice story Sady. Here is your dress. Smells a lot better. How is your head?"

"I've got this terrible headache, but my stomach sure feels a lot better. That's the end of my drinkin' Alec. No more."

"Sady, you guzzled it down too fast. But some people can't drink, they do get sick. You'll never be a confirmed drunk. Look, we have to get going. I have to get to work and I'm hoping we can get you to your room before Sister Theresa notices anything."

Alec and Sady did manage to sneak into the mission, but Sister Theresa stopped Alec on the way out. "Alec, what are you doing here this early in the morning?"

"I just thought I'd ask Sady if she wanted to go to breakfast so I could catch her up on what is going on with her case, but she's not feeling too well this morning."

"I thought you might just be going to morning mass," Sister Theresa said teasingly.

"Sister Theresa, now you know better than to assume that. See you later."

"We'll get you back one day Alec. Have a nice day."

Alec wiped his brow and said to himself, "that was a little too close."

Alec went to work and Sady went to bed hoping to feel better before the day was over.

chapter 25

A FEW DAYS went by and Sady hadn't heard from Alec. She had hoped she didn't ruin what little relationship between the two of them that had developed, because she got drunk and threw up all over herself. Sady couldn't worry about whether or not Alec was mad about her drunken adventure, because it was her night to work at the mission serving food to the homeless and poor.

Sady was amazed at the crowd for a Monday night. There was a huge variety of food to be served. The doors opened at four o'clock and closed at seven.

Sady kept her eyes on the containers. When they were empty, she would hurry to the kitchen and fill them again.

It was getting late and the kitchen was getting ready to close. Sady noticed a gaunt, young red-haired girl come in. She was one big mess. Sady stared at her because she looked so familiar. It was the fire-red hair that threw her off. Sady couldn't believe her eyes. It was Becky.

Sady got out from behind the serving table and went over to her and grabbed her arm. "Becky, it's me Sady. Where is Grace?"

Becky looked at Sady as if she saw a ghost. "Get off of me you bitch!"

"No, you're gonna' tell me where my Grace is!"

Sister Theresa ran over to see what was going on.

"Sister Theresa call Alec, please hurry and call him!" Sady said in a panic.

Just then Becky threw her plate of food at Sady, pushed her down and ran out the door.

Becky took off running and Sady tried to run after her. It was almost seven at night. It was dark and cold. When Sady ran out the door she did not grab her coat. Sady chased Becky but couldn't catch her. Becky was finally out of Sady's sight altogether. Sady had no idea where she was and walked in circles for at least an hour. She did see a sign that said Pennsylvania Avenue. She remembered Alec talking about the Royal Theatre. She thought, "if I could only find the Royal Theatre, maybe I could tell them I know Alec and they could call him to come and get me."

Sady didn't realize it, but she was at the lower end of Pennsylvania Avenue, one of the worst parts of the city. The Royal Theatre was blocks away towards the upper end. Sady was lost. She was lost and cold and scared once again. She could hear gun shots. She could hear a woman screaming. She thought to herself, "if only I could hear a siren from a police car or ambulance, I could wave them down."

It was so cold. There were a few people standing on grates coming out of the sidewalk. Sady went over, stood on the grate and noticed the warm air blowing up. It did warm her legs a little but the frigid cold, loneliness, and fear of the streets just overwhelmed her. She crouched down on the grate, started crying and just gave up.

Just then she heard a voice ask her, "lady, lady, you ok?"

She looked up and it was an older colored man.

"No, no, I'm not ok. I wish I was dead. I wish I never left home! No, I'm not ok!"

The old colored man had a blanket and put it around Sady. It had the smell of whisky, cigarettes, and old garbage on it, but she didn't care. The blanket kept her warm and probably kept her from freezing to death.

"Ma'am, you don't want that wish about bein' dead to come true. That's a bad wish to make around here. Miss, this ain't no place for a white woman to be. You better go back where you came from."

Sady with tears streaming down her face answered the man. "That's my problem sir. I'm lost. Can you tell me where a church called Our Lady of the Rosary is?"

"No ma'am, I never did hear of that church. All I know is you got to get off this street. A lot of bad things go on here. I ain't ever seen many white folk down this end, especially a woman."

Just then a gang of young colored boys, fifteen to eighteen or older, start walking towards the old man and Sady. They were busting beer bottles, ranting and raving and drunk or high on drugs.

The old man hollered to Sady. "Lady, get under the blanket. Don't make a sound." He threw some clothes and junk he had scattered around him over the blanket.

One of the boys stopped right in front of the old man and demanded money. He even pointed a gun at him. "Ok Pops, hand over any money you got, or I'm puttin' a big hole in your head today."

"Please son, you see I got nothin' but junk here. I got fifty cents and this half bottle of whiskey. Here, take it. Please don't shoot me!"

"What am I supposed to do with fifty-cents? How am I supposed to buy my "white junk" with fifty-cents Pops? And you can take this bottle of whiskey and take a bath in it 'cause you sure do stink." The young boy poured the whiskey over the old man's head.

The gang member took the fifty-cents and hit the old man in the side of his face with the butt of the gun. "I'm comin' back tomorrow Pops and you better have another fifty-cents for me."

Bleeding and confused the old man said, "I will son, I will. Promise you I will!"

After the gang left, Sady stuck her head out of the blanket. For once that day, she never thought about her problems. She tore one of the shirts the old man threw on top of the blanket and tried to wipe the blood from the side of his head.

"Mr., you can't stay here. If they come back tomorrow, they'll kill you. What is your name? You saved my life and I don't even know your name."

"Lady, please get down. They might turn around and come back this way. You see what they did to me. This ain't even a scrap of what they would do to you. You got to get out of here, and my name is Calvin, Calvin Washington. What's your name lady?"

Sady put her hand out to shake Calvin's hand. "My name is Sady – Sady Milsap, and I'm honored to meet you."

"Miss Sady, I'm glad to know you too, but you got to leave now. I do know some Arabbers two blocks down. They probably know where this church is."

"What in the world is an Arabber, Calvin?"

"You see them all day long with their horses pulling their wagons. They sell fruits and vegetables up and down the streets. There is a fella' I can trust that can hide you in his wagon and take you out of here. Those gang members won't bother him because they make him pay them some of his money he makes selling his goods."

"I'm not goin' anywhere unless you go because they'll be back tomorrow. You heard what they said that they will do to you."

"Miss Sady, I'm an old man. I sit here all day, all year, hot, rain, cold, snow – doesn't matter. I've watched these boys grow from babies to what you heard today. They'll never live to be my age. I used to have a life, a family and even had a job at a big hotel downtown. I lost it all. I drank it all away. I don't deserve anything nice in my life. I just deserve to sit here and accept what the Good Lord sends my way. If it is a bullet in the head, then that's what I deserve. I gave up bein' a man years ago."

"Well, the Lord I pray to must be a different Lord, because He would never let one of his children settle for what you're settlin' for. You go get that man you were talkin' about, but you're goin' with me."

"I'll be back a few minutes, just stay covered up."

A few minutes seemed like hours to Sady. She was well hidden under the blanket but still terrified. "Dear God, please keep watch over me until Calvin comes back. I know some day I have to die, but I don't want it to be today. I don't want to get beat up and raped. Give me strength to get through this."

Just then she heard some bells and a horse's hooves on the street in front of her. She peeked out of the blanket and saw Calvin riding with another colored man on the front seat of the wagon.

"Miss Sady, Miss Sady, come on, hurry. Get in back of the wagon and cover yourself up. This here is Jacob. He knows where that church you asked me about is. He's goin' to take you there. Hurry!"

"But Calvin, please come with me. The church has a mission and they can help you too. Please come with me. That gang is going to come back and hurt you. Please Calvin!"

"Miss Sady, all I know is the streets now. There ain't no hope for me. You just get back there and get under all those baskets of vegetables and fruits. Nobody will see you. Thank you for carin' about this old man Miss Sady. God bless you."

It took Jacob almost an hour to get to the church. Traffic was stopped on the main street with police cars all over the place. Sady had no idea these police cars were looking for her. It had been almost three hours that she had been missing.

Jacob made it to the church and beat on the back of the seat of the wagon. "Miss Sady, we're here. You're safe. You can come out now."

Sady climbed down out of the wagon. "Jacob, I owe you so much. Thank you. Please take care of Calvin. See if you can get him to come down here for help. I'm really concerned about him."

"Miss Sady, I'll try to talk to him, but he's set in his ways. And his ways are the streets."

"Well, you can try anyway. Thank you again."

Sady was a mess. She was covered in dirt from the wagon and really did smell bad. She noticed one of the police cars raced over to her. A policeman got out of the car and asked her, "are you Sady Milsap?"

"Yes sir, I am."

The policeman rushed back to his car and radioed in that he found Sady Milsap and that she is in front of the church. It wasn't five minutes and Alec's car, brakes squealing and almost hitting the other police car, stopped short in front of Sady.

Sady ran over to Alec and put her arms around him. "Alec, I was so scared!" Sady could tell something was wrong because Alec didn't return the hug. "Alec, what's wrong?"

"What the hell do you think you were doing? I told you we knew where they lived and we were following them. All you had to do was go in the kitchen and call me and stay hidden from her. We would have been there before she could have gotten her plate filled. After Sister Theresa called me, we had every patrol car out looking for you. I told them to drop everything and look for you! What's wrong, why can't you listen? You could have been killed tonight!"

"Nothin' is wrong with me, nothin'. I saw Becky, followed her and lost her, and wound up on Pennsylvania Avenue. An old black man named Calvin hid me under a blanket until one of those men he called an Arabber, named Jacob, brought me here; and don't holler at me!"

"Sady, you're the reason we lost Becky. Blame yourself. It's been over three hours. I'm sure Becky met up with Leroy and they both took off and are hiding out somewhere. Hopefully, they dropped Grace off with somebody, but we'll never know that will we. Sady, I know how you feel, but we have to start from scratch all over again."

"Alec, please find Grace. I'm sorry. And you don't know how I feel, you can't. I'm not goin' back home without Grace if I have to walk these streets every night until I find Becky. That's what I'm gonna' do whether you like it or not."

Sady turned her back and started to walk around the church to the back where the mission was.

Alec took his coat off. "Sady, please put this coat around you. It's a long walk out back to the mission and you're shivering. Look, I'm sorry I talked to you this way, but you're so bull-headed. Sady, I don't want to lose you. That could have happened tonight."

Alec put his coat around Sady's shoulders, hugged her, and then said, "I'm falling in love with you Sady. I never thought this would happen to me again. I never thought I would let it happen."

"You asked me the other day why I have so much guilt. I'll tell you why. I wasn't supposed to fall in love again either, and Alec, I love you too!"

Just then Alec got an urgent call on his radio. He had to go to a homicide further into the city. "Sady, you get a good night's sleep. We'll talk tomorrow." Alec then laughed and said, "and, please take a bath. Hey, Sargent Powell, walk Sady to her room. Thanks."

"Alec, please be careful."

Alec and the other police left the premises. Sady watched as they all left then walked to the mission with Sargent Powell by her side. Sargent Powell watched as she walked up the steps and unlocked the door. He hollered up and asked if everything was ok and Sady nodded yes. Sargent Powell walked away knowing she was safe. Sady was happier than she had been for a long time.

chapter 26

SADY WAS SO tired, she just wanted to hurry and take a bath and jump in bed. The first thing she did was to go over to her dresser and pick up a picture of her family. The picture was of her, Jack, Donny and Eddie from years back. "I miss you guys so much. Please don't be mad Jack. Alec is a good man just like you."

Sady took her dirty dress off and went into the bathroom and started running the water to take a bath. She still had her slip and underwear on. She went over to the mirror and took the hairpins out of her bun to let her hair down so she could wash it. Under her breath she uttered, "boy do you stink Sady!"

Sady bent over to get a clean towel out of her clothes basket. When she looked up into the mirror, staring back at her was Leroy. She screamed, pushed him aside and managed to get into the other room.

She noticed Leroy was sweating profusely and was covered in blood.

"Leroy, get out of my room. How did you get in here anyway? Get out now before I call the police."

"What are you going to use a tin can? I don't see any phone. What's the matter, you got nothin' to say? Do you feel trapped Sady? That's just how I've been feeling ever since you got to this city. The cops have been on my tail every day because of your mouth. You owe me something woman."

"You got that wrong. You owe me. Where is Grace?"

"Don't know, don't care. Come over here Sady. I'll let you make up for all the trouble you caused me."

"I'm not afraid of you Leroy. You're scum. Tell me where Grace is and I'll forget you were here."

"That, my dear, is never going to happen." Leroy grabbed Sady by her hair, pulled his gun out and started rubbing the gun across her slip and the outline of her body. "Who's in charge now Grandma? You know you got a real nice body for a grandma. Take your clothes off. NOW!"

"You want my clothes off, you take them off!"

"No problem, Grandma. You want to be a hard ass and play tough. That's ok with me. I like that rough stuff. Becky liked it too. It must be a thing with you mountain women. I love playin' rough."

"You make me sick! Where is Becky?"

Leroy rips Sady's slip and bra strap. "Let me say that she won't be a burden to me anymore. I don't have to share my heroin with her anymore. Now take your clothes off bitch!"

Leroy backed up towards the door and stared at Sady while she slowly pretended to lower her slip and bra strap on the other shoulder. While Leroy was in a trance watching her and high on heroin, Sady, surprisingly kicked Leroy in the groin.

Leroy was bent over and in pain. "You bitch, you bitch! You're one dead broad now!"

Sady tried to run and Leroy shot her and just grazed her in the arm. She tried to run again and tripped and fell on the floor face down. Leroy rolled her over to face him. He stood over top of her with the gun pointed at her head.

"Beg bitch, let me hear you beg bitch!"

Sady closed her eyes and told him to shoot. "Do it, do it, get it over with you bastard!"

Just then Sady's apartment door started to open slowly.

Leroy turned and shot.

One shot was fired from Leroy's gun.

Sady opened her eyes only to see and feel the back of Leroy's head lying on her chest. Sady glanced up and saw Willow standing at the doorway, her left arm bleeding pretty badly.

Sady pushed Leroy off of her and noticed a big familiar Bowie knife sticking out of his chest.

Willow helped Sady up and hugged her. "Sady, are you ok? Let me see your arm girl."

"Willow, I'm ok, but you're not. You are really bleedin' pretty badly. You need to get to a hospital. What are you doin' here? When did you get here? How did you find this place? Let me wrap your arm to stop the bleedin'."

"One answer at a time Sady. Yep, he's as dead as a rusty old doornail. You need to oil those rusty old hinges on that door. Now to answer your questions. I got Mr. Tibbits to give me a ride to Boone. I caught the bus, rode all day and night. I asked where this here church was when I got to Baltimore City and walked from the bus station here. I heard a scream and just had this awful feeling it was you. And, here I am."

"Willow, if it wasn't for you, I'd be dead. But if you don't leave now, you'll be arrested for murder!"

"I don't run from anybody or anything Sady. Girl, you should know that by now. I'm an old lady, ain't goin' nowhere. I promised your pa before he died that I would look after you. I hope he's lookin' down here and sees I kept my word."

Willow walked over to Leroy's body and pulled her knife out and washed the blood off of it, then put it back in the knife holder on her side under her coat.

"Willow, it's too late. Somebody must have called the police. I can hear the sirens."

The sirens stopped right outside of the mission and much rumbling and people running up the steps could be heard. Finally there was a heavy knocking on the door. "This is the Baltimore City Police- open the door – NOW!"

Sady put her bathrobe on and opened the door. Sister Theresa ran in and asked Sady if she was ok. "Sady, your arm is bleeding. And who is this lady, her arm is bleeding too. Please, somebody call an ambulance for these two women."

An older policeman walked over to Sister Theresa and said, "Sister, an ambulance is already on its way, but these two ladies have some explaining to do. Somebody like to tell me what happened?"

Sady told the policeman a lie so that Willow wouldn't get into any trouble. "This man tried to rape me. He held a gun to my head and was ready to shoot me. He already shot me in the arm. My friend Willow came through the door and he shot her. I grabbed a knife and stabbed him while he was tryin' to put more bullets in his gun."

"Lady, where's the knife? Did you know him?"

Willow looked offended at the policeman and said, "This lady has a name. Her name is Sady Milsap, and she didn't . . ."

"Willow, Willow, please he needs a statement from me."

The policeman said, "that's right Willow. Willow, and you're last name?"

"My name is Willow Moone."

Just then the ambulance driver came and so did the Medical Examiner.

Alec also came running into Sady's room. Sady and Willow were already being tended to by the ambulance attendants and were to be taken to Johns Hopkins Hospital.

Alec told the policeman in charge that this was his case and he would take any information from here on in. He didn't want Sady or Willow talking to the police until he found out exactly what happened.

The first thing Alec did, of course, was to find out how bad Sady was shot and make sure she was not in any danger. "Sady, I'm so sorry I wasn't here. Right after I got to the homicide that I heard on the radio, I called headquarters to put a guard at your door."

"Why, Alec?"

"I hate to tell you this Sady, but Becky was murdered about two hours ago. She was beat up real bad and her throat was cut. But she managed to write LC in blood next to her."

"Alec, I'm goin' to be sick. This will kill Eva. What about Grace? Did you find her Alec? Please don't tell me somethin' terrible happened to her."

"Sady, that's the only good thing that came out of this mess. A tenant in the building was taking care of Grace. When she saw the commotion, she panicked and brought Grace to us. Sady, she is fine. Not a hair on her head was touched. She's at child services being examined right now. You will be getting her sometime tomorrow."

Sady quietly muttered something under her breath. "From one mother to another, thank you."

Alec asked Sady, "what did you say Sady?"

"Nothin', just that all of us mothers and grandmothers have to stick together."

Alec noticed Willow and said, "I already know who this young lady is. This has to be Willow."

"You sure do have a good eye, son. Who is this good-lookin' man Sady?"

"Alec, you guessed right. This is Willow Moone from Harmony that I told you about, and Willow this is that friend I told you about on the phone that was helpin' me find Grace. And he found her! Willow I'd like you to meet Detective Alec Karastaupolis of the Baltimore City Police Department. Did I pronounce it right Alec?"

"You sure did Sady. Nice to meet you Willow. I see you were shot in the arm too. It doesn't look too good. You're going to Hopkins with Sady."

"I don't need a hospital to fix me up. I can doctor myself up. I had worse than this happen to me before and come out like new. I'll just ride with Sady to make sure she gets fixed up."

Alec shook his head and said, "no, you're going to get looked at also. Looks like you lost quite a bit of blood Willow. The hospital might have to put some blood back in you."

"I ain't taken somebody else's blood. It might have little critters or bugs in it. No way!"

"Alec took Willow's hand and said, "let's go to the hospital first and see what they say."

Willow enjoyed Alec holding her hand. She usually never let a man touch her, but she could tell Alec was special. Willow smiled at Alec. "You promise to hold my hand if they go to put blood in me?"

"Yes, Willow, I certainly do promise to hold your hand."

While riding in the ambulance Alec held Willow's hand. He really wanted to hold Sady's hand but he felt Willow was out of her environment and scared. Sady kind of thought that was cute and very nice of Alec to show affection to someone like Willow who had such a hard life in her earlier days.

Willow asked, "Alec, are you married?"

Sady said, "Willow, that's a personal question."

Alec responded, "No Willow, I'm not married. Are you interested?"

Willow giggled and asked, "got a girlfriend?"

Sady interrupted. "Willow, this ain't the time or place to be askin' those kinds of questions. You're talkin' like you got shot in the head instead of the arm."

Willow responded. "I just figured a handsome man like Alec should've been taken by now."

"I was married a long time ago Willow. Just didn't work out."

"You just have to find the right one son. It will be like magic. You'll look into each other's eyes and know you both have somethin' special to give each other. Before you know it, you'll be growin' old together."

Alec gazed into Sady's eyes and she gazed into his. Willow was smarter than they both knew. She already knew there was something there between them. She always wanted to see Sady happy again. She just had a hunch that Alec was going to be the man to make Sady happy.

Willow started to slur her words and lose consciousness. She had lost a good bit of blood and was very weak.

Alec hollered for the driver to speed it up, because Willow did not look good at all.

chapter 27

THE AMBULANCE PULLED into the emergency bay and transported Sady and Willow to the emergency room. Doctors were alerted by the police about the severity of the gunshot wounds before the ambulance left the mission.

Sady was at one end of the emergency room, and Willow was at the other. They both were treated right away. Sady's bullet was only a graze. She was treated but made to lie down for a while to make sure the bleeding stopped. Willow, on the other hand, had a more serious wound. The bullet lay close to an artery in her arm.

Willow was given oxygen and was a little more alert. She absolutely did not want to part with her clothes, more importantly, her Bowie knife. All of her clothes were put into a bag and Alec requested that he be given the knife. Willow was finally put to sleep and taken to the operating room to remove the bullet. Sady remained in bed while Alec waited for Willow to come out of surgery.

Alec had to question Sady. She told him the same story that she told the other policeman. She didn't realize Alec had the knife. He knew Sady was lying for Willow. He knew a Bowie knife had a concave curve at the tip so that when the knife was pulled out it made more damage to a person. He also noticed there were no knives at all in Sady's room. There was no need to have any knives because there was no kitchen. Sady came into town with a derringer. No knives were on her or in her suitcase. She really didn't have to lie for Willow. Alec knew that Leroy's death was a case of self-defense. If Leroy wasn't killed, the scene would have been a lot different. Alec would have been looking at Sady's and Willow's body.

Right now, Alec's main goal was to get both women together, talk to each one, and find out what really took place. But at the moment, Alec wanted to make sure both women were ok. He could tell Willow was tough, but at her age, being shot, losing a good deal of blood, then going under anesthesia was pretty dangerous.

Willow was finally out of surgery. Doctor Aspen told Alec that she lost quite a lot of blood. Alec volunteered to give Willow blood. Doctor Aspen asked, "what is your blood type Alec?"

Alec replied, "the last time I received blood was in Sicily when I had a grenade thrown at me and I was pretty well torn up. I believe it was A positive.

"Alec, Willow is AB negative. That is the rarest form of blood and hard to find. We are giving her our last two pints of blood now, but she needs at least one more. We're calling all around the city to see if any of the other hospitals have some that we can borrow."

"I'll check with the guys at the precinct. Maybe somebody there either knows someone or has that type of blood. Can I see Willow?"

"She's still asleep from the anesthetic. I noticed that her back is full of scars that have healed from years ago. It looks as if she was abused very badly by someone. I think you should question her about those scars. Whoever did it used a whip. I'd like to know myself what kind of animal did that to her. Well, I've got to get back on the phone and see if I can get that blood."

"Thanks Doctor Aspen. What will happen if she can't get the blood?"

"That's something we don't want to even think about. We'll get that blood."

Alec went in to see how she was. Willow was asleep. Her white hair was up in a cap for the operation. Her black eye patch was removed and a large white gauze patch with tape over it was put in its place. Alec went to put her blanket up around her when she turned on her right side. He was taken back by what he saw. Her back was full of scars that had healed just like the doctor described. He could tell these were very old scars from years ago and they were old whip scars, because he had seen this type of abuse before in many of his cases. But there was something at the base of her neck and close to her left shoulder that really amazed him. There was a birthmark in the form a heart, just like Sady's, even in the same spot.

Alec asked the nurse to come in. "I know that this is a birthmark. But what are the odds that another person, a person that she is close to has the same birthmark in the same place?"

The nurse replied, "very unusual. I would say this lady and the person you're talking about are probably related. I would venture to say they are more than likely mother and child. Do you know if she had any children? She sure could use a pint or two of their blood right now. I do believe that one of her children would probably carry the AB negative blood type. If she needs me or wakes up, just holler."

"Ok, I will."

Alec was shocked. Apparently Sady knew nothing about this. He thought, "no wonder Willow has been with her since she was a baby. She is Willow's daughter. She probably gave her to Sady's parents because she couldn't take care of her or because of this person who beat her so badly and ripped her skin to shreds at one time. How could anyone abuse another human being like that?"

Alec really didn't feel that it was up to him to tell Sady that Willow might be her mother. He really wanted to know Sady's blood type before he said anything to either one of them. He felt that knowing Sady's blood type would confirm, along with the birthmark, that Willow was her mother, and hopefully, save Willow's life.

Alec walked over to the nurse's station and told the head nurse that he needed a sample of Sady's blood because of the homicide she was just involved in. He needed to know right away what her blood type was. He told the nurse he would need it for court purposes. After getting permission from the emergency room doctor that treated Sady's wound, the nurse sent a tube of Sady's blood downstairs to the lab to be analyzed.

A couple of hours went by and the nurse had Sady's blood test results. When Alec read the results, it confirmed what he thought previously. Sady's blood type was AB negative.

Alec had the nurse page Doctor Aspen immediately.

Dr. Aspen met Alec in the hallway. "Doctor Aspen, we have a blood donor for Willow. I had a blood sample taken from Sady Milsap, the other woman that was also shot along with Willow. The blood was analyzed and it was confirmed that Sady is AB negative. I did lie a little. I told the head nurse I needed a blood sample because Sady was involved in a homicide. I don't want the nurse to get into trouble."

Doctor Aspen said, "Alec, this is between you and me. Why in the world did you have that hunch?"

"If you look at both of their necks towards the left shoulder, they have the same birthmark that is in the shape of a small heart – the exact same shape and size."

"Very good Alec, I guess that's why you're in the profession you're in."

"Sady doesn't know that Willow is her mother. She won't hesitate to give Willow blood if you ask her because of their close friendship. So, please say nothing to her. I feel when Willow gets on her feet; it should be up to her to let Sady know – that is if she wants to."

"Alec, this conversation won't go beyond the two walls we're standing in front of. I'm just thankful we found a blood donor for Willow. I'll have the nurse in the emergency room explain to Sady that Willow needs blood and it was just noted from Sady's earlier blood test that she would be a good donor for Willow. I'll leave it up to her. I'll tell her she doesn't have to give blood to Willow, that we can have someone else donate their blood. That way it doesn't look so suspicious. If she says ok, I'll get the nurse to start getting her ready. How's that sound to you?"

"Thank you Doctor Aspen. I have a strong feeling she won't say no. If she does, I'll just have to tell her that I believe Willow is her mother. I'll go and sit with Sady while she is having her blood drawn. She probably has never given blood before. She might be a little anxious. I've got some questions to ask her anyway."

"Alec, as soon as Willow gets that blood, she should be ready to get up and dance. She'll be here overnight so that we can monitor her vital signs, take care of that bullet wound, and make sure the transference of blood is all she really needs. She should be able to go home some time tomorrow. I'll talk to you then."

Alec walked down the hallway to Sady's room. She hadn't seen him for quite a while and finally felt a lot calmer and less apprehensive when he walked into the room. Of course she didn't think he was going to question her, but he had to find out what really happened that night in Sady's room.

"I see they are getting you ready to donate blood to Willow. Have you ever given blood before Sady?"

"No Alec, but if anybody gives blood to Willow, I want it to be me. That way she won't worry that somebody put somethin' in her blood. You know how she is just by that little introduction you had."

"That's pretty nice of you Sady. It's not that bad. I give blood at least every two months. It will be over with before you know it and Willow will be feeling a lot better because of it."

"How is Willow doin' Alec. They won't let me out of this bed. I would like to go see her."

"I did go see her Sady. She is very weak from losing a lot of blood. She was sleeping when I went into her room. Sady, what happened to Willow years ago? The doctor and I saw all these horrible scars from being whipped on her back. Did she ever confide in you or your parents as to what happened?"

"Alec, I've never seen Willow's bare back. What you just told me makes me feel sick. I've never known her to have any friends other than my parents. I really don't know what happened to her eye. I do know when she was a little girl her father was hung in front of her and her mother. My parents told me that. Her mother went crazy and was put away and died at a young age in an asylum. My grandmother took and raised Willow as her own. My mother and her were like sisters. When Willow got older she went back up to her home in Blackheart Mountain. After my mother had me, Willow would come down to help her with her chores on the farm. My mother was always very sickly. Willow was just part of my life. She was always there to help my parents."

"If that is a private part of Willow's life that she doesn't want to talk about, then we should respect it. But Sady, about what happened tonight – you do know I am a detective – right?"

"Of course, Alec. What are you tryin' to tell me?"

"I'm trying to tell you in a nice way that I don't believe your story. I saw the knife wound in Leroy. It matches the Bowie knife that Willow had on her when she was admitted tonight. You didn't even know Willow was coming to see you. I think she heard you scream, and heard the shot, then raced upstairs to help you. Leroy turned and saw her and shot her. She threw that knife at him and "bullseye" got him right in the heart. That's exactly what happened Sady."

"How do you know that everything happened the way you think it did?"

"I'll tell you how I know. Sister Theresa heard the scream and the first shot. She ran over to the convent to make a phone call to the police. She also saw an older woman run up the steps right after she heard the shot. She didn't have a knife in her hand. The woman used both handrails to help her get up the steps. And Sady, more importantly, there was a big glob of blood in the front of your nightgown as if somebody fell on top of you."

"I don't care what anybody saw. I grabbed Willow's knife and I killed Leroy!"

"Sady, I saw where Willow kept her knife. Leroy would have killed both of you before you could get that knife out of the case on her side. Anybody could see that it was self-defense. I don't know why you just don't tell the truth!"

"The truth is, I don't know about your laws here, but back home a woman's word is very seldom respected in court."

"You're not back home Sady. This happened here. Yes, I have to write a report and keep the knife as evidence. Yes, there will be a review of what happened. But as far as I'm concerned, like I told you, it is a case of pure self-defense. Leroy killed Becky. She even wrote his initials on the floor. Willow did society a favor. Now please reconsider the story you just told me. Nothing will happen to Willow. You have my word."

"Ok, ok, Willow threw the knife, but it was to keep Leroy from killin' me. He had the gun pointed at my head and was gettin' ready to shoot me. She saved my life! Alec, you can't let anything happen to her!"

"Sady, I haven't lied to you since the day you walked into my office. Why would I start lying to the woman I love now? You and Willow might have to stay around for a few extra days until the facts are investigated and cleared, then you, Willow and Grace can get on the bus and go back home."

"Alec, Instead of actin' like I'm takin' everything out on you, I should be thankin' you so much for gettin' Grace back for me. I owe you so much!"

"You're welcome, my lady and you owe me nothing. I don't look forward to you going back home, but I know you can't stay here forever. I know Eva needs you Sady. I had to call Eva right after we got here. To be told over the phone that your daughter was murdered had to be terrible for her. Thank God she is at your house with her son. Dewey said he was going to get Mrs. Tibbits to be there for his mother until you get there. Sady, I have a lot to think about and I will be coming to Harmony to see you soon."

"Alec, I know how busy you are here, but please come to Harmony as soon as you can."

"How do you think I feel Sady? Being with you has been the best thing to happen to me in my life. You best believe I'll be there as quickly as I can."

Sady, very sad over Becky's death said, "poor Eva. I don't know how I will comfort her. Losin' a child to me was like losin' part of my heart. There are no special words anyone can say to take that sorrow that you carry around away. I can't explain it. The years pass, but the terrible day your child died is a memory that you play over and over in your mind. You go on livin' because you have to. You really don't live a normal life; you exist because it's not your time to go. You know when the first time after all these years that I didn't feel like I was just existin'? It was when I fell in love with you Alec. You let me feel like I want to actually live again, not that I don't think about Donny or Jack, but I feel that new love I felt when I was young and in love. My heart is still broken, but it's like a new part of my heart started to grow."

Alec said, "I've never heard anything so beautiful put into the words you just spoke. You let me work on getting us together. You work on getting yourself and Willow better. Here comes the nurse to get you ready to give blood. I'll sit here with you while you're giving blood."

The whole time Sady was giving blood, all she could do was look at Alec. Her mind went in circles again and all she could do was think. "I'm so happy with this man. For once in my life I feel alive and happy again. Please God don't let this end!"

chapter 28

THAT NIGHT SADY stayed in Willow's room. She didn't want Willow to be alone when she finally came out of the sedation. The hospital provided her with a nice reclining chair so that she could also get a little sleep if possible. Willow came out of the sedation but was quite drowsy. Sady was there to give her a little water and to rub some ice on her lips when needed.

Sady hardly got any sleep. She closed the door as far as she could to keep the noise out. She dimmed the lights so that just maybe she could get a little sleep, but that was impossible. Sady noticed that Willow was restless and tried to turn on her side but couldn't. Sady went over and propped pillows behind her back to make her more comfortable. Willow's gown was open in the back and Sady saw those horrible scars that Alec told her about. Sady couldn't help but cry when she saw the scars. "Oh my God. What kind of monster would do this?" She then tried to close her gown because she couldn't stand to look at her back anymore. When Sady went to tie the strings together on her gown, her fingers just froze. Sady saw the birthmark below Willow's neck.

"How can that be? It's just like mine, exactly the same. I don't understand. Are we related in some way or is this just a coincidence?" Sady sat back in her recliner and her mind was full of unanswered questions. Her skin was darker than her parents. Her hair was a very dark brown, not blond like her mother's or light brown like her fathers. Her mother was never a strong-willed woman like Sady or physically strong like Sady was. Her father was a small man, layed back and very easy going. As a matter of fact, none of her parents or relatives matched Sady's disposition or looks. Sady remembered what Eva told her the night that she put a knife in Roby's heart. "Eva said that me and Willow were just alike. Could it be that Eva knew somethin' that I didn't? No, I don't believe that."

Sady just blurted the words out, "Is Willow my real mother?" Sady covered up the birthmark and just sat back in the recliner and waited for the sun to come up and another day to begin so that she and Willow could get out of the hospital and she could go get Grace. She just couldn't or wouldn't think about this anymore.

The next morning, Alec came to the hospital to pick up Willow and Sady and take them back to the mission. He peeked in the room and Sady was fast asleep in the recliner. Willow was up and put her finger in front of her lips for Alec to be quiet.

"Alec whispered, "Willow, you look so much better. I have to wake Sady up; I have a surprise for her." He stepped outside of the doorway and brought in Grace. Willow had a smile from one ear to the other.

Alec tried to wake up Sady. "Sady, Sady, wake up. I've got a present for you."

Sady still a little drowsy said, "Present, present, what are you talkin' about Alec?"

Alec held up Grace. "This little present Sady. Do you want me to take it back or do you want it."

Sady jumped out of the chair, picked Grace up, and couldn't stop hugging her. "I can't believe it. I've got my baby back. Grandma will never let you out of her sight again Grace."

Grace hugged Sady and wouldn't let her go. "Grandma, love you."

"Oh, my beautiful girl, I hope someday you love someone as much as I love you! Alec, can we go home now! Please, I want to get out of this place."

"I just talked to the nurse and she said both you and Willow can leave. She said if you go home before the end of the week, make sure Willow has a follow-up at her hospital to make sure that wound is healing. She also needs to wear a sling and keep her arm elevated."

Willow said, "I don't need no sling. I just want my clothes and my knife."

Alec said. "Sorry Willow, I have to keep that knife until the District Attorney goes over the case. I hope to give it back to you before you leave Baltimore."

Sady reluctantly admitted, "Willow, Alec knew what really happened that night. It was all self-defense. He was too smart to tell a big fat lie to. Sorry Alec, but Willow wanted to tell the truth. It was me who interfered, not her."

Willow said, "doesn't matter none, that boy was bad. He's in Hell now with the Satan and his lot."

"Willow, I'm glad to see you're feeling a lot better. Wouldn't you say so Sady?"

"Yeah, Alec, she is back to her old self. Can we please get out of here?"

Alec could see something was bothering Sady. He shrugged it off and figured it was because of what Leroy had put her through the night before.

"Let's go girls and get out of here before one of these doctors or nurses changes their mind.

On the way back to the mission, Alec knew something was wrong with Sady. She was very quiet, except for giving Grace a lot of hugs and kisses.

Willow seemed back to her old self. "Alec, you sure are a right fine fellow and a handsome man too. You're gonna' make somebody a fine husband someday. I wish I was 'bout ten years younger."

Alec had to laugh. "Only ten year's younger Willow? Well, you know, some men do like older women."

"You're just playin' with me Alec. I see how you look at Sady and how she looks at you."

Sady, embarrassed, turned around and said, "Willow, now stop that, you didn't notice nothin' of the kind."

"Sady, I ain't seen that glow in your face for a long time. I know what I'm seein'."

Alec just shook his head. Sady gave up and turned around.

Sady went into her purse and pulled out some money. "Alec, I don't have any way of gettin' to the bus station. Do you mind pickin' up three tickets for Boone, North Carolina when you get a chance?"

"Sady, put your money back. My department will pay for your tickets home. That is the least the City of Baltimore should do for you."

"No, no, I pay my own way! I always have."

Alec asked Sady, "why do you have to be so hard-headed. Has she always been like this Willow?"

"One thing you gotta' learn 'bout a mountain woman Alec, they're tough, they gotta' warm heart, and they are stubborn and proud of it! Right Sady?"

Sady turned around, looked at Willow and said, "you got that right Willow."

Alec finally gave in. "Ok, ok, Sady, I'll take your money and buy the tickets!"

Alec helped Willow up the steps to Sady's apartment at the mission while Sady carried Grace. While Sady was getting Grace settled down, Willow had a last few words to say to Alec before he left for work. Willow whispered in Alec's ear, "don't let her go Alec, she needs you more than she's ever goin' to admit it."

Alec whispered back in Willow's ear, "don't worry about it Willow. I need Sady too. I want to be in her life, and I want her in my life."

Willow replied in a louder voice, "good boy, Alec."

Sady overheard Willow's reply to Alec. "Who's a good boy Willow?"

"I told Alec he was a good boy for bringin' us home."

Sady replied, "yeah, Alec, thank you. I know you get so tired of me sayin' that I won't be able to repay you, but I won't."

Alec answered, "you don't owe me a thing Sady. Look I have to get to work. I'll get those bus tickets for you and drop them off. You girls take care now."

After Alec left, Sady got Willow settled in the apartment. She let Willow sleep in bed and she and Grace slept on the couch. Sady didn't get much sleep that night. So many questions and thoughts about Willow being her real mother overtook any chance of a good-nights' sleep. "Should I ask her, or shouldn't I say anything and leave well enough alone?"

No, Sady knew she had to know the truth. When to ask Willow was the question. Sady always loved Willow and would never want to hurt her. But things were different now. Sady just had to wait for the right time.

chapter 29

BEFORE THE END of the next week, Willow was back to her old self and feeling much better. Believe it or not she and Sister Theresa became good friends in that short time. Willow had her singing "Wabash Cannonball" in no time. Even Father O'Shesky became fond of Willow. She just had a down to earth personality that grew on a person.

What Willow couldn't understand was why Reverend Marshal, in Harmony, would often talk about priests and sisters of the Catholic faith as if they were a distant cousin of Satan. Willow even went to mass with Sister Theresa. Even though she couldn't understand the Latin part of the mass, she could see the love the parishioners had for the Lord. It was the same love she saw on the faces in her church in Harmony, just different faces and a different way of showing their love for Jesus. She had to admit, she did like the beautiful voices in the choir at Holy Rosary compared to those way-off-key voices at Harmony Baptist Church; but Harmony was a much smaller church and had a much smaller congregation.

Two weeks had gone by since that dreadful night that Leroy was killed. Sady and Willow missed Becky's funeral. Alec had her remains sent by train. The train only went to Johnson City, Tennessee. Boone had no train station. The funeral director in Boone picked Becky's body up from Johnson City and prepared it for viewing. The casket and the funeral were paid for by Alec. The funeral director was told to tell Eva that a very wealthy couple in Boone paid for the funeral. No one, not even Sady knew that Alec paid for Becky's funeral. Sady was told by Dewey that Eva really took Becky's death very hard and blamed herself for everything. He told Sady that she stayed in her room all day crying. That's when Sady knew she had to get herself, Grace, and Willow back home. Christmas was only a few weeks away. Sady though that if Eva could hold Grace again, that it might take away just a little bit of the sorrow she was feeling.

Sady knew that dreaded day would come when she would be leaving Alec, not knowing when she would ever see him again. She felt so vibrant and alive again, even after what she went through two weeks before. She felt she had everything. Her life was fulfilled. There was only one thing left in her life to make things right again, and that was to get Eddie back home.

Alec felt the same way. He couldn't bear to let Sady go. He had never felt this way in years, even with his first wife. It was a Thursday night, rainy and cold. He stopped by Sady's apartment to give her the bus tickets for the return trip to Boone. The bus would be leaving that Saturday very early in the morning. "Here are your tickets Sady. Do you realize how hard it is for me to hand these over to you?"

"Alec, do you realize how hard it is for me to take them from your hand?"

Grace and Willow were both asleep. Alec and Sady sat on the couch holding each other.

"Sady, I'm going to find a way. I can't let you walk out of my life. I won't!"

"Alec, I feel the same way. Do you think I want to get on that bus knowin' I might never see you again? If I had no family or no home, you would be lookin' at this face day after day. I don't know what to do either! I'm sure God will get us through this."

"Ok Sady, you're starting to sound like my good friend Father Joe. I don't have to rely on God. I'll find a way we can be together. I hate to say it but I have to get back to the precinct. I won't be able to see you until Saturday when I pick you up to take you to the bus station. I've got a case I have to present to the District Attorney tomorrow."

"Alec, how long have you known?"

"How long have I known about the case?"

"No. How long have you known that Willow might be my real mother?"

"Sady that is something you both have to talk over. I saw your birthmark, and I saw her birthmark. Not only that, but the night Willow needed blood, I asked the nurse to draw your blood to find out what type of blood you had. Sady, Willow had a rare type of blood, AB negative. You also have AB negative."

Sady said, "when were you goin' to tell me that last part?"

"I wasn't. Willow could have died without the right blood. You should know that because you also have that type in case something happens to you. When the time is right, talk to her about it. Sady she has been there for you all your life, you just never called her Ma."

"I should be a little mad – about the blood thing – but I'm not. Thanks for being honest with me Alec. You better go. I'll see you Saturday mornin'."

"Sady, come here." Alec kissed Sady as though it were their last kiss. "Sady, I love you."

"Alec, I love you too, maybe even a little more."

"I doubt that. Goodbye Sady. Oh, wait a minute. Your derringer and Willow's knife are in this bag. Do me a favor, and don't give her this knife until you're home."

Sady laughed. "I won't give it to her until we're home. Don't worry about it. Bye, Alec."

Saturday morning came quicker than Sady wanted it to. Alec came in the apartment to help the girls with their suitcases or in Willow's case a big plastic bag. Willow had on the coat that Sady got her from the homeless shelter with all the bright colors in it.

Alec looked at Willow and said, "Willow, may I say you look beautiful this morning. Sady's not going to lose you at any of the bus stops! That coat will glow in the dark!"

"Ain't it beautiful Alec. Just like Joseph, in the Bible, and his coat of many colors. I ain't ever had nothin' so pretty. Alec, you see this here color blue – that's how pretty our sky is in Harmony. Sady is just too good to me."

There is a tear in Willow's eye.

Sady noticed the tear and said, "Willow, is somethin' wrong? Looks like you're cryin'."

"No, I ain't cryin'. Since I only got one eye, this other one waters up every once in a while."

Alec looked at his watch. "We better get going. This is the last bus until next Wednesday going to Boone, and if it snows, there won't be one for a week or more."

Alec loaded the bags while Willow, Sady, and Grace got into the car for the ride to the bus station.

Sady just stared at Alec wishing the trip to the bus station would never end, but it wasn't that far from the mission. She knew it would have to end sometime.

They all said their goodbyes before getting on the bus. Alec had one more thing to say. "Now I'm going to warn you. As soon as I get a chance, I'm coming to Harmony Creek. I've got to meet all these people you have been telling me about Sady. And I want to see this blue Carolina sky you told me about Willow. I can't believe it's any different than the sky I'm looking at now."

Willow just laughed and said, "you'll see, you'll see."

Alec tenderly kissed Sady. He then leaned over and kissed Grace and Willow on the cheek.

Alec then turned to Willow and said, "you keep everybody on the right path Willow."

Willow looked at Alec. "That's exactly what I been doin'. You pay us a visit real soon Alec."

Sady waved to Alec until the bus was out of sight.

The three of them sat on the longer seat in the back of the bus so that they could all sit together and Grace would be able to lie down.

Willow noticed the sadness in Sady's eyes. She knew exactly why she looked so sad.

"Sady, what are you gonna' do about it?"

"Do about what Willow?"

"All I know is that kiss Alec gave you weren't the same kind of kiss you give your aunt."

Sady held her head down. "I don't know what you're tryin' to say Willow."

"Sady, I'm old and only got one eye, but I'm not blind. You love that man."

"Willow, I should have known I couldn't fool the likes of you. I feel guilty Willow. I grew up with Jack. I knew him all my life. I've only known Alec almost a month and I have these feelin's for him I can't explain. I feel like I'm betrayin' Jack because I feel this way. Yes, I love that man Willow. There, I said it."

"Sady, do you know how many women never have that special feelin' for a man that you have for Alec? That is a gift. You un-wrap that gift and keep it close to your heart. The past is gone, Sady, and it was a good past with Jack; a wonderful life, but don't throw away a chance you have to be happy again."

"Boy, I never know what's comin' out of your mouth Willow. I have to admit, you are right about that special gift. Sady gave Willow a big hug and so did Grace. I don't know what I would do without you Willow. There is somethin' I want to ask you though. I think I'll lay Grace down first so she can take a nap."

After Sady got Grace situated beside her, she moved closer to Willow so they could talk without waking up Grace.

"Willow, I am just goin' to come out and say what I have to. While you were in the hospital and unconscious, I noticed the terrible scars on your back. I also noticed you have a birthmark that is exactly like mine. That's not all Willow. You needed blood. You have a rare blood. I have that exact same rare blood. Willow, are we related in some way? Look, Willow, I don't want to hurt you. If you would rather not talk about it, that's ok with me."

Willow put her head down and said, "Sady, I don't want you to hate me."

"Willow, how could I ever hate you. You're always there for me and you were always there for my parents."

Willow began her story. "Sady, I was raped a long time ago. After he raped me, I spit on him and he took a cigarette and put my eye out. Then he tied me to a tree and whipped me on and off all day and all night, then raped me over and over. That monster finally left. I was a mess, bleedin' everywhere, I couldn't see. I was in so much pain Sady. I don't know how, but I managed to crawl and slide back down the mountain to your parent's house. They wanted to call the Sheriff, but I wouldn't let them. I was so ashamed. I never trusted the Sheriff anyway. Things back then were worse than they are now. Bein' a Cherokee Injun was even worse. Your mama and daddy bandaged me up and took care of me for about a month."

"I'm so sorry Willow that you went through that."

"There's more Sady. You know how sick your mama always was."

"I sure do Willow."

"You're mama and daddy always wanted a baby, but your mama was too sick. About a month later, I knew I was with child. I stayed with your parents until the baby was born. Your mama delivered the baby. After the baby was born and I felt better, I went back up to the mountain with the baby. I had a lot to think about."

"Willow, I never knew. I'm happy that my mama and daddy were there for you. What happened to the baby?"

"It was a little girl Sady. She was beautiful. Your mama never missed a day comin' up that mountain to help me with the baby. Your ma's face would light up and she would sing and talk to the baby. Your pa was just as happy as your ma. Sady I knew I couldn't keep that beautiful little girl. I had no money; the people in Harmony shunned me like they do now. I didn't want that to happen to her."

Sady asked in a suspicious voice, "Willow, where is that little girl now?"

Willow looked up at Sady. "She's sittin' here next to me on this bus."

"Willow, I don't know what to say."

"Sady, whatever you do or say, please don't hate me. Nobody in the community knows I birthed you. You're ma and pa kept that to themselves. You're ma had a little weight on her in those days before she got really sick, and when she saw some people in town and you with her, she just said she had no idea she was with child, she thought she was eatin' too much. And Sady they believed her."

"I could never hate you Willow. I would have been just as proud if you would have kept me. I want you to know that. I can't imagine livin' all these years and seein' me almost every day was doin' to your heart. Willow, who raped you? I have a feelin' I know, but I want to hear it from you."

"It was Silas Prestel, Roby's Pa, Sady. I was the last woman he raped. I made sure he never raped another woman. He was also one of the men who hung my Daddy. I was five, but I remember his face and the other fella's face. To me he murdered both my ma and pa. I was only five, then he comes back twenty some years later and almost murdered me."

"Willow what happened to him?"

"Let's just say him and his boy Roby are sharin' a room in Hell. He came back to Blackheart Mountain for me, about two months after you were born, and this time I was ready for him. I set a trap and caught him like the animal he was. I cut off a few pertinent things a man needs to be a man, drug him up the mountain and threw him screamin' and alive down that minin' hole. He's keepin' Roby company."

"You know Willow, it doesn't bother me so much as what you did to him because he deserved it, it's the idea that I'm related to Roby."

"Sady, don't pay that no mind. You don't look like him, act like him or even have his blood- the hospital people found that out for you. You are just like your ma and pa, goodhearted, kind, and a carin' person. Just get all that nonsense stuff out of your head. Roby was a wicked, wicked man like Silas."

"Willow, I know this was hard for you, but thanks. I had to know. This won't go any further then the two of us. We're not goin' to look back anymore at the bad things that happened. We're gonna' look at what good came out of the past. Let's try and get some sleep Willow. It's a long ride home."

chapter 30

THE BUS PULLED into the bus station in Boone about two o'clock early in the morning. Sady didn't want to call anyone that early, so the three of them sat in the waiting area and tried to get some sleep until morning. Sady wasn't sure who she should call. Dewey wasn't old enough to drive, even though he did many times. Eva really never had a chance to learn to drive, Roby never let her. Sady thought about Mr. Tibbits, but she didn't want to call him so early in the morning. Her mind went back to Dewey. He knew how to drive. He had been driving for a few years even though he wasn't supposed to, but many farm boys drove their father's trucks in order to do what farm chores that had to be done. Sady made her mind up. She would call Dewey as soon as the sun came up. But before she would make a call to Dewey, she gave Willow her Bowie knife that Alec gave Sady to hold.

Willow said, "Sady, you made me one happy woman. I didn't think I'd ever see my knife again. Now you thank Alec for me."

The sun finally came up and Sady made her call to Dewey. He told her he would be there in about an hour and a half.

When Dewey arrived, he was so happy to see everyone, especially Grace. "Miss Sady, I'm so glad you're home. Ma is taken Becky's death real hard. She lies in bed and cries most of the day. She's blamin' herself for everything. Maybe seein' Grace will help her some."

"I'm so sorry Dewey about Becky. I did get to see her before she died. Dewey, she really looked bad. She was on that heroin and was really lookin' sick."

Willow spoke up. "Dewey, I'm sorry she died the way she did, son, but that sickness she had turned her into a Becky that none of us ever saw before."

"I know Willow, but you can't convince Ma of that."

"Well Dewey, me and Sady, were gonna' try our best to help your ma."

On the way back from Boone, Sady couldn't help but to feel so happy coming home. She could breathe in that fresh cold mountain air now instead of all those fumes from the cars and factory's. The pines stood so tall and straight, but it was the smell from the pines that let her know she was home. There were no cars and buses and people hanging on the street corners shouting obscene or rude remarks. No, she saw absolutely no one on the streets of Boone or walking on the country road on her way back home. She was finally home, and felt a peacefulness that just filled her heart and soul. She accomplished her goal – she got Grace back. She only had one more goal to achieve, and that goal was to have Eddie back home. She had to admit though that for her first time being in a big city like Baltimore, she saw and learned a lot about people and history that she never knew before. But it is always good to be back home.

In the process of getting Grace back, Sady was able to meet a wonderful man that she fell in love with. Her life changed those weeks in Baltimore. She grew quite a bit; she learned how to accept others that believed a little differently than she did. She under-stood criticism and having more patience was necessary in order to accomplish what your mind and heart set out to accomplish. The most important thing Sady learned was that happiness is up to the individual. If you want to be sad and feel guilty all the time about wanting to be happy, you will never find happiness. Sady was fortunate; she finally found that happiness – in Alec. The problem was how could they ever be together?

The snow started to fall. The ground was covered in no time. Christmas was only a week away. Sady was finally going to be home in time for Christmas. She could see the smoke coming out of her chimney as they rounded the mountain. She was so excited. This Christmas would be one of the best she had in a long time. She was finally home.

Sady even noticed how happy Dewey was. He looked healthier than ever. She noticed how much he laughed and kidded around. What happened to Roby that night was the best thing that could have happened for Dewey and his mother. Sady was thinking, "what is really sad is that Dewey will never know that I'm related to him." No, Sady promised Willow no one would ever know, and she was not one to break a promise. The only other person that had an inkling that Willow was Sady's mother was Alec. Sady knew he was an honorable man and would never divulge that information to anyone. Alec knew nothing, of course, about Sady and Dewey being related.

It felt so good to open the front door. It was getting colder outside and the heat coming from the woodstove felt so good.

Wolfe ran out and jumped all over Willow and almost knocked her down. Willow couldn't hug Wolfe enough. She was so happy to see him. That bond the two had for each other was enough to make a person cry. Willow treated Wolfe like the child she never had.

Dewey hollered upstairs for his mother, "Ma, they're here, Grace is here!"

Sady said, "that's ok Dewey, I'm goin' upstairs anyway. Come on Grace. You've got another grandma to see. Hurry!"

When Sady got upstairs, she noticed Eva wasn't there either. She came back down and got her coat on. "Maybe she went to the barn to get wood. I'll be right back, you all just get warm."

Willow told Sady to take Wolfe with her just in case any wild animals were outside looking for food.

Sady went to the barn, but Eva wasn't there. Sady hollered her name, but she never answered.

"Come on Wolfe, maybe she took a short walk to clear her head."

Wolfe started to bark. "What is it boy. You got good eyesight, because I don't see anything."

Wolfe ran and layed down out in the open field. Sady could hardly see because the snow was really coming down and blowing and blinding her. When she got to Wolfe, she couldn't believe what she saw. She saw Eva, sitting up against an old locust tree in the field. Eva was frozen. All she had on was a nightgown and no shoes. She was blue; she was dead.

Sady knelt down beside her and just screamed. She screamed and cried. "Why Eva, why? You had so much to live for now, Grace, your son, finally peace in your life. No more beatins'. . . why Eva?"

There was no way Sady could carry Eva back to the house. She would have go to the barn and get a sled to bring her body to the house. She didn't want Dewey to see her like that. Sheriff Hardin would have to come and get her to the funeral home somehow. All Sady could think about was "if Sheriff Guy Hardin would have done his job the night Grace went missin', Becky and Eva would still be alive, and Leroy would have been locked up for kidnappin'."

Sady slowly opened the front door. Dewey walked over to her and said, "Miss Sady, did you find Ma?"

Sady had to ask Dewey a question. "Dewey when you left this mornin' to pick us up, did you tell your ma?"

"No Miss Sady. I didn't want to wake her up. She's been feelin' so bad lately, I just left her sleep. Why, Miss Sady, what's wrong?"

"Sit down Dewey. I have somethin' to tell you."

Willow could see the terror in Sady's eyes. She knew something happened to Eva.

"I ain't sittin' nowhere Miss Sady. Where's my ma?"

"Wolfe found your ma Dewey. She's down by the locust tree. It looks like she's been there a long time Dewey. I think somethin' terrible happened to her mind when Becky died."

"Why didn't she come back with you? She's got to be cold?"

"Dewey, your ma passed on. She has been out in this cold a long time. She only had her nightgown on and no shoes. Dewey, Dewey ...don't go..."

Dewey ran out of the house and into the field where his mother was.

Willow turned to Sady. "Let him go Sady. He needs to be with her. You call the Sheriff. Eva just now didn't lose her mind. It's probably been comin' on from the way Roby treated her all these years. I'll go to the barn and get a sled so we can bring her here to the house."

Willow went out to the barn, but didn't get the sled. She saw Dewey carrying his mother through the snow covered fields. The sight of this boy carrying his mother was too much for Willow to bear. She stayed in the barn for a few extra minutes. She didn't want anyone to see her crying. Willow was a tough old bird, she wasn't supposed to cry.

Dewey sat with his mother on the back porch. The porch was enclosed so the snow couldn't blow in. There was a small wood stove on the porch. Sady loaded it with wood to keep Dewey warm until the Sheriff and undertaker, Mr. Dodd, of Dodd's Funeral Home, could come and pick up Eva's body. Willow, Grace and Sady sat in the front sitting room, along with Wolfe, to give Dewey privacy to be with his mother.

Sheriff Hardin arrived with Mr. Dodd about two hours later. The snow and blizzard like conditions held them both up. One of the farmers used their tractor to clear the road for the Sheriff.

The Sheriff took Dewey in another room and questioned him about his mother's death. Dewey was quite upset and could hardly answer any of his questions. Sady couldn't understand why the Sheriff had to question Dewey at a sorrowful time like this. She made her mind up to be with Dewey and find out exactly what he expected Dewey to say.

"Sheriff Hardin, I'm the one that found Eva, not Dewey, so maybe you should be questionin' me."

The Sheriff turned around and said, ""Oh, that's right. I forgot. You've got all the answers Detective Sady. If I have any questions for you Sady, I'll ask you. Now why don't you go in the other room and make yourself useful."

Dewey hung his head and Sady knew that he really shouldn't be subjected to hearing over and over again what happened to his mother.

Sady said, "Dewey, please go out to the sittin' room. I want to talk privately to Sheriff Hardin.

"Yes ma'am. Dewey left the two of them to talk and went into the other room. Willow tried to console him as much as she could.

Sady couldn't believe how he talked to her. "Sheriff, I don't like the way you just talked to me, and in front of Dewey. This is my house and you will respect me in my house. Can't you see Dewey is upset and grievin' over his mother. I told you I found her. I'm sure you know Becky was murdered in Baltimore. Eva hasn't been herself since her death. I talked twice to her on the telephone. She blamed herself for Becky's death. When Dewey left this mornin' to pick us up from the bus station, he didn't want to wake his mother. I think as soon as Dewey left, Eva left the house, walked out to the field, sat down and just gave up. She finally gave up. She just couldn't carry that guilt any further than that locust tree."

Sheriff Hardin said, "don't you ever undermine me again when I'm questionin' a person. Do you understand Detective Sady? Next time you interfere with an investigation, you're gettin' locked up. Understand me woman?"

"You want to call me Detective Sady, Sheriff, that's up to you. I think I did pretty good without any assistance or help from you. You really didn't care if I got Grace back, did you? Maybe if you would have tried to go after Becky and that guy, her and Eva would both be alive today. The boy just lost his mother. She froze to death. She lost her mind and went out in the snow, sat down, and froze to death. He doesn't need any more of your badgerin' questions. Understand me MAN?"

"Let's get one thing straight Sady. You don't tell me who to ask or what questions to ask of anybody. See this badge. It's not on you. It's on me. Don't forget it."

"Well Sheriff Hardin, maybe it's been on you a little too long."

At that point, the Sheriff was mad and didn't want to be confronted by any more of Sady's remarks. He walked over to the room where Eva was and tried to help Mr. Dodd get Eva ready to go to the funeral home.

Dewey kissed his mother as she was on the stretcher on her way out of Sady's house.

It was a sad, sad ending to the happiness Sady felt earlier that morning as she waited for Dewey to pick the three of them up at the bus station.

Sady knew she had to let Alec know what happened. She called his number at the precinct and told the operator to leave him a message to call her as soon as he got a chance.

Eva had no money left to take care of her burial and Sady hadn't received any money yet from the tobacco crop that Mr. Tibbits and Dewey sold at the tobacco warehouse in Boone while she was in Baltimore. What little bit of money she had in savings, she took into Boone to Mr. Dodd to see if he would accept that for her burial. Mr.

Dodd told her it wouldn't cover a decent casket or any other necessities needed for the funeral.

Sady and Dewey left Dodd's Funeral Home knowing Eva wouldn't get a decent burial unless they came up with the rest of the money Mr. Dodd asked for. Sady had the impression that no matter how much money they had, Mr. Dodd just didn't want anything to do with burying Eva. She couldn't let Dewey know how she felt. Being told that would hurt his feelings and he didn't need to feel any worse than how he was feeling now.

"Miss Sady, I'm pretty good at buildin' things. I'm gonna' build my Ma a nice coffin. Can I please bury her by that locust tree. I don't want her to be buried next to Becky in the church cemetery. She sat under that locust tree for a reason. Please!"

"Of course you can Dewey. I wouldn't have it any other way. I'll call Mr. Dodd when we get home and see if he will keep your Ma for a few more days until that casket is built. How does that sound? We can take the casket to Mr. Dodd. When he is ready and you are ready we can bring your Ma back here for burial."

"Thank you, Miss Sady. I'll make it up to you somehow. I know I'm not family, but I think Ma would be happy bein' close to people who treated her good."

"Dewey, you don't have to make anything up to me. Me, Grace, and Willow – we're your family now. When Eddie comes home, our family will be complete." Sady thought to herself, "poor Dewey, he doesn't know how much of a family we really are. Maybe someday, when the time is right, I'll have to tell him."

Eva's death spread throughout Harmony pretty quickly. Mr. and Mrs. Tibbits were waiting at Sady's to be there to find out what they could do for Dewey. No one from Harmony First Baptist Church, where Eva attended, even paid a visit to Sady's home. Henry and Lena Tibbits came, not only to offer their help, but also gave Dewey a two hundred dollar collection that their church took up. At first Dewey would not accept the gift.

"Mr. and Mrs. Tibbits, I can't accept this money."

Henry spoke up. "You will accept it boy. We thought a lot of Miss Eva. She treated us and our colored friends like we were human, like Miss Sady does. You take this money and give Miss Eva a nice burial."

Sady looked at Dewey. "Mr. Tibbits is right Dewey." She then spoke to Mr. Tibbits. "Mr. Dodd wanted a lot more money than we had to bury Eva. Henry, Lena – Dewey can use this to buy some good wood. He's goin' to build a casket for his ma. Thank you."

Henry looked Dewey straight in the eye. "I'm goin' to help you build that casket for Miss Eva. I got some good lumber at my house. We'll start later today. How's that sound?"

"I don't know what to say Mr. Tibbits." At that point Dewey started to cry and hugged Henry and Lena.

Henry said, "you don't have to say nothin' boy, you don't have to say nothin'!"

There were good people in Harmony Creek. Eva's sudden death brought these good people from Mr. Tibbits' church to be there for Dewey. Dewey realized at this time who these people were and who he could count on at this low point in his life. All the years Eva went to the Harmony Creek First Baptist Church, where were these so-called Christians? Eva did nothing for these people to shun her. Was it because of Roby and the way Becky turned out?

Dewey told Sady later, "I don't want anything to do with those so-called Christians at Reverend Marshal's church. I'll never go back there again!"

Sady said nothing. There was nothing to say. Dewey was right.

chapter 31

EVA WAS BURIED two days later beside the locust tree where Sady found her. The wooden casket was beautiful. Dewey also made a cross with Eva's name, with her birth and death date inscribed on it. The pastor from Henry and Lena's church performed the ceremony over the gravesite. After the small service, Sady invited everyone to come in and eat.

Time went by pretty fast that day. Night came and everyone went to bed early except Sady. She sat in the sitting room thinking to herself, "I can't understand why Alec hasn't returned my call. I hope everything is ok."

The week went by and Christmas Eve was the next night. It would be a sad Christmas for Dewey. Of course, Grace was all excited about Santa Claus coming down the chimney. All she wanted was a doll baby and a carriage. Sady tried to bring a little bit of cheerfulness into her home, but it wasn't easy. She was so grateful Willow was still staying with her. She was a lot of help and really was a lot of company for Sady. Willow's arm was healing up nicely. She even went partially up Blackheart Mountain and cut a small, but beautiful, blue spruce tree for Christmas. Everyone decorated the tree. Even Dewey helped string the popcorn around the tree. Sady was so glad to see a little smile on his face.

Sady, Willow, and Grace went to Christmas Eve services at their church. Dewey wouldn't go and Sady didn't blame him. Several people came up to Sady and said they were sorry. They wanted to pay their respects but were hesitant to drive on the snow covered road at that time. Sady was civil with them but not understanding. She felt they could have gotten together and followed each other. If the Tibbits made it to her home, along with some of the people from their church, then

Mary Wagner

there was no reason that the people Eva sat next to in church for years couldn't come and pay their respect.

Reverend Marshal walked over to talk to Sady after the service was over. "Sady so good to see you here, and little Grace too. You know we prayed for your safe return, and God blessed us with your presence here today."

"Reverend Marshal, do you not see Willow standin' right beside me. Why do you ignore her?"

Willow tried to cut in the conversation. "Now Sady, that's ok, it doesn't bother me none."

"No, Willow, it bothers me. Did you forget Reverend Marshal that Willow is a child of God too, or is her skin not white enough for this church? Did it ever occur to you that her people were here way before anybody even knew Harmony Creek existed?"

"Now Sady, you know we all love Willow and . . ."

"And what? I can tell you one thing. If it weren't for Willow here, I'd be one dead woman. You should have seen how she threw that knife right through Leroy's heart. Bullseye!"

"Sady, I really don't want to hear . . ."

"Hear what, the truth. That you and most of the people who come here are hypocrites?"

Reverend Marshal's eyes got as big as walnuts. He didn't expect Sady to tell him how she really felt.

Sady said, "tell me why you couldn't come and pray or at least pay your respects for Eva. She's been a member of this church most of her life. Don't you think that hurt Dewey? Well it did, because he will never come back here again and I don't blame him. What did Eva do to anybody in this church to hurt them? Mr. and Mrs. Tibbits' church took up a collection toward her funeral. Their preacher even presided over the funeral."

Reverend Marshal said, "Eva did nothing wrong. It was Roby and his carryin' on. It was the sin that went on in that house. If he comes back here, we don't want no trouble. Becky was a sinner like her father."

Sady said, "you are a hypocrite and a poor excuse for a man of the cloth. If you knew what was goin' on in Roby's house and didn't do anything about it, you're goin' to hell, Reverend or no Reverend. Come on Willow." Sady picked Grace up and the three of them went home.

Sady felt bad arguing on Christmas Eve, but she also felt a lot better. She had seen how the church treated Willow for years, and how the church ignored Eva was all she could take.

On the way home, Willow looked at Sady and said, "yep! You sure are my baby!" They both started to laugh.

Sady had the house decorated from the inside to the outside. There were wreathes in every window that Sady and Willow made from pine tips that they cut from pine trees. Even the two Frasier Fir trees below Sady's front porch were decorated with big Christmas lights. There was the old manger in front of one of the fir trees that Sady's father carved years ago. In the manger, of course, were Mary, Joseph, and little Jesus. Sady thought it was her duty to make sure most of the sadness and heartbreak didn't overshadow the joyous occasion that Christmas was all about.

Christmas morning came and everyone opened their presents. Sady bought Dewey and Willow each a nice flannel shirt from the Emporium in Boone. Grace got her doll baby and carriage. Willow gave Sady four little gold nuggets that she found in the creek behind her house. She put a little hole in each one and put a chain through the holes to make a necklace. It was quite beautiful. And to everybody's surprise, Willow gave Dewey her prized Bowie knife that was handed down through many generations.

Dewey said, "Willow, I can't accept this. This belonged to your daddy's daddy. There's nothin' like this knife this side of Harmony or Boone."

Dewey didn't realize it, but he was part of her family and that's who she wanted to have her knife. "Yes sir, you will take it. That is my gift to you. I don't think I'm goin' to be needin' it anymore."

"Thank you Willow, thank you Miss Sady. "I don't know what I would have done without either one of you bein' here for me. Thank you."

Early Christmas afternoon the Tibbits arrived for dinner. Mr. Tibbits brought the main course – one of his biggest hogs that he butchered and Lena cooked. The smells in Sady's home were overwhelming. The aroma of the pumpkin pies, cornbread stuffing, gravy, buttermilk biscuits, summer squash with onions and her bell peppers just floated throughout the house. Even though it was a sad time because of Eva's death, having family and friends together helped brighten the spirits of everyone, most importantly Dewey.

Mrs. Tibbits finished warming up the sweet potatoes and placed them on the table. "It's time to eat everybody while everything is still hot." There was a long table brought into the sitting room which Sady used for such occasions.

It was time to eat that delicious meal and Mr. Tibbits said grace and everybody ate.

Sady said, "I don't hear a sound, so I guess I won't hear any complaints about the food."

Everyone laughed and just continued to eat.

In Sady's heart she knew what was missing that Christmas. It was Alec. She never got a chance to tell him about Eva's death. He never called back. Sady figured he was either busy, didn't get the message, or maybe he found somebody else. She thought, "If he did find somebody else, I want to know, so that I can get over the hurt that I'm goin' to feel."

Sady's thoughts also were consumed in thinking about Eddie that day. "Wouldn't he be just tickled to death just to see how happy little Grace is? If you can hear my thoughts Eddie, I love you son. Please come home to us soon."

After supper, Sady started to clear the table when there was a knock on the door.

Sady had no idea who it could be. She opened the door and couldn't believe who it was. It was Alec.

"Are you going to let me in, or just stand there with your mouth open and let me freeze to death?"

Sady shut the door behind her and jumped in Alec's arms and kissed him. Alec, I need to tell you something before you come in."

Jokingly, Alec said, "oh no, don't tell me your boyfriend is in there."

"Alec, I left you a message to call me over a week ago. When you said "freeze to death" it upset me because after I came back from Baltimore, I found Eva in the field and she did freeze to death. I didn't want you to mention those words in front of Dewey. I'll tell you more later on. Dewey is takin' it hard. I just wanted you to know before you came in the house."

"Sady, I'm so sorry. I've been in Washington D.C. since I left. I just got back two days ago. Nobody told me you called. I'm so sorry."

"Come on in. I want you to meet everyone."

"Everybody, I'd like you to meet Detective Alec Karastaupolis. This is the detective I told you about from Baltimore that found Grace. Where did Dewey go?"

Mr. Tibbits answered Sady. "Sady he went out back to get more fire wood." Henry put his hand out to shake Alec's hand. "I'm so glad to finally meet you Mr. Alec. I'm Henry Tibbits and this is my wife Lena."

Mrs. Tibbits said, "we heard so much about you, Mr. Alec, everything good. God sent down an angel and called him Alec and he brought our Grace back home to us. Thank you so much."

"Please call me Alec. I really don't deserve the Mr. I heard a lot about you and your husband. Can I call you Lena?"

"Of course you can, but we're still goin' to call you Mr. Alec. After what you did, a man deserves a special title with respect."

"Sady told me how much both of you help her and what good friends you both are. Lena believe me I'm no angel and certainly not special. I just did my job."

Mr. Tibbits said, "Sady is a good person with a good heart Mr. Alec. You probably know that already. It's been a privilege to be a part of Sady's life all these years."

Alec walked over and hugged little Grace. He then saw Willow and went over and gave her a great big hug. "Willow, you saved Sady and I'll always be grateful to you. You know that don't you?"

Willow said, "Alec, I could have saved people a lot of trouble. If I would have been here the day the Sheriff refused to go after that devil boy and Becky, I would have saddled up Sady's horse, Jenny, and went after 'em myself. But then Alec, you never would have got a chance to meet Sady."

"You've got one hell of a point there Willow! And this beautiful creature must be Wolfe." Wolfe actually got excited when Alec started to pet him. Wolfe didn't take to many people. Wolfe just had that inborn instinct and knew Alec was a good person.

"Oh, and by the way Willow, Sister Theresa wanted me to give you this little gift. She said you admired the bigger one in the church. She wanted you to have this to remember her by. And Sady, Sister Theresa said to tell you a man who was just hired as the caregiver for the church said to say hello. His name is Calvin Washington."

Mary Wagner

"Thank God Alec. He's the man I told you about that kept me safe on the street that night until he found someone to take me back to the mission. I'm so happy for him. That is a Christmas gift."

In the meantime Willow unwrapped her gift from Sister Theresa. Her eyes lit up. She was so happy. It was a small crucifix. She held it close to her heart and said, "I've never seen anything so beautiful. Look Wolfe. When I go back up on the mountain, I'm goin' to hang it over my bed."

Sady grabbed Alec's arm. "I know you're hungry. Come on in the kitchen and let me fix a plate for you." Alec was no sooner around the kitchen door when Sady jumped up into his arms. Her weight slammed him against the wall and they just kissed and kissed. The kissing stopped when the back door slightly opened.

Dewey walked in carrying the wood for the woodstove.

Alec looked at him and said, "this has got to be Dewey."

"Yes sir, I'm Dewey."

Sady introduced them. "Dewey, this is Alec, the detective from Baltimore that saved Grace's life and mine a few times."

Dewey was so excited, he dropped the wood. This was the most lively and really happy Sady had seen Dewey since his mother died.

Dewey put his hand out to shake Alec's hand. "I'm honored Mr. Alec to meet you. I can't believe I'm shakin' the hand of a real live detective from Baltimore."

"One thing is for sure Dewey, I am alive. We've got a lot of smart and really good detectives in my precinct, not just me."

"Mr. Alec, is it hard to become a detective?"

"Well Dewey, it takes a lot of studying and determination not to give up. You see, you also go through a lot of physical training and have to pass a lot of tests, mental and physical. Think you're up to it?"

"I'd sure like to give it a try. Was it hard for you?"

"I don't think it was as hard on me as it was on the regular guys right out of high school. You see, Dewey, I was a lawyer for years and I knew a lot about the law. I gave it up to be a detective. I joined the Army as soon as War was declared by President Roosevelt. I wanted to serve my country to preserve our freedom here and overseas."

"How come you're not still in the Army like Eddie is?"

"About two years ago, I was driving a tank in Italy when a group of Fascists, under that dictator Mussolini threw a grenade at my feet after

168

I jumped out of my tank to pick up one of our guys that was hit. Let's just say I was severely wounded. When I returned home, I wasn't sure I would get my job back at the police department, but the department was good enough to take me back. So if I can do it, you can too."

"But, Mr. Alec, do you think they would take a gimp like me?"

"Take a what?"

"I'm a gimp, Mr. Alec. That's what my pa used to call me. I was born with one leg shorter than the other. Do you really think they would take me?"

"You're no gimp, Dewey. Your pa never should have called you that. Sure, you may have to work a little harder than the rest of the guys, but if I'm around to help you, you better believe you're going to work your hind end off. From what Sady tells me about how hard of a worker you are, you shouldn't have any trouble being a police officer Dewey."

Dewey got this huge smile on his face. "Mr. Alec, I sure do hope you're around here to make me work my hind end off. You'll see how hard of a worker I am."

"I have no doubt about that Dewey."

Alec and Dewey started to pick the wood up off the floor. "I'm real sorry, Mr. Alec, about what happened to you in the Army, but I sure am glad you went back bein' a detective. You sure did make Miss Sady a lot happier and me too when you got Grace back."

"Thanks Dewey. Who knows, if you ever make detective, you'll do a lot of great things to bring happiness to a lot of families who depend on your skills to solve a crime or find a loved one. But you have to serve as a policeman or deputy first. And Dewey, I'm real sorry to hear about your mother, I really am. If you need to talk to somebody, I'll be there to listen."

"Thank you Mr. Alec. I miss my ma, but sometimes I get so mad at her for givin' up like she did. She finally had a nice life here with Miss Sady, then she goes and . . ."

Dewey starts to cry and is embarrassed that Alec sees him crying.

"You know Dewey, I think your mother was content and happy just knowing that your father ran off and wasn't going to beat on you anymore. She knew Miss Sady would take care of you and that your life would be safe now. I think she died knowing that. Now you owe it to your mother to make her proud of you. Think you can do that?"

"I sure can Mr. Alec and I'm goin' to make her real proud of me! Like you said my pa never should have called me a gimp, but Mr. Alec that was the nicest word he ever called me."

"Dewey as long as I am around here, and if your pa happens to come back, I'll make sure he never calls you anymore names or beats you. Got that?"

"Yes sir, I got that! I'm hopin' he never comes back."

While Sady was warming up Christmas dinner for Alec, she heard every word of the conversation from afar and knew that Dewey just needed those words from a man that he admired and looked up to. Alec was that man. How proud Sady was of him.

"Alec, your dinner is ready. Dewey go on in and put the wood in the stove. I do believe it's gettin' colder outside. Can I talk to you for a minute Alec?"

"I haven't been here that long Sady, what did I do wrong?"

"You didn't do a thing wrong Alec. I just overheard you talkin' to Dewey and I really think you gave him confidence and hope. Hope is somethin' that boy ain't had in a long time. It's just that you're tellin' him if his pa comes back, you won't let him be mistreated anymore. Alec, you have to be here to do that. If you're not here, you can't protect him."

Alec never answered her. "Boy that smells good Sady. Let's go in the front room. While you and your company are eating dessert, I'll eat this delicious-smelling dinner."

"But Alec . . ."

"Come on Sady, these people want some of those wonderful desserts you baked."

Sady knew Alec didn't come all that way on the long trip from Baltimore for nothing. She was soon going to find out why he was paying them a visit.

chapter 32

AFTER EVERYONE ATE their dessert, and Alec ate his dinner and dessert, he had something to tell everyone. Was it good news, or was it bad news? They would soon find out.

Alec finally spoke up. "I not only came to see Sady and to meet her friends, but I also came to bring some news about Eddie and Thomas."

Mrs. Tibbits grabbed Mr. Tibbits hand and started to shake. Sady just stared at Alec and started to look a little pale. All either parent could do was think of the worst thing that could have happened to their child – death.

Alec could see how upset they were and said, "please don't be upset. Let me tell you both and you Sady what I found out about your boys while I was in Washington. I do have good news and not so good news. Both boys are alive. They are on a naval ship leaving France sometime within the next two months. That soldier you talked to on the bus Sady was right. Their division was sent to the Ardennes Forest in Belgium and France. They got there sometime after Thanksgiving. There was a big battle with the Germans that started the first part of December. I was told in Washington, they called this battle the Battle of the Bulge. The boys were in the back of a transport truck. The truck ran over a land mine and blew up. They were hurt, but survived. Right now they can't be moved. They are in a very good hospital in France."

Mrs. Tibbits was crying and shouted out, "thank you Lord for not taken our boys, thank you!"

Sady looked at Alec with tears in her eyes. "There's somethin' else Alec. Tell us. Tell us the truth. Why two months?"

"Eddie had severe head trauma. He has broken ribs and a broken leg. He can't be moved at all until he starts to heal." Alec knows Sady must be heart-broken inside and he can't really console her; he can only hold her hand and be there for her.

"Henry and Lena, Thomas is the one who is really in bad shape. Thomas lost a leg and broke his left arm."

Henry and Lena both started to cry uncontrollably. At this point Alec was helpless. He didn't know what to do. Dewey came over and put his arms around Lena. Willow tried to comfort Henry. Sady got up and ran in the kitchen. Alec ran after her. She ran out the door into the snow and fell on the ground and just screamed and screamed. Alec picked her up, held her as tight as he could.

"Alec, I can't go back in there. I can't take it, I can't, I can't."

"Sady, listen to me. Eddie will be coming home to you. You're such a strong woman Sady, everything will be ok. It will take time, but Eddie is going to need you. Grace is going to need you. You're going to have to be there for Henry and Lena too, for Thomas. Come on; let's go back in, you're going to get sick if you stay out here any longer." Sady started to calm down, listened to Alec and went back into the house. Alec had more to say to them about their boys.

"I was told when they come home, both boys will go to Fort Howard Hospital in Baltimore, Maryland to recuperate. They could have been sent somewhere else, but this way I can visit them and I will bring them home to you."

Lena spoke up. "Alec, you don't understand. Thomas will never be able to accept what has happened to him. No leg, It's goin' to be so hard for him! He always dreamed of operatin' and ownin' his own construction business one day."

Alec started to unbutton his shirt.

Sady questioned his action, "Alec, what are you doin'?"

He opened his shirt in order to expose some of the scars left from the severe burns from the war to Henry and Lena.

Henry and Lena were surprised to see the extent and degree of damage that Alec suffered from his war injury. Henry said, "Mr. Alec, we're sorry, we didn't know."

Alec said, "I'm sorry, but these are just some of my wounds. I was lucky. I came home with all my limbs, but I will always be ashamed of what my body looks like. I just want you to know that Thomas will be able to get a new leg, walk again, and do whatever he wants to. That shouldn't keep him from owning a construction company. He won't be able to run a marathon or climb a ladder, but he will be able to and tell others how to build whatever it is he instructs them to build. Thomas is not dead. I'm not dead. If you encourage him and let him know that he can do whatever he wants to do, he will succeed at anything he puts his heart and mind into doing. And Sady, time will heal Eddies head injury and his broken bones. They are both alive. That's all that counts right now. There are parents out there now who are being told their sons are never coming home."

Sady said, "you're right Alec. They both could have been killed. We are lucky, Henry and Lena, very lucky, because they are comin' home to us."

That brought a little smile from Lena. "Thank you Alec. Just knowin' he's alive. God answered our prayers." Lena wiped her tears, looked at Henry and said, "It's gettin' dark, Henry, and that snow might get too deep for our truck. I think we better be goin'."

Alec said, "no, no, don't go home yet. Dewey can you hand me that big bag I laid over in the corner?"

"Dewey, Sady told me you were a pretty good hunter. Think you would like this?"

Alec hands Dewey a gift that is wrapped.

Dewey excitedly unwraps and opens the gift. "Oh my goodness, Mr. Alec, a Winchester 94 huntin' rifle. Look Mr. Tibbits. This thing will bring down deer, squirrel, rabbit, wild turkey, anything. Thank you, Mr. Alec, thank you."

"Willow this is for you. I thought it would go really well with that coat from Sady."

Willow was so surprised that Alec gave her a gift. She unwrapped the box and opened it and said, "Sady, isn't this scarf beautiful. Red, my favorite color. It's so warm. Look, it wraps around my neck. Oh boy, all those ladies with their noses up in the air at church will be jealous when I walk in. Alec you sure do know what a woman likes, thank you."

Alec said, "you are welcome Willow. I have to say that color red really makes you look a lot younger than you are."

Dewey said, "Willow, maybe you might find yourself a man lookin' pretty like that."

"There ain't no man this side of Blackheart Mountain or even in this whole state that I even want to look at. Don't need no lazy man to cook for, pick up after or listen to his mouth run off about things I don't even care about. No sir. Don't want no man!"

Everyone just laughed.

"Of course another doll for Grace."

Sady said. Alec, it's bigger than Grace. "Say thank you to Mr. Alec, Grace."

"Thank you."

"You're welcome sweetheart."

"Henry and Lena, Sady told me about your delicious pies. I found these new glass baking pans. They had clear and sapphire blue. I thought the sapphire blue was so pretty. And Henry, I got you this nice bottle of wine right from a vineyard in Maryland. It's nice and sweet with berries and spice.

"Mr. Alec, me and the Mrs. didn't get you anything. You shouldn't have spent your money on us. Our gift from you was lettin' us know about our Thomas."

"Henry, if I didn't have the money, I wouldn't have gotten anything. I really don't have a family, so I adopted all of you."

Dewey spoke up. "Mr. Alec, you forgot Miss Sady."

Alec pulled a bulky package out of the bottom of the bag. "This is for you Sady."

"But Alec, I'm like everybody else here, I didn't get you anything."

"Just open it Sady. Don't be so bullheaded."

Sady unwrapped and opened the present, and it was a camera.

"Alec, I can't accept this."

"You will accept it and I don't want to hear any more about it. The whole time you were in Baltimore, you kept saying "wish I had a camera so I could show my friends how beautiful some of these buildings and churches are."

"Yeah, but I didn't mean for you to buy me a camera Alec. You know what I'm goin' to be doin' all day tomorrow. I got a lot of memories to put in this camera. I love it. I love it!"

Alec said, "Let me get a picture of everybody while you're all here together, then I'll show you later how to use the camera Sady."

After Alec took the picture, Henry and Lena really had to leave; it was getting late. Alec promised to keep in touch with them about Thomas' condition.

Alec looked at his watch and said, "Sady, I better get going. I'll be back tomorrow morning if it is ok with you."

Sady said, "just where are you goin'?"

"I thought I'd go into Boone and get a motel to stay in tonight."

"No sir, I won't allow that. You can stay right here. You can sleep in Eddie's room with Dewey. There are twin beds in there. I won't have it any other way."

"I don't want these neighbors around here to talk Sady. I don't mind staying in a motel."

Dewey insisted, "Mr. Alec, please stay here. I've got a lot of questions to ask you, please!"

Willow said, "Alec, these people around these here parts would talk about you even if you gave them everything you got. Soon as you turn your back they're stickin' you with a pitchfork. They're all pretenders, 'cept for the Tibbits. I've seen these menfolk and even a few so-called ladies of the Church Council, Christian people of course, go into the barn and reach in the feed barrel where their booze is buried and drink every last drop. If they ain't drinkin' they're meetin' somebody else's wife or husband in the holler down the road. So you're stayin' with us while you're here."

Sady shook her head. "Alec, you can't argue with Willow. Go get your suitcase and Dewey will show you where you're goin' to sleep tonight. I'll see you in the mornin'."

Alec kissed Sady and went to the car, got his suitcase and went upstairs with Dewey. He was tired and was really glad he didn't have to drive on that icy crooked road thirty miles to Boone.

chapter 33

THE NEXT MORNING around eight o'clock, there was a loud knock at the front door. Sady and Willow were in the kitchen cooking breakfast. Sady said, "who in the world could that be this time in the mornin' Willow?"

"It's an awful loud knock Sady, hope it don't wake up Alec. I guess you better go see who it is."

Sady pulled the curtain and saw Sheriff Guy Hardin staring back at her. All she could think of was that she hoped something didn't happen to Dewey. She couldn't take any more bad news. She knew he took his new gun up in the mountain to target practice earlier. "Please Lord, don't let it be Dewey." Sady finally opened up the door.

"Sheriff Hardin, what brings you out here so early in the mornin'?" Sady asked.

"Aren't you gonna' ask me in Sady, it's kind of cold out here?"

"Sure Sheriff, come on in."

Willow came over and stood beside Sady.

The Sheriff looked at Willow. "You still here Willow? Thought you'd be gone by now."

Willow said, "What's it any of your business where I'm at?"

Sheriff Hardin gave her one of his dirty looks.

Sady asked the Sheriff, "so what do you want Guy?"

"That's not a nice way to speak to your Sheriff Sady. I was just ridin' around and noticed a strange car out front. Wanted to make sure you all were ok."

Sady sneered at him. "I bet you were real worried about us. Well it's a friend that is visitin' with us so you can be on your way Sheriff, everything is ok."

Just then Alec came down the steps. "So you're Sheriff Hardin." Alec put his hand out to shake the Sheriff's hand. "My name is Alec Karastaupolis. I'm a detective from Baltimore, Maryland. That's my car out front. Is it in your way or something? There are one hundred and fifty acres here that Mrs. Milsap owns. I thought it would be ok to park in front of her house."

Alec already didn't care for the Sheriff. He knew he wasn't a very nice person and didn't treat Sady with any respect when her husband and son were killed or cared at all when Grace was kidnapped.

Willow and Sady just had to laugh. They never expected Alec to confront the Sheriff like that.

"Don't you get smart with me, Mr. Baltimore Detective. That's what you are, a smart ass."

"I sure am. And you're a stupid ass. Why do you care who's car is parked out front. You let a couple get away that assaulted a woman and kidnapped a baby. I sure am a smart ass and proud of it. Now you're worried about a stranger being parked in front of Sady's house? Sady where is Dewey?"

"He's up in the woods target practicin'. Why?"

"Because I don't want him to hear what I am about to say to your good Sheriff."

The Sheriff got in front of Alec's face and said, "just who do you think you are, talkin' to me like that?"

Alec answered him. "Who do I think I am? I am a real man, Sheriff - a man of the law that's supposed to protect law-biding citizens like the Tibbits and Sady whether they are black, white, or purple. You didn't do your job Sheriff. You caused an innocent girl's death. You almost got Grace, Sady and Willow killed because they had to do your job because you wouldn't."

"Don't pin Becky's death on me. Becky was a whore and a drug addict anyway. I did her mama a service by lettin' her go off with that boy."

Alec balled his fist up and started to grab the Sheriff. "You son-of-a-bitch. I ought to ..."

"Go ahead, Mr. Detective. I'll have you locked up and thrown in jail today. What do you got to say about that?"

Alec just stared him down. "Another place, another time, another way ... but not here. I have too much respect for these people."

The Sheriff turned and laughed and started to walk out the door.

Alec shouted at him. "You just didn't kill Becky, you killed her mother too. That's on your head."

The Sheriff turned around and said. "Eva's been dead for years livin' with that drunk and puttin' up with him beatin' on her."

Willow was furious. "I told you Sady he knew she was bein' beat on and did nothin'. I told you."

The Sheriff started to turn to walk away again, and then turned around again because he had something else to say. "Oh, I actually forgot why I came all the way out here. It concerns Willow. In about two months the Eastman Road Company is goin' to be blastin' on top of Blackheart Mountain. A new road is goin' in. Instead of goin' way around these here mountains, it will be a straight shot from Harmony to Boone. It's called Condemnation Proceedings. So clear your shack out Willow and find a place to move to."

Sady said. "You can't do that. Willow owns fifty acres on top of Blackheart Mountain. And it's a lie. Blastin' the top of the Mountain won't make it a shorter route; it will be more curves and crooked roads to take."

Willow said, "I have a deed where my daddy was given rights to that land."

"Maybe if I was treated with a little more respect today, I would fight for you at the Town Council meeting next month. But that didn't happen. See you good folks later."

Sady and Willow just looked at each other. If the top of Blackheart Mountain gets blown up, that old mine where Roby and his father were thrown in will also be blasted. Sady and Willow were both thinking, "what if their bodies are found, or rather what is left of them?"

Sady asked Alec, "can they just take Willow's property like that?"

"I'm not sure Sady. If it were the government condemning it, that's one thing. If this is just a money deal between the Town Council, Eastman Road Company and the Sheriff, then they are trying to pull a fast one over on an older woman – no, they can't do that. Willow, can you get your deed, I would like to read it."

Willow said, "I'll go up to my place tomorrow. I need to get a few things anyway. And what does he mean my "shack"?"

Sady said, "Willow, he is an ignorant excuse for a human. Forget what he said. I'll go with you tomorrow. Your arm is still a little weak."

"Sady, I'll be fine."

Alec looked at both of them. "No, I'll accompany you two ladies tomorrow. I don't trust that Sheriff."

Sady said. "I like that idea a lot better. You never know. There have been many times when I haven't trusted the Sheriff either."

Alec looked out the door and up at the sky. "Willow, you were right. Look at that sky. I've never seen one that blue with not a cloud in sight."

"I told you Alec how beautiful our sky was. Never saw a sky this color in Baltimore."

"You got me there, Willow. You're right."

The next day, part of the morning was spent showing Alec the farm and some of Sady's tobacco leaves that were left over from the sale of her tobacco. Alec was amazed by the work it took from tobacco seedlings until it was shipped to the market for sale. He couldn't believe how much work was involved in farming, from taking care of the animals, putting out a big garden, canning, to doing her own repairs on old equipment that breaks down. Sady was always taking her father's antique tractor apart and working on it so that she could plow the tobacco fields and her huge garden. As a matter of fact, Sady was the best mechanic in Harmony. Her father taught her everything she knew. It was either fix the tractor or use her two mules to plow.

After lunch, Alec, Sady, Willow, Dewey and Wolfe climbed Blackheart Mountain so that Willow could get her deed to her property. Mrs. Tibbits came to get Grace for the day, and took Grace back to her house.

As Alec climbed the mountain, he looked back and noticed how beautiful the valley and hollers were. There were no beautiful spring flowers, but the pines, laurels, and the huge vines throughout the woods entangled with winter greenery that glistened with snow showed the mountain's real beauty. Alec took a deep breath. The fresh, cold air was so exhilarating and coupled with the scent of pine, that it cleared his mind. The climb up the mountain was a little strenuous; there is no mountain climbing in Baltimore. Once he got to the top, he felt better than he had in a long time.

Willow stopped suddenly about one-hundred feet from her cabin. Sady said, "Willow, what's wrong? Are you ok?"

Willow said, "Somebody's been up here. I can tell. Look at those briars over there, they have been cut and trampled on. Seein' how I ain't been up here for quite a while, those there briars should be all together and not layin' flat on the ground like they are."

Alec pulled his gun from his holster and said, "Everybody step back. Somebody might still be in the house. I'll check it out first."

The door was ajar. Willow kept her house locked. Someone had broken into her home. Alec slowly opened the door and went inside.

About two minutes later Alec hollered out, "come on in, it's clear in here."

Willow gasped when she went through the door. "My house, my little home, it's a mess, who did this?"

Willow's house was ram- sacked. What pieces of furniture she had were over-turned. The walls were gutted as if someone was look-ing for something. Her mattress was overturned and cut to shreds.

Alec said, "whoever was in here, Willow, was looking for some-thing special. Can you think of anything of value you may have had here that someone would go to this extent to find?"

"No, Alec. What little I have isn't worth half of a penny."

Sady put her hand to her neck and felt the little gold nugget neck-lace that Willow gave her for Christmas. "Willow, did anybody know about these here gold nuggets you gave me for Christmas?"

"Why no Sady. I got those nuggets over a month ago. I did take them to town to the jewelry store for Mr. Little to shine them up for me."

Alec said. "Willow, he not only shined them up for you, he must have told somebody about them, thinking that you have a lot more gold up here in this mountain."

Sady gave Alec a questionable look. "Come to think about it Alec, Mr. Little is on the Town Council, and him and the Sheriff hunt together in deer season."

Willow was beside herself. She found another knife lying on the floor, picked it up and said, "I'll fix Mr. Little's carcass. Ain't nobody goin' to wreck my home, then try to steal my land. I'll fix that Sheriff next. He'll be huntin' alright, huntin' for a way out of Hell. I never did like Guy

Hardin, Sheriff or no Sheriff. More than hatin' Guy, I hated his daddy, Ira even more. He's all crippled up now and in a wheel chair where he rightly deserves to be. And I knowed Sady, Guy lied about that night Jack and Donny were killed, I knowed he did."

Alec said, "hold on Willow. You don't need to be doing something you'll be sorry for later. Let's get that deed. I'm sure whoever was in here was looking for that too."

Dewey turned to Willow to ask her a question. "Miss Willow why has the Sheriff's daddy been in a wheelchair all these years?"

"I'll tell you why boy. The only way I can tell you is with the straight truth. You're Grandpa Silas was the older man who scalped my daddy then hung him on that old Buckeye tree over yonder when I was a little girl. He also came back years later when I was a young woman and put my eye out and gave me a whippin' ain't nobody should have to take. Guess who that young boy was that was with him that helped Silas pick my daddy up to hang him on that tree was? Go ahead guess."

"I don't know Miss Willow, tell me."

"It was the Sheriff's daddy, Ira Hardin. But he got what was due him. Years later, he climbed up this here mountain and a big ole' black bear came up from behind him and scared the tar out of him. He fell and rolled all the way down the mountain, hittin' every boulder 'till he got to the bottom and lay beside Harmony Creek. I found him the next day. He was still alive but his legs were twisted all kind of ways. That was the prettiest sight that I saw in years. He got what he deserved. I pulled him away from the creek because it was risin' from the rain that was comin' down. I went down the holler and got somebody to help me. Henry Otler put him in his pick-up and took him into Boone to the hospital. He never could walk after that. Sometimes I question myself. Why didn't I just leave him there to drown? But he ain't the one who killed my daddy, your grandpa was."

"Willow, I can't even tell you I'm sorry, 'cause I'm too ashamed. I ain't nothin' like my daddy or my grandpa. You know that. I hated my daddy for what he did to us. I heard about how evil my grandpa was from others. Please don't hate me Willow for what they did to you."

"Son, look at me. The only thing I got inside for you boy is love. Roby and Silas were two evil men. You have a good heart. You had to live with that evil man all your young life and there ain't one part of you that took after him. You battled Satan and came out on top. Ain't too many people can claim that fight boy. I love you boy and respect you. Don't you ever forget those words."

Alec was dumbfounded. He didn't know until now who put Willow's eye out or gave her all those terrible scars from a beating on her back, because Sady never told him. "You know Willow, you're one of the strongest women I have ever met. The respect I have for you after what you have been through in your life, I just have no words for. You knew all these years since you were a little girl who killed your father. Why didn't you go to the authorities? They both would have been locked up."

"Alec, look at me. I'm an old Injun lady now, then I was a little Injun girl. It was hard 'nough bein' a girl or a woman in those days much less a Injun woman, and it ain't changed that much in these new times. Nobody would believe me back then or even now. No, the Good Lord took care of the ones who wronged my daddy and mama and me. I just try not to look back."

Sady said, "Willow, I am so sorry for the way you were treated. But you know you can still have old Ira locked up and you can make him tell what Silas Prestel did to your daddy."

"No Sady. I'm grateful to be alive and feelin' good. Look at Ira. He's in pain every day. Lord only knows what happened to Silas Prestel. And I got blessed to have all of you to care about me. That's all I need in my life."

Willow walked over to the old Buckeye tree, with a shovel, where her father was hung by Silas Prestel years ago. She started digging and pulled an old box out of the dirt. "This box has everything that is important to me in my life. Here is my daddy's deed Alec."

Willow handed Sady the picture from the box. Willow whispered, "Your mama took me with her when you were a baby to have your picture taken. She let me hold you and had the man take a picture of you and me. This is all I had of you. I want you to have it now that you know the truth."

Sady couldn't say anything. She hugged Willow. The tears streamed down Sady's face when she looked at the picture. Willow looked so happy holding Sady in the picture, and she was so beautiful when she

Mary Wagner

was younger. "Willow, this picture will always be close to my heart. Thank you so much."

Alec said, "Everything ok Sady?"

"My life could never be better Alec. Let's get back down this mountain, have some supper, and read Willow's deed. Let's go."

chapter 34

THAT NIGHT AFTER supper, Willow was tired and went up to bed a little early. Dewey went upstairs to his room to listen to the radio. His favorite shows "Abbott and Costello" and "Amos n' Andy" were on the air. Sady and Alec finally had a chance to be alone.

"Alec, I want to show you this picture. Willow gave it to me when we were up on the mountain today."

Alec looked at the picture and said, "I see a little baby that I think is you, and a beautiful young Indian woman with a patch on her eye, that I am pretty sure is Willow. Am I right?"

"I know the patch gave her away, but wasn't she beautiful as a young woman Alec?"

"Yes, she was Sady. She was as pretty as her grown daughter is today. Am I right?"

Sady laughed a little. "Of course you are Alec. That's because you're a good detective. Alec, she finally told me that she is my real mother. She gave me to my parents because she really couldn't give me a life up on the mountain. She knew how hard it was for her to be accepted and she didn't want that for me. But Alec, she never was out of my life. It seemed as though I always had three parents."

"How many people out there are lucky to be loved and cared for by three parents, Sady?"

"I know, I know, Alec. The part that I am havin' a problem with is the man who is my father."

"Again, I have a feeling that I know who it is. It was Silas Prestel. Sady, he doesn't define who you are. All he did was biologically contribute to you forming a body. Think about it. You're a loving, compassionate person with a heart of gold. You get that from the three people who instilled those beautiful qualities in you. Now at times you are a little stubborn and feisty like Willow, but I love that part about you too. Just think about it. I'm right. Look at the horrible man Roby turned out to be. He was raised by a brutal father – Silas. Thank God, both of them are out of the picture now as far as Dewey is concerned. Dewey is more like his mother. And he has got to be the luckiest boy in the world, because he has you now to instill those same virtues in him."

"Wow, Alec, that was a nice complement and I appreciate your words, but it is goin' to take time for me to adjust to all these changes in my life."

"And, Sady, I think Willow knows what happened to Silas and Roby. Maybe you do too. That's not my concern. Wherever they are, they both belong there. I'll never question that."

"I appreciate that Alec. I really don't want to talk about either one of them ever again, and Dewey has no idea that Silas is my father. I promised Willow I would never let him know that."

"I won't mention them again Sady, and never to Dewey. I do have to tell you that I have to get back to Baltimore within the next couple of days. I don't want to, but I have to."

Sady lays her head on Alec's chest. "Alec, I'm goin' to miss you. Why can't you stay a little longer?"

Alec put his hand under Sady's chin and lifted her head up. "Sady, I have some things to straighten out at home and in the precinct. I have some cases that are open and need to be closed. I'm also going to look into Willow's deed so that when that Council meets next month Willow will be able to prove the land is legally hers and they can't take it away. There is probably nothing we can do about her house being broken into. We have no proof or witnesses that saw anybody break into her house. I am sure it is about the gold nuggets. I'm sure the Sheriff, Mr. Little and the Eastman Road Company have a deal going on after finding out those nuggets came from Willow's property."

"Alec, will you be comin' back?"

"You're darn right I am. I'll be here for that Council meeting. I wouldn't miss that for the world."

"Hold me Alec. I don't want you to go, but I know people are countin' on you at work."

Alec kissed Sady. "Sady, I love you. You just don't know how much. I will be back, I promise and we're going to have to talk about a few things."

"You just make sure you come back Alec. I just don't want this night to end. I never thought I could have these feelins' for another man. But I do have them and I feel guilty because they are feelins' greater than the ones I had for Jack. You're a different man than Jack was. He was a good, decent husband and father, but he just never made me feel the way you do. What's wrong with me?"

"Nothing is wrong with you. Jack and I are just two different men. I have those same feelings about you. I thought I loved Julia, but the love I have for you surpasses every definition of love that I have ever known. Let's just sit here Sady and hold each other."

Before long, a little glimmer light from downstairs woke Willow up. She went downstairs to turn the lights out and noticed Sady and Alec both asleep in each other's arms. She got the afghan behind the couch and covered them up. She thought the world of Alec and knew that this was what Sady needed in her life at this time – a man who truly loved her. She turned the lights out and went back to bed.

The next morning Alec and Sady woke up in each other's arms. They were both surprised that they fell asleep that way. Willow was already in the kitchen getting breakfast ready. She brought them both in a cup of coffee.

"Here ya' go sleepy heads. Nice cup of strong coffee to wake you two butterfly's up."

Sady was a little embarrassed. "Willow, we didn't know we fell asleep ..."

"Now Sady, I'm the one who covered you two up. There ain't no explanation needed. Just drink your coffee. Right Alec?"

"You're right Willow. I'm not saying a word."

The next two days went by too fast. Alec went over Willow's deed but needed a lot more specific information about the rights in the deed. He knew he could find out a lot more in Baltimore searching through the court records as far as Indian territorial claims went. His law books were back in his apartment anyway. He had one more question for Sady that was on his mind since she was arrested in Baltimore when he questioned her. It was about her husband and son's mysterious accident.

"Sady, I hate to bring up a memory that I know hurts you to talk about, but didn't you tell me at one time that it was Sheriff Hardin that took almost an hour to get to the accident scene the night your husband and son died?"

"Yeah, it was Sheriff Hardin. He said somebody called about a truck bein' stolen and he had to investigate."

"Did you believe him?"

"Hell, no! I don't know where he was. I vaguely remember him sayin' somethin' about a vehicle that got stolen. Two people died that night and he used the excuse for not showin' up that he had to report a stolen vehicle. I couldn't believe it. I figured he was out with a woman and used that as an excuse. I was too upset to even think about anything. I felt like I lost my mind. I couldn't think. I didn't want to talk to anybody, I couldn't sleep. Alec I never want to go through anything like that again.

"Sady, I can't imagine what you went through. I'm so sorry. Did he investigate the accident at all?"

"He said it was probably an out of state driver goin' through and we'll never know who it was."

"That was his answer? You should have gone over his head Sady."

"You don't understand Alec. Havin' an accident here is different than havin' an accident in Baltimore, when it involves the law. There's no head to go over if you want to stay here and live your life. I was worried sick and so concerned over Eddie that I didn't care about the law. He almost died. If Mr. Tibbits wouldn't have come along when he did, Eddie would have died. Mr. Tibbits did find a funny lookin' piece of metal at the accident. I showed it to the Sheriff, but he said it could belong to several cars, because there were several accidents in that same spot."

"Do you still have it Sady?"

"Of course I do Alec, I'll go get it."

Sady came back from her bedroom with the object that Mr. Tibbits found at the scene of the accident and gave it to Alec.

"This is a hood ornament Sady. It goes on the front of a hood. It's a Ram. This is usually on a Dodge pick-up. Didn't you say Eddie said it looked like a truck was following them?"

"He sure did."

"Well, what did Sheriff Hardin say about that?"

"Nothin', nothin' at all. He didn't want to hear anything. He just acted like he wasn't interested. I didn't know what else I could do. I was worried about Eddie. I was so afraid I was goin' to lose him, Alec."

"Can I take this hood attachment back to Baltimore with me?"

"Sure, it's not doin' me any good. Maybe you can have some luck with it."

That night Alec packed his suitcase and went to bed early. Everybody went to bed early so that they could all get up to see Alec off the next day.

The next morning came too quickly. It was a sad day. Alec didn't want to leave and Sady didn't want him to leave.

"Now Dewey, you take care of Sady, Grace and Willow."

"Oh, I surely will Mr. Alec. While you're in Baltimore, will you get me some information about becomin' a policeman or a detective?"

"I sure will Dewey. Maybe you can go downtown to Boone one day to the courthouse and see if they have anything there about becoming a deputy here."

"I never thought about that Mr. Alec. I'll do that as soon as I can."

"But don't forget Dewey, you have to stay in school and get good grades. Promise?"

"Yes sir, I promise!"

Alec went over to Willow and hugged her. "Now you be good Willow and stay out of trouble."

"Now Alec, you know I'll stay out of trouble, at least until you come back."

They both laughed.

"Grace, you be good for Grandma, ok?"

"Ok, I be a good girl."

Alec gave Sady a kiss. "Don't you worry Sady, I'll be back here before you know it and hopefully with good news."

Sady said, "we will be waitin' Alec, we will be waitin'. You take care and keep in touch with a phone call once in a while."

"Sady, you're going to get sick from hearing from me so much."

"Never, Alec, never."

Alec got in his car and drove off.

Mary Wagner

Sady said, "Willow, do you think he's comin' back?"

"What's the matter with you girl? The man is in love with you. Get your head out of the mole hill it's in. You know he loves you. Start acceptin' that. A woman like you should always have a man by her side that loves her the way he does. You know he's a comin' back. Now let's get inside, it's cold out here. No more talk like that anymore."

Sady just smiled and said, "yes ma'am, I should know better than to argue with you."

"How about we go back in the house and get us another cup of coffee, Sady. I sure could use one. Might warm these old bones up some seein' how it's gonna' be another cold day."

chapter 35

THE MONTH OF January was going by pretty quickly. Alec had been gone almost a month. He did call as often as he could, but Sady still worried that he would run into some pretty girl in Baltimore and forget all about her. She just couldn't wrap her mind around the fact that someone like Alec actually could love her. She was so in love with him, she didn't want to be hurt again. The sudden death of Jack and Donny was just too much to bear.

The Council meeting dealing with Willow's property being condemned by the town of Harmony was postponed until the second week in February. As a matter of fact the meeting was to be held on Valentine's Day, February 14th.

There was an odd call from Alec asking Sady questions about a young girl that may have been a friend of Becky's. Her name was Emma Caldwell. Alec read the old newspaper archives from Harmony for the week of Jack and Donny's death to see if anything suspicious happened around the same time. He came across an article about Emma Caldwell's disappearance within a day of the fatal accident. He told Sady he would tell her more when he came to Harmony for the hearing about Willow.

Two more weeks had passed and it was February 13th. There was no Alec to be found.

Willow could tell Sady was quite nervous and tried to calm her down when it really should have been the other way around.

"Sady, what's wrong with you? You pace back and forth like a caged bobcat."

"Where is he Willow? The hearin' is tomorrow. I can't talk to those Council people, I don't know what to say. He promised he would be here."

Mary Wagner

"And he will be here Sady. What's wrong with you? Alec is a man of his word. You need to have a little more trust in him Sady. If he said he was comin', he'll be a comin'."

Just then there was a knock on the door. Dewey ran to open the door.

Dewey shouted, "he's here, he's here everybody!"

Sady and Willow ran into the front room. It was Alec. Sady couldn't help herself. She just ran over and hugged him. "I've been so worried Alec. Come on in and get warmed up. I'll get you some hot coffee."

"Sady, did you lose confidence in me? Sounds like you did. I had a lot of cases to tie up before I could leave and believe it or not, the biggest one was a case from here."

"I never for a moment thought that you wouldn't come back Alec." Sady looked at Willow. Willow just shook her head and laughed.

Willow said, "what case are you talkin' about Alec?"

"That missing girl, Emma Caldwell. Were she and Becky friends, Dewey?"

Dewey said, "not really Mr. Alec. They were kind of friends. Emma was about three years older than Becky. I think they talked to each on the bus when they went to school, but that was about it. From what I heard, Emma's daddy was a big drinker like Pa was and he wasn't very nice to her either. It was hard for me to believe that because when I saw him at church he always looked like a real gentleman. He was always dressed in the best suits. You see, he owned Caldwell Textiles in Boone. His family had lots of money, but after Emma ran away from home, he sold his company and him and his wife moved to Burlington, North Carolina. His wife took Emma's runnin' away real bad and lost her mind. She died about a year ago."

"Thanks for the quick rundown about the Caldwell family Dewey. There were a few things there I didn't know about."

Sady said, "what is all this interest in Emma about? Does it have anything to do with Willow's property or her hearin' tomorrow?"

"No Sady. It has a lot to do with your husband and Donny's accident. I did a little research, while I was away. I looked into old archives of newspapers from your area the night of the accident. There was a short account of Jack and Donny's accident. I then brought up the next

192

day, the 21st of November and it seems a girl named Emma Caldwell went missing from Harmony. She supposedly ran away. I'll explain after Willow's hearing. I have to check out a few things first. I'm going to need some detective help Dewey. Think you can help me out a little?"

"Help you out? Are you kiddin' me? Mr. Alec just let me know when or what it is you want me to do and I'll be there!"

"I'm glad I can depend on you Dewey."

Sady said, "you know, Alec, you sure are a mysterious creature at times."

"Sady, that's my job. A little mystery goes a long way to solving a crime."

"Dewey, you mind takin' Alec's suitcase upstairs? After you come down, we'll eat some supper."

"Yes ma'am I will, I'll be right back."

Alec gave Sady another hug. "I missed you so much. I love you so much Sady."

"Alec, I really don't think I can stand to be apart again. I'm gonna' go back to Baltimore with you, that is, if you want me to."

"That's something else we have to talk about Sady. Right now I have to go over my brief that I wrote for the hearing tomorrow. That's my main concern now. I don't want anybody to take Willow's property from her. I have to win, I just have to. I can't let her down."

"Alec, Willow thinks the world of you. Even if things don't turn out the way you want them to, she has a permanent home here with me. Let's go eat some supper, you can go to bed early and be ready for those people on the Council tomorrow morning."

"You're right Sady. All I can do is give it my best shot. Let's eat, I'm starving."

chapter 36

THE SUN CAME up bright and early the next day. Sady and Willow fixed a big breakfast consisting of bacon, eggs, biscuits and hominy with grits. Everybody piled into Alec's car and headed into the small courthouse in Harmony to confront the Town Council.

Willow looked at Wolfe from the car window and said, "don't you worry none Wolfe, Alec ain't gonna' let us lose our home. You be a good boy 'till I get back."

All twelve Council members were present and, of course, Sheriff Guy Hardin was there with bells on ready to pounce on Willow's property. To Alec's surprise, every seat in the galley was taken. People were standing in the aisles. Most people in town were nosy and it wasn't too often they got to meet a real detective who is also a qualified real lawyer from Baltimore. Yes, this was to be an event for the townspeople of Harmony to watch.

The President of the Council was a woman, Mrs. Pansy Willard. She led the Council and the people that were present in the Lord's Prayer and the Pledge of Allegiance to the United States Flag.

Mrs. Willard introduced the case and introduced Alec to everyone and told him to make his case.

"My name is Alec Karastaupolis and I am defending Miss Willow Moone who lays claim to fifty acres, more or less on top of Blackheart Mountain."

"None of you have the right to condemn Miss Moone's land and make her move. The only body that can do that is the United States Government. I quote "Condemnation is the formal act of exercising eminent domain to transfer property from its private owner to the government." Your little Town Council here doesn't have the right to condemn Miss Moone's property for your own personal use. You have no right to make a contract with the Eastman Road Company for Miss Moone's property. As a matter of fact, Miss Moone can turn around and sue the town of Harmony for the emotional distress and worry you have put her through. That is exactly what I may advise Miss Moone to do as her lawyer."

The Sheriff got up and shouted, "show the Council her deed. She is an Injun, and no Injun around here owns any land or should own any white man's land."

Council Woman, Pansy Williard asked for Sheriff Hardin to sit down and shut up.

Alec turned to face Sheriff Hardin. "Sheriff, I think you have got your information backwards. The Indians were here way before your great-great-great Grandfather settled in these mountains. The white man took the land from the Indians, not the other way around. You're infringing on Indian property. It was President Andrew Jackson who initiated the Indian Removal Act of 1838-39. The Indians were forcibly removed from their land – I'll say it again, THEIR land and sent out west. The Indians were marched like cattle for six months. Many died of diseases, hunger, violence from the frontiersman, floods, and the harsh winter that they weren't prepared for. Over 4,000 Indians died on that march. Read about it when you get a chance. As a matter of fact, I challenge every one of you on the Council to read about the "Trail of Tears". Maybe it will bring a tear to your eye, that is if you or anybody on the Council has a heart."

Council representative Charles Little said in an unconcerned voice as to what the Indians went through years ago, "Mr. Karastaupolis, we do want to see Miss Moone's deed."

"As a matter of fact, I made a copy for every one of you sitting behind that table. Before I hand it out, does anyone in the room have any idea who broke into Miss Moone's home and vandalized it? There is a small reward if anybody knows anything about that."

Mr. Little glanced towards the back of the room at Sheriff Hardin. The Sheriff just gave him a hard look and a little twist of the head in the no position. Mr. Little put his eyes down and did not glance anywhere else in the room.

Sady looked at Willow and Willow looked back with a slight smirk on her face. The reward was a surprise for both of them.

Alec handed a copy of the deed to the Council members.

Alec went on to address the Council. "Many of the Cherokees remained behind and hid in the mountains during this horrendous Indian Removal Act that President Jackson initiated. They didn't want to give up the land that their forefathers left them. There was a white man named William Holland Thomas, who was recognized by the Cherokee Indians as their Chief. He fought for the Cherokees for them to be able to keep their land. He bought 50,000 acres of mountainous land and offered it to the remaining Indians. Even though they felt the land was their land, he gave them a chance to buy the acreage they wanted at a very cheap price and it would become their land when they paid him in full, and they would get a signed deed. Well, Chief Wohali Moone, Miss Moone's Grandfather, worked and paid Mr. Thomas in full. He was the only blacksmith in town and was able to save enough money to pay for his fifty acres. This is the original deed signed by William Holland Thomas. The deed also states that the land would automatically go to all descendants after Chief Wohali Moone. When he died the land went to William Thomas Moone, Willow's father. Chief Wohali Moone thought so highly of Mr. Thomas that he named his son after him. Willow's father was declared and granted citizenship by the North Carolina General Assembly in 1855 which also makes Willow a citizen of this great country of the United States of America. Willow was an only child. The land rightfully belongs to her.

Councilman Little said, "are you finished Mr. Karastaupolis?

"No, sir I'm not finished. If I have to, I will get in touch with the Senator of this great state and let him know that the town of Harmony, the Town Council, illegally attempted to declare Willow Moone's property condemned, not by the Government, but by a select few in order to take her land from her for personal gain. And I will tell you from many cases that I have tried in the past, Government agents will be in this town arresting anyone involved in this incident before supper time tonight." Are there any questions?"

The Council was stunned. They didn't have a leg to stand on. Some members still had their mouths open in disbelief. They didn't expect the eloquent speech and defense that Alec presented.

Council Woman, Mrs. Pansy Williard said, "from what I have heard from Miss Moone's Legal Counsel, this inquisition into the condemnation of Willow Moone's property is over. She is the rightful owner of fifty acres of property on Blackheart Mountain along with her home. Thank you Mr. Karastaupolis, your client Miss Willow Moone, and members of the town of Harmony for being here this morning. You all witnessed our Democracy in action today. The meeting is over. All persons involved in this hearing are dismissed. Please enjoy the rest of the day."

There was loud clapping from the audience that stunned Willow. They were clapping for her. She hugged Alec along with Sady. People came up to Alec and congratulated him and Willow. They were amazed at how intelligent Alec was and how great of a defense he had for Willow.

There was a commotion at the entrance to the courtroom. The Sheriff's wife was pushing Ira Hardin, the Sheriff's father, into the courtroom in his wheel chair. Ira had not been seen for years. The only time he could be seen was when he would push his curtain aside to peek out the window at people walking down the street. The Sheriff was startled but more mad at his wife Eliza.

The Sheriff shouted at his wife, "are you crazy? Why did you bring him in here?"

"Guy, don't be mad. He begged me to bring him here today. I don't know why."

Ira looked up at the Sheriff and said in a voice that was almost inaudible to understand, "shut up son. Leave me be. I ain't crazy like you make me out to be, I'm just a crippled, broken man."

Ira looked around the room. His eyes locked onto a person he hadn't seen for years, the person he was looking for – Willow. Ira called out to Willow. "Willow, Willow, please come here!"

Willow hesitated. She looked at this man, who as a young boy, no older than Dewey, watched as Silas Prestel beat her father then hung him. Silas made Ira help carry Willow's father to the tree. Even though he took no part in the beating or the hanging of her father, Willow knew he was there. He came with Silas and left with him. She hated him almost as much as she hated Silas. She remembered the last time she saw Ira when he had his accident. She always wondered why she saved him, and asked herself many times why she didn't leave him lay in the creek to drown. Why? That was a question she pondered every day of her life but couldn't answer. Was it because Willow had a heart and conscience and was no murderer? Willow's Indian parents and Sady's parents who later raised Willow were peaceful people, good Christian people, who taught Willow right from wrong. What little she knew of Ira was that he got beat every day of his life, thrown out of his home and went to live with Silas. Yes, she knew how lucky she was to have been surrounded by people who loved her.

Willow looked down at this brow-beaten old man and said, "just what do you want Ira?"

Tears fell from Ira's eyes. He put his hand up and held Willow's hand.

Sheriff Hardin, Ira's son, ran over and said, "old man, are you crazy? What are you doin'?"

Ira ignored his son. He looked up at Willow with tears streaming from is eyes and said, "please forgive me Willow, please."

The Sheriff said, "forgive you for what? For lettin' a Injun live in Harmony? I always thought it weren't no accident you had. I know this old lady pushed you off that mountain!"

Ira looked at his son. "No, no, she saved me. I saw Silas Prestel murder her daddy years ago. I did nothin' to help him. I was too terrified to do anything. Please forgive me Willow, please before I die."

Willow said, "Ira, I saw the fear in your eyes when Silas hung my daddy. I know you saw me with Mama hidin' amongst the laurel bushes. You looked right into my eyes, but you didn't tell Silas we were there. If you would have told him, I wouldn't be here today. And if you would've told him not to do what he did that day, he would have hung you right beside my daddy. Silas was worse than any wild animal up on Blackheart Mountain. I thought I hated you all these years, but I really didn't or I would have let you drown in the creek years later when you fell off the mountain. I forgive you Ira."

Ira cried like a baby. "Thank you Willow, thank you."

The Sheriff backed up, looked at his wife, and then put his head down. He never knew what Silas did to Willow's father, nobody knew but Willow and Ira. For the first time Sheriff Hardin felt ashamed of the way he treated Willow all these years, but he still was too proud to say he was sorry.

Sheriff Hardin turned his father's wheel chair around and started out the door with him. He turned around and said to Willow, "I'll try my best to find out who tore your house up Willow. If it's ok with you, I'm sendin' some men from the community up to your place to fix what got destroyed."

Willow said, "It's ok with me Sheriff. Thank you." Willow knew the Sheriff had something to do with her home being vandalized, but she also knew it took a lot for him to turn around and say what he did to her. She thought to herself, "forgiveness really does lift your spirits and give you a peacefulness that just can't be explained."

All Willow knew was that the burden of hate was lifted from her shoulders. It felt good to forgive Ira and to know that his last days on earth would be free of the terrible guilt he must have carried around all these years. What a waste of precious life to carry in your mind and heart what Ira carried all these years. What a waste.

Alec had one more difficult matter to take care of – what really happened the night Sady's husband and son were killed.

chapter 37

AFTER EVERYONE GOT back to Sady's house and ate lunch, Alec asked Sady if she would go out to the barn with him because he wanted to talk in private.

"Alec it's kind of cold out here. I want to tell you though how proud I was of you today. I don't think the town of Harmony ever met a really one-hundred percent smart lawyer like you. Now what is so important that we had to come out to the barn to talk?"

"Sady, I had my "sources" run down every car dealer in every county in North Carolina to find out which car dealers sold a 1939 Dodge truck and who it was sold to. That hood ornament you gave me belonged to a 1939 Dodge truck. That was the year Dodge changed over to the Ram as a hood ornament."

"Alec, you did dig deep. What did you find out?"

"Two trucks were sold from a dealer in Winston Salem and one truck was sold from a dealer in Hickory."

"So what does that prove?"

"Sady I found out that the person who bought the truck from the dealer in Hickory was Mr. Rufus Caldwell, Emma's father. She's the girl I told you that ran away from home the next day." Maybe it means nothing at all, but I've got to look into this a little deeper."

"Alec, are you sayin' that Mr. Caldwell ran into Jack that night?"

"Sady, I really don't want to jump to any conclusions yet. What I really need to do is find out just where that truck is right now. There may be a few clues in it even after all these years. I hate to do it, but I really need to talk to Sheriff Hardin. I'll get Dewey and we'll go over there around four or five o'clock."

Four o'clock came and Alec and Dewey drove into Harmony to see Sheriff Hardin.

Alec and Dewey walked through the doorway and there sat Sheriff Hardin. He looked up and said, "did you come here to rub it in my face some more Alec?"

"I came here to ask you a few questions about the night Sady's husband and boy were killed. Sorry that you took what happened today at the hearing to heart, but I was helping Willow keep her home and property and would do it all over again if I had to. Now I'm here on business and I need a few answers."

"Ok, how can I help you?"

"Do you have any idea what happened to Mr. Rufus Caldwell's 1939 Dodge pick-up truck? Being a small town, I thought maybe you could tell me who he sold it to."

Sheriff Hardin said, "he never sold it. The night Jack and Donny died, I got a call from Mr. Caldwell tellin' me somebody stole his truck. That's why I got to Jack's accident scene so late. I was over at the Caldwells' takin' down all the information. But you can't tell Sady that; she'll tell you I was up to no good. I can't talk to her about that night whatsoever. Anyway, the next day is when Mr. Caldwell called to tell me his daughter Emma was missin'. Sady blamed me because I got to the accident scene a little late and they both died. From what I saw of the bodies, they looked like they died instantly. But I can't change what Sady feels in her heart. I told her where I was, but she didn't believe me anyway. Did I answer your question?"

"Sheriff didn't all that seem odd to you, the accident, the truck and Emma both wound up missing? Sady said she also showed you a hood ornament that Mr. Tibbits found. It was a Ram. It went to a Dodge pick-up truck just like Mr. Caldwell's truck."

"I had a lot goin' on that night. I was goin' in two directions with no help. My main concern that night, even though Sady wouldn't believe me, was gettin' Eddie to the hospital so we wouldn't lose him too. What's your point Alec?"

"Sady is not going to rest and have peace of mind until she finds out just who was involved in that hit and run. I'm sure if it were one of your loved ones you would want to know."

"You're right, I would want to know and every day I would probably be out there lookin' for any kind of clue I could to find the person or persons who caused the accident. I'll ask around about the truck and see if anybody here knows anything about it."

"I appreciate it Sheriff. If I find out anything, I'll get back to you."

They both awkwardly shook hands. Alec and Dewey got back in Alec's car and drove away from the Sheriff's office.

"Dewey, something is just really wrong about that night."

"What do you mean Mr. Alec?"

"Well, the truck missing that night and Emma missing the next day, it just doesn't add up. Can you remember what was going on in Harmony on the night Jack and Donny were killed?"

"There's not much that goes on in Harmony. But I do remember that was a Wednesday night. The only thing around these parts most folks do on Wednesday nights is go to Bible study."

Alec said, "we better head on back to Sady's. It's getting dark anyway. Tomorrow is another day. We'll come up with a plan tomorrow Dewey."

"Mr. Alec, why can't you just call Mr. Caldwell and ask him if anybody ever found his truck. If he moved right after Emma and the truck got missin', and if the truck got found, he probably didn't see any reason to let the Sheriff know anything."

"That's the detective work I'm talking about Dewey! I just know some day in the future you're going to make a fine detective."

Dewey's buttons almost popped off his shirt with pride. Finally there was a man in his life that gave him confidence, guidance, a moral compass, and most of all a belief in himself that he wasn't that stupid, no-account gimp that his pa called him day in and day out. He didn't deserve the vile words from his father's mouth and the horrible beatings his father gave him almost daily. No, Alec brought hope and kindness to a young boy who gave up any desire or dream of being recognized as an intelligent, useful citizen in the town of Harmony.

"Thank you, Mr. Alec."

"Thank me for what Dewey?"

"For showin' me that there are good men like you in this world. In my world, I only knew men like my pa. I want to be like you Mr. Alec when I get older. I want to be just like you."

Alec had to turn his head to keep Dewey from seeing him get all teary-eyed. He blocked out a lot of feelings after he was hurt in the

Battle of Sicily and lied to by his ex-wife. He turned a lot of his feelings off. Sady ignited a fire in him that he couldn't put out. Dewey just opened his heart up a little more – the part of his heart he kept closed because he couldn't stand to be hurt anymore.

With his voice quivering somewhat, Alec said, "yeah, tomorrow we'll pick up where we left off."

Sady was glad to see both of them come home and had a nice meal waiting for them.

"Alec, a man called today from the Veteran's Hospital in Johnson City, Tennessee. What is that all about? Is it about Eddie or Thomas?"

"Hold on, hold on. I thought about what would be better – when Eddie and Thomas are shipped from the hospital in France, would it be better to be at the Fort Howard Veteran's Hospital in Baltimore or the Veteran's Hospital closer to you, about sixty miles to be exact, in Johnson City? The hospital in Johnson City is just as equipped to care of them as the hospital at Fort Howard."

"Oh, Alec that's just wonderful. This way I can visit Eddie and the Tibbits can visit Thomas. We can ride together. Thank you, thank you."

"I'll call him back. He probably wants to let me know what kind of rehabilitation they will be getting and an idea of when they are coming home."

Sady was so excited waiting for Alec to call the man back that she couldn't eat supper.

Alec made the phone call and let her know what the Director had to say. "Sady, he wanted to know if you and I would like to visit the hospital and actually see where Eddie and Thomas will be staying and go over the schedule of their routines and the rehabilitation they will be receiving."

"Yeah, of course. Should we call the Tibbits too? Willow would you mind watchin' Grace when I go?"

"Of course not. I'm a fixture here now, at least until I get my house fixed back up. Me and Wolfe love playin' with Grace."

Alec said, "the Director can't see us until late next week. So you can ask the Tibbits if they would like to go with us. I know Dewey would like to go too."

"Oh, I know Dewey will be excited when I tell him. The Tibbits don't have a phone Alec, so I'll drive over tomorrow and ask them.

Are you sure it's ok with your boss in Baltimore that you stay another week? I don't want to see you get fired."

"Sady, that's my worry. Dewey, you ready to hit the sack, we got a lot to do tomorrow."

"I sure am Mr. Alec. Now you get me up when you get up. Good night everybody."

Sady said, "good night Dewey." Sady then turned to Alec and said, "I see such a change in Dewey since you came back Alec. He was so withdrawn before, now he's eager to get on with his life and most importantly he seems so happy."

"Sady, that boy had a rough life with Roby. He has opened up a part of me that I kept closed for so long. Let's just say him and I are good for each other. I'm going to bed a little early tonight too. See you in the morning." Alec kissed Sady then went upstairs to bed.

Willow walked over and sat down beside Sady. "Sady, don't let him get away. That's a good man. He sure has changed everybody in this house for the better. He is a keeper isn't he Wolfe?"

Sady hugged Willow. "I know he's a keeper Willow, I know that."

chapter 38

THE NEXT MORNING Alec asked Sady if she minded if he made a long distance call to Burlington, North Carolina, but first he would have to get a phone number for Rufus Caldwell.

Sady got on the phone with Leanne, the operator. "Leanne, this is Sady. I'm doin' fine, how are you?....Good, glad your Mama is feelin' better. Is it possible to get a long distance number for Mr. Rufus Caldwell? It's kind of police business and should be kept to ourselves, if you know what I mean. I knew you would ... of course, I'll hold."

Sady put her hand over the phone so Leanne couldn't hear her. "Alec, she thinks she has a number for Mr. Caldwell."

"That's great Sady. Just say it and I'll write it down. No, wait. Ask her to put you through, and then give me the phone."

"Ok Alec. Repeat that again Leanne, Bu-555-25. Thanks. Oh, Leanne, how about dialin' it for me so the detective here can talk to him. Remember, hush, hush. Thanks. Alec, it's ringin'. Here."

"Hello, Mr. Caldwell. My name is Alec Karastaupolis. I'm a detective investigating an old cold case for a friend here in Harmony. I know you remember an accident that happened around five years ago when a man and his son were killed. Yes, that's right, Jack and Donny Milsap, good you do remember. I believe that was the same night your truck got stolen and I believe your daughter ran away the next day. Am I correct? The two incidents may be related, I'm not sure. The accident happened between 8:30 or 9:30 at night on Wednesday, November 20th, one week and a day before Thanksgiving. Can you tell me where your daughter was around that time and when did you notice your truck was missing? .. ok ...ok ... I see, well thank you for your input Mr. Caldwell. Bye."

"Sady anxiously asked Alec, "what did he say Alec?""

"He said that his daughter was home before 8:30 p.m. and the truck was sitting out in his driveway. He said she went to Bible study that night at the Harmony Creek First Baptist Church. She came home and went to her bedroom. He said about a half hour later he noticed his truck was missing. He went upstairs to see if Emma was in her bedroom. He saw her in bed sleeping and didn't think it was necessary to wake her up. He called the Sheriff and reported the incident. He never did see her come down the steps. But he did finally admit he had quite a bit to drink and may have dozed off. He didn't notice until the next morning that his daughter was gone. When he went over to Emma's bed, he noticed she had piled a bunch of pillows in a row and threw a blanket over them. He said if I find Emma, tell her she's to blame for her mother's death and he never wants to see her again."

"That's so sad for him to feel that way Alec. Do you think she was involved in the accident?"

"Sady, I don't know. Right now I feel that Mr. Caldwell's truck was involved in that hit and run, but determining who was driving is the hard part. For all I know, Mr. Caldwell may have been driving the truck. He did admit he was drinking too much. Dewey, let's you and I go to Reverend Marshal's house and ask him if he remembers Emma being in Bible study that night."

"I'm ready, Mr. Alec whenever you are. You're gonna' have to take Miss Sady's truck, 'cause I don't think your car will make it up that mountain."

Alec asked, "ok to take your truck, Sady?"

"Alec, you know you don't have to ask me."

"Let's go then Dewey."

Dewey knew exactly where the Reverend lived. His home was pretty far from town, secluded on top of about thirty acres of dense woods on old Buzzard Mountain.

Alec said, "Dewey, why in the world would he live so far from town and on this jungle of a mountain. At least Blackheart Mountain is close to Harmony."

"He's been here for years. I heard he got it pretty cheap."

"Cheap, cheap. I'd live in Willow's house, on Blackheart, any day of the year compared to this. Finally, here we are. I hope he's home."

Reverend Marshal came out to greet them. "You should have told me you were comin'. I know this isn't the easiest place to get to, but it's so peaceful up here and the air is so fresh and pure. I feel surrounded by nature and the hand of God. I write my best lectures for church sittin' right over there on that rock – that is when it's not covered with snow. Come in, come in, it's too cold to stand out here."

Alec and Dewey went into the living room to talk to Reverend Marshal.

"What brings you out here Dewey, and I know you must be detective Alec Karastaupolis. The whole town is talkin' about what you did for Willow. I commend you for that."

Alec shook hands with Reverend Marshal. "Thank you Reverend. I'm really here to try and jog your memory about the accident that killed Jack and Donny Milsap about five years ago."

"Oh my, that was a sad time indeed. Poor Sady just lost it. She was in deep depression and full of sadness for so long. How can I help?"

"Do you happen to remember that night if a girl named Emma Caldwell was in your Bible study? I know it was a long time ago, but when something horrific happens in someone's life, they tend to remember every detail of that day. Her dad said she went to Bible study that night and came home around 8:30. Can you remember anything?"

"First of all what does Emma have to do with anything. She was such a sweet, sweet, girl and her father was nothin' but an alcoholic with a lot of money and a big company. He treated Emma and her mother terribly."

Just then Reverend Marshal's little poodle came running out with a ball in her mouth. She wanted Dewey to play with her.

"Bebe, these nice men don't want to play with you."

Dewey said, "that's ok, I can throw her the ball while you talk to Mr. Alec."

Alec continued his conversation with Reverend Marshal. "Do you remember if Emma was in Bible study at the church that night?"

"I pride myself on my memory Alec. Yes she was in Bible study that night. I remember that night like it was yesterday. That night stood out in my mind for so long. I actually had a few nightmares. I would never say anything to Sady, but her boy, Donny, was so cut up it was hard to tell who he was. Yeah it was bad. Why, do you think it was the Caldwell truck that caused the accident?"

"A Ram ornament that goes on the hood of the truck was found at the scene of the accident. It matches the same year as Mr. Caldwell's truck. That was the first year Dodge used that Ram as a hood ornament. You don't have any idea what happened to the truck, do you?"

"All I heard about it was that it was stolen. Sorry Alec. Wish I could be of more help."

As Alec and Reverend Marshal continued talking about the night of the accident, Dewey played with Reverend Marshal's poodle, Bebe. Dewey loved all animals; but he cared more for dogs as a pet. He was never allowed to have a dog. His pa saw no use for them. As a matter of fact, Roby killed many dogs or cats that belonged to the neighbors.

Dewey threw the ball to Bebe and the ball went into a closet in the kitchen that had a sheet for a door. "Go get it Bebe. Go on get the ball. Ok lazy, I'll go get it." When Dewey opened the sheet to get the ball out of the closet, his eyes were fixed on something he recognized from years back. He thought, "it can't be, no, it can't be." Right in front of his eyes was a pair of black and white snakeskin boots. One of the snakeheads was missing on one of the boots. These were the same boots that he recognized on the feet of the unknown man that would stand there and watch his pa do the dirty things he did to Becky. He knew they had to be the same boots that he would look at while hiding under his bed.

Dewey got the ball, threw it to Bebe and ran out the door and threw up. Alec and Reverend Marshal heard the door open and walked to the back door to see what the commotion was about.

Alec could tell there was something wrong with Dewey. "What's wrong Dewey? Your face is whiter than that sheet over there."

"Sorry, Mr. Alec. I guess it's 'cause I didn't eat this morning. I just got sick. Do you mind if I wait in the truck?"

"I'm finished here anyway Dewey. Thank you Reverend Marshal for your time."

"Any more questions just come on back or see me after church. Hope you feel better Dewey."

Dewey didn't answer him and Alec knew that wasn't like Dewey to ignore anyone or have bad manners.

Alec got in the car and started driving. Dewey didn't talk. "You can tell me the truth now. You ate breakfast. What's going on Dewey?"

"Mr. Alec, when I was a little boy, I slept in the same room with my sister, Becky. Pa would come in most nights and do terrible, dirty things to her. I always hid under the bed until he was finished. Sometimes there was another man that Pa would bring into our bedroom. He didn't do nothin'; he would just watch and make all these awful sounds. All I could see was his boots. His boots were black and white snakeskin boots with a snakehead missin' on one of them."

Dewey put his hand in his pocket and pulled out a snakehead. "I found this snakehead on the floor of our bedroom beside Becky's bed years ago. I've carried it around with me for years hopin' to find these boots so that I could find the man and kill him. Tonight when I threw the ball to Bebe, it went into a closet in the kitchen where the white sheet was hangin'. Those same boots were in there Mr. Alec. It was him. It was Reverend Marshal that was watchin' Pa do all that dirty stuff to Becky and makin' those noises. I should have brought my gun with me tonight. I want to kill him. He's no better than Pa was."

Dewey just cried uncontrollably. The tears just flowed. He stopped after a while and apologized to Alec. "I'm sorry Mr. Alec. I guess you think I'm actin' like a baby, but when I saw those boots, I thought about what Becky went through almost every night. It was so sick."

"Dewey, never say you're sorry because you have feelings and sometimes those feelings come out in the form of tears. That just means you have a heart. If you only knew how many times I lay in a foxhole in Italy and hid my face because I didn't want the other guys to see me cry. I was scared. I didn't know if I was going to die that night or the next morning. And you know the irony of it all; I wasn't the only one with a few tears coming down my face. At night I could hear other sniffles and they weren't mine, and they weren't sniffles from a cold. Never be ashamed to cry and let it out."

Dewey said, "but I always said if I ever knew who that other man was, I would kill him. What did I do? I threw up."

"Dewey, if it means anything to you, I didn't believe a word he said. The one thing you don't want to do is take the law into your own hands. You'll wind up in jail for the rest of your life if they don't give you the electric chair first. I've seen electrocutions boy, and you don't want to go that way. Do you know of anybody else that we can talk to that would remember if Emma was at Bible study that night?"

"Old Mrs. Hamby used to take attendance. If you never missed Bible study for so many Wednesdays, she would give you a little prize. She lives down the road from Miss Sady. She might not remember too much though, she's probably close to a hundred."

"Let's go, it won't hurt to try."

Mrs. Hamby lived with her daughter who took care of her. Alec asked to talk to Mrs. Hamby. Her daughter went in and helped her to the kitchen table. Alec introduced himself, but she remembered Dewey right from the start. Alec was surprised at how good her mind still was. "How can I help you Mr. Alec?"

Alec asked Mrs. Hamby, "Dewey said you used to keep attendance records of those people who came on Wednesday nights to Bible study. I'm interested in one particular night, November 20th, 1939. It was the night Sady Milsap lost her husband and son in that terrible accident. Do you remember if Emma Caldwell was at Bible study that night?"

"I don't believe she was Mr. Alec. Dewey, would you get that big old book over there on the shelf? Thank you."

Alec couldn't believe she still kept her attendance book after all those years. Mrs. Hamby gave the book to Alec and told him just to go through it until he found November 20th, 1939. He found it and went down the list. There was no signature for Emma Caldwell.

"Mrs. Hamby, does this absolutely mean that Emma was not at Bible study that night?"

"Yes, Mr. Alec. Everyone signed in when they came in. Nobody wanted to be left out of the attendance contest."

"I may need this book later. Do you mind if I come back to get it? And please, Mrs. Hamby, don't let anyone else know about this book or let it out of your sight."

"I surely won't. Now you come back Mr. Alec and bring Dewey with you."

"I intend to Mrs. Hamby. Thank you again. Let's go Dewey."

Mrs. Hamby called to Alec as he started walking out the door. "Mr. Alec, Mr. Alec, I need to tell you somethin'."

Alec leaned down while Mrs. Hamby whispered very quietly in his ear. "I never did care too much for Reverend Marshal. He liked all the young girls and he lies. Please you and Dewey be careful."

Alec wasn't exactly shocked at what Mrs. Hamby told him, especially after what Dewey told him. He knew he couldn't tell Dewey because that would fuel the fire and the hatred he had for Reverend Marshal. No, he knew he had to listen to all the facts before he made a judgment.

After supper that night and after Dewey went upstairs to listen to his favorite radio programs, Alec told Sady and Willow what Dewey said about the man with the snakeskin boots. He told them that Dewey found the boots, without one of the snakeheads, in Reverend Marshal's kitchen closet. He told them that Reverend Marshal lied about Emma being in Bible study that night, and what Mrs. Hamby said about that night and what she whispered in his ear.

Sady said, "Alec, I've known Mrs. Hamby for years. She is tellin' the truth. She is as straight as an arrow. If Emma didn't sign that book, then she wasn't there that night. What does Reverend Marshal have to gain from lyin'? Maybe he wants you to think that when she left Bible study, she may have caused the wreck. He must have forgotten that Mrs. Hamby kept good records. Apparently, Mr. Caldwell admitted he was drinkin' and probably didn't notice the damage to the truck that night. As far as Dewey noticin' those boots, Reverend Marshal was probably there when Roby was doin' those horrible things to Becky, but what can you do after all these years?"

Willow gave her opinion of what should be done. "What can ya' do? He ain't no man of the cloth. He should be put in the middle of town and stoned! If he was doin' that peekin' to Becky, there are probably a lot of other young girls in that church that he done worse to and they are too scared to say anything. He was probably doin' somethin' to that Emma."

Alec said, "now Willow, we don't know that for sure. You can't jump to conclusions until you have all the facts. And we have very little facts as of today."

Willow got a little loud. "Very little facts. The man's a got part of Satan in him just like Roby. That one fact of him watchin' Roby doin' all that dirty stuff to Becky is all I need. Why if that was my little girl, I'd cut off his ..."

Sady said, "Willow, now we know what you would do, but let's prove one thing at a time. Anyway, Grace is over there playin' and I really don't need for her to hear that kind of talk."

"I'm sorry Sady, but if he did that to Grace, you can't tell me you wouldn't go after him with the biggest butcher knife you could find."

"You're right Willow. I remember I threatened Roby a time or two when he mentioned he wanted to hold Grace. I already knew what he did to Becky. Thanks for remindin' me. I'm the one should be apologizn' to you."

"You two ladies are too much. I hope I never do anything to offend either one of you ladies. I'm tired and I'm going to bed. See you all in the morning."

That night Alec just couldn't sleep. Everything ran through his mind. He thought, "Sady had a point. Why did the Reverend lie and say Emma was in Bible study? Sady's right. He wanted to plant the idea in my mind that Emma probably hit Jack's truck on the way home from Bible study. What kind of man, religious or not, would stand and watch a grown man, a father, have sex with his daughter while he had sex with himself? What kind of pervert was he? How could he preach the word of the Lord every Sunday knowing what he was doing? Was he seeing Emma as a girlfriend? Mrs. Hamby said he liked young girls. Did he know about the accident that night? Things just don't add up. Willow hit it on the nose. If he was in some uncivilized country, the Reverend and Roby would have been castrated."

Alec almost fell asleep when something just hit him. He noticed part of a roof of an old barn about 200 yards from the Reverend's house when he was there earlier. He sleepily said to himself, "that's a tomorrow job."

The full moon and light from the glistening snow shone right through the bedroom window. Something didn't look right in Dewey's bed. Alec turned the light on. Dewey was not in his bed and his rifle was gone. Alec immediately got dressed and pounded on Sady's door. "Sady, Sady, wake up."

"Alec, what's wrong?"

"Dewey's not in his bed, and I think I know where he went. Call Sheriff Hardin and have him meet me at Reverend Marshal's place as soon as he can."

214

"Alec, I'm goin' with you. What if your car can't make it to the top?"

"Then that will leave both of us stranded and in danger. No Sady. It might be too dangerous for you. You finally got Grace back and she needs you. Everything is going to be fine. Don't worry and don't open the door to anyone. Understand? Maybe now is the time I need a little prayer. Just say a prayer for me."

"Yes Alec I will, but please be careful."

All the way up the old dirt road to Buzzard Mountain, Alec kept thinking, "I actually asked for a prayer for help. Father Joe would be proud of me. I'll have to let him know this old boy asked for a prayer to be said for him. Yeah, this would be a proud day for Father Joe."

chapter 39

DEWEY PUSHED SADY'S old truck out of the driveway earlier that night so no one would hear him start it up. He did this right before they all came upstairs to go to bed. He knew Alec wouldn't turn the light on because he wouldn't want to wake him up. He had a good half hour start on Alec.

He thought if he could get the boots and take them to the Sheriff, that he might believe him. Why would he lie about the boots belonging to the man who would come into Becky's room, since he had the other snakehead that matched the other boot that he carried around for years? But maybe the Sheriff just wouldn't believe him. He had to take that chance.

Dewey finally made it up Buzzard Mountain. He parked Sady's truck about a half mile from the Reverend's house and quietly climbed to the top and entered through a side window in the kitchen that, to his surprise, was open. He thought, "thank God, all I have to do is get in that closet and get the boots and get out of here."

Just then the lights came on. Bebe ran over and licked Dewey. Dewey looked up and there stood Reverend Marshal with a sawed-off shotgun pointed at him. "What are you lookin' for boy?"

"I dropped my knife earlier when I was playin' with Bebe."

"Get up boy, you're lyin". I hate a liar and so does God."

Dewey said, "yeah, do you know what God hates more than a liar? He hates a grown man that does dirty things to little girls like you and my father did to Becky."

"No boy, you got that all wrong. God wants men like me, men of the cloth, to train these little girls on how to please their husbands when they marry off. He brings them to me through prayer. They even thank me for showin' them the true way. Your sister wasn't nothin' but practice for me. She wasn't nothin' but a whore when she got older."

"You're sick. You're the reason my sister is dead. You and my Pa killed her mind years before she ran away."

"Had a lot of fun doin' it too boy!"

Dewey, madder than he had ever been in his life started to charge at him.

"Go ahead boy, I got the gun. Try it one more time and you know what I'm goin' to do. I'm goin' to shoot Bebe first!"

"No, no, don't shoot Bebe. I won't do it anymore. Just let me go. I won't tell anybody anything."

"You really think I believe that boy? Get that lantern over there. I'm takin' you where nobody is ever goin' to find you."

"What about Miss Sady's truck. When they see it, they'll know I was here. They'll come lookin' for me in the mornin'."

"Mornin', you won't be here come mornin'. You must think I'm stupid boy. That truck's never goin' to be seen again after tonight. Now get gone out the door, I'll tell you when to stop."

Reverend Marshal took Dewey to the old barn that Alec had remembered. It must have been years since anybody went that way. The overgrowth of briars and trees hid the barn pretty good. The only thing that stuck up somewhat was part of the roof. The Reverend made Dewey clear a way in the snow and tear some of the briars down to get into the barn while he had his rifle on him. Reverend Marshal opened the doors and removed a tarp that was over a very large object. Dewey couldn't believe what he saw. It was the Caldwell's truck with front end damage to the left side and the hood ornament was missing.

"It was you who hit Mr. Jack and Donny. You killed them."

"Not really Dewey. You see me and Emma were real close. You know what I mean. Soon as Bible study let out she picked me up. We were comin' up here, but we didn't make it. I drove the truck that night. We were on that mountain road right behind Jack Milsap. She started foolin' with me; you know what I mean son. I know you do. Anyway, she excited me so much, I ran into the back of their truck and it went down the mountainside. You see, she caused the accident, it was her fault."

"Why didn't you stop and see if they were ok?"

"Now what would that look like if I was caught with Emma in her daddy's truck?"

"You're not human. People stop for dogs, or animals crossin' the highway. You're a sick man. You belong in jail."

"You know boy, you got a mouth on you I don't like."

"What did you do with Emma?"

"Oh, that's a funny story. I drove the truck back to her daddy's place and laid low in the front while she went in just so her daddy would think she was home. Her daddy was always drunk anyway. About ten minutes later she snuck out; we got in the truck and come up here. Her daddy never knew she left. He thought she was up in bed sleepin'."

"So where's Emma?"

"You ask too many questions boy for somebody that ain't got long to live."

"Open up that door and get inside that truck."

Dewey opened the door and let out a yell. "Who is this? Whose bones are these?"

"You been askin' me about Emma. After I put a hole in your head like I did her, you two can keep each other company. Now get in."

Dewey pushed the truck door into the Reverend knocking him down and started to run. The Reverend got up and started shooting every way he could hoping he would hit Dewey.

In the meantime, Alec walked up the mountain about fifty feet to get to Reverend Marshal's house. He didn't want to alert the Reverend that he was close by letting him hear the motor running in the car. He remembered where the old barn was and headed for it. He heard the gunshots, and he ran faster toward the barn and ran inside with his gun cocked. One of the bullets from the Reverend's gun hit Alec in the upper chest. Dewey saw him fall and came running over toward him trying to help Alec up. Dewey heard the rifle cock behind him. He knew it was the Reverend. He couldn't reach Alec's gun; the Reverend was right there. He laid Alec back down.

"What you goin' to do now you smart mouth gimp. Ain't that what your Pa always called you - gimp. Now I got to get rid of two more bodies."

Dewey still had his back toward the Reverend. He cautiously got up and slowly turned around. He carefully grabbed the Bowie knife Willow gave him for Christmas from the knife case under his jacket. This was his only chance. He knew he could shoot better than he could throw a knife. He was no Willow, but he was going to fight for his life and Alec's life. He pulled the knife out and threw it at Reverend Marshal. The Reverend's gun misfired as the knife pierced his heart. He had no idea Dewey had that Bowie knife on him.

Dewey went up to the Reverend while he was dying, pulled the knife out, and said, "when you see my pa and grandpa in Hell tonight you tell them the gimp's mama raised a good boy with a good heart and a good soul, and I hope that fire that's burnin' them for eternity reminds them of all the horrible things they did to the people here while they were alive."

Alec watched everything while lying on the ground bleeding. "Dewey, you're going to be the man that other men want to be. Thank you for saving my life."

While Dewey was putting pressure on Alec's wound he said, "Mr. Alec, I'm sorry I snuck out of the house. I just wanted to get those boots. The Reverend told me he caused Mr. Milsap and Donny's accident, and he murdered Emma. But you know Mr. Alec, killin' him didn't make me feel any better. I knew it was either us or him. I didn't have a choice, but it just didn't make me feel any happier like I thought it would. I guess I'm a little mixed up. I'm kind of glad I feel this way. It means I have feelins' and a conscious and I'm nothin' like my pa."

"Dewey, you hit that one on the nose. You know good from evil. Your pa didn't. Evil was in your pa's heart from the time he could walk. It was instilled in him by your grandpa. You're a kind person like your mother. That's not a trait you're born with, that's a trait you learn by watching someone, your mother, be kind to others. Dewey, you're going to be a fine man one day that a lot of people will respect. Well what do you know, here comes the Sheriff."

"You ok Alec? Got here as soon as fast as I could. Looks like your bleedin' pretty bad. I'll take you and Dewey to the hospital in Boone.

I'll have my deputies drive your vehicles home so Sady can know what happened. I see you found the Caldwell truck."

"No, Dewey found it. He saved my life."

Dewey said, "Sheriff, Emma's body is in that truck. Reverend Marshal shot her years ago and left her in the truck. He was goin' to kill me and Mr. Alec. I threw this knife and killed him first. Am I goin' to jail?"

Alec spoke up. "You - go to jail! I'll see to it just about everybody in this town goes to jail with you." You're a hero boy and don't forget it."

The Sheriff said, "no Dewey, you're not goin' to jail. I'll get your statement at the hospital."

Alec said, "Sheriff, you'll have to call Rufus Caldwell in Burlington. He told me that if I saw Emma to tell her never to come home. Let him know she died the day she went missing and she won't be coming home to bother him."

The Sheriff looked inside the truck at Emma's bones. "What a sad end to a young life. That Reverend really played this town like a banjo. I'll have this truck and Emma removed from this barn tomorrow. If Mr. Caldwell doesn't want Emma's remains, we'll have a service for her here and bury her in the church cemetery. We'll have a new Reverend from Boone come in and conduct our services until we get a permanent Reverend. Let's get out of here. This place creeps me out."

Alec had to stay in the hospital overnight. Sady drove to Boone and stayed with him all night. A nice hospital chair was brought in for her and she slept there throughout the night.

The next morning Alec was feeling a lot better and was told he would be discharged that morning. He told Sady about her husband's and son's accident and how and it happened and who was driving the truck that knocked Jack's truck off the mountain.

Alec said, "your prayer must have worked Sady, because my car never stopped on that dirt road going up to the mountain for a second. Father Joe would be proud that I even asked for a prayer."

"Alec, I even had Willow sayin' prayers for you. It is really hard for me to accept who the person was that was responsible for Jack and Donny's death. The night of the accident and all the next week,

Reverend Marshall did nothin' but console me. He even cried with me. And all the time, he knew he caused the accident and murdered Emma. How could he emotionally put on that act? That is really a sick person. I don't know how he could have even faced me. But it's over. I know now what happened and I can live with this. I feel like a weight has been lifted from my shoulders. If it wasn't for your persistence in findin' out who the hit and run driver was and what happened that night, the misery of never knowin' what happened would be playin' in my mind over and over until the day I die."

Alec said, "I'm glad you got to find out the truth about that night, but it's sad that Emma had to lose her life the way she did. And I think it's going to take Dewey a good while to get over killing another human being, even though I don't consider Reverend Marshal a human being. I know it took me a long time after I shot a bank robber who was holding a bank teller as a shield when I first joined the force. It never leaves you. I guess this war changed me a whole lot. After a while you get used to the killing because it's either kill or be killed by the enemy. The funny thing is I knew the enemy felt the same way."

Sady said, "Dewey is still a teenager Alec, but he's a strong-willed boy who has been through so much in his short life. I think he'll be able to sort this thing out. He thinks the world of you, and I'm sure if he has anything that is botherin' him, he'll talk to you about it."

"I hope so. Sady, I forgot to tell you. I got a phone call yesterday from the Veteran's Hospital in Johnson City. Tomorrow is the only day that the Director can give us a tour and show us how the rehabilitation process will work for Eddie and Thomas. Do you still want to go?"

"Of course I do. But what about you? Do you think you will be able to make the trip?"

"I wouldn't miss it for the world. We'll take Dewey and Grace with us. Dewey can drive my car, that is, if he wants to. I know he doesn't have his license, but if we get stopped, I'll just say it is important police business. Do you think Willow would want to come?"

"Alec, I know she would. On our way home from the hospital, let's stop by and ask the Tibbits if they want to follow us tomorrow mornin'."

"Finally, here comes my wheel chair. They won't let you walk out of this place. I want to thank you Sady for staying by my side and being here for me."

"Don't you ever thank me Alec. It's an honor to be able to know a man like you."

"That's enough of that kind of talk Sady. My shoulder is already swelled; don't need my head to match it. Let's go."

chapter 40

THE NEXT DAY everyone got up extra early and ate a big breakfast. Willow and Sady packed a big lunch for the ride to Johnson City. The Tibbits pulled up, excited of course, and waited for everyone to get into Alec's car.

It took about two hours to get to the hospital. The Tibbits parked alongside of Alec's car in the parking lot. Mr. Tibbits got Dewey aside and told him that he had heard what happened and how proud he was of him.

Dewey said, "thank you, Mr. Tibbits, but how can I be proud because I killed a man, a man of the cloth?"

"A man of the cloth? He wasn't a man of the cloth. Dewey he killed three innocent people who never done a darn thing to him and had nerve to preach the Gospel every Sunday knowin' what he did. As far as I'm concerned he was Satan dressed in a Reverend's clothin'. No, you get that out of your head. If you didn't do what you did that night, Mr. Alec and you wouldn't be here today. We'd be goin' to two funerals instead of comin' here."

"Mr. Tibbits, I know you're right. Mr. Alec is right. I just got to get right. Might take me sometime but I'll get there."

"That's what I want to hear son. You got a lot of good people on your side. When you need one of us to talk to, just say the word."

"Thank you Mr. Tibbits."

The Director of the hospital met everyone in the lobby and started showing them around. They got to see the gym where the boys would be doing all different types of exercises and the equipment that would be able to help them regain their upper and lower body strength again. The Director let them know that it would be a long recovery for Thomas who had lost a leg.

Sady couldn't take her eyes off of the soldiers who were in rehabilitation. So many soldiers were without arms or legs. She felt so blessed that Eddie didn't lose a limb; then she felt so guilty because Henry and Lena's Thomas lost a leg. She did notice the soldiers who had been there for a while had a wooden prosthesis for a leg. They were learning to walk again. She felt Thomas had a chance after seeing those boys.

The Director took them up to the second floor to look at the rooms their boys would be staying in once they got back to the States. Lena and Sady noticed how clean they were. Most of the rooms had wide windows that allowed the sun to shine in. Sady thought the rooms would be drab, dirty and depressing. Everything she thought was the opposite. She was quite content and accepting that Eddie would be here for at least a month.

Alec suggested that they go down to the sunroom where most of the boys would go either before lunch or in the early afternoon to relax.

They all sat down, looking out the window when one of the soldiers, on crutches, came up from behind Sady, tapped her on the back, and said, "Miss, this is where I usually sit every day."

Sady was embarrassed to even look up and said, "I'm so sorry, I'll move . . . oh, my God, Eddie, Eddie. It's you." Sady hugged and hugged Eddie so hard that Alec had to pull her away a little.

"Alec, you knew this. You knew this the whole time. When did you get here Eddie?"

"I got here about a week ago. I wanted to be able to use these crutches before I got to see you. I left France over a month ago and was sent to Fort Howard Hospital in Baltimore. That's where I first met Alec. He organized everything from leavin' France to being brought to the states so that I could be closer to you Ma."

"Alec, that's why you stayed a little longer in Baltimore. I don't know what to say, but thank you. Seems like lately I'm always thankin' you for somethin'."

"Sady, he's here now. I don't need any thanks. Just enjoy the peace in knowing your son is home."

Eddie sat down and stared at Grace. Tears rolling down his face, he grabbed her and hugged her saying, "my baby, my baby." Grace was startled. She was upset a little because she really didn't get a chance to know Eddie before he left. She was just a baby.

Sady said, "give her time Eddie, it won't take long."

"I know Mama, I know. It's just I can't believe I'm here and finally lookin' at my baby."

Eddie looked at Dewey. "This fella' here has got to be Dewey. You got so tall. I heard a lot about you Dewey. I'm sorry about your ma and Becky. But I want to thank you for bein' there for my mother. You're my little brother Dewey. Hope I can be your big brother."

"I always wanted a big brother, Eddie."

Henry and Lena hugged and shook Eddie's hand. "We're so glad you're home Eddie. So glad."

Alec noticed the look on the Tibbits' face. They were happy for Sady but he could tell inside they were sad that Thomas wasn't there.

"Henry and Lena, I want you to go to Room 234, there's a young man in there that has been waiting to see you both for a long time."

Lena said, "Mr. Alec, you don't mean Thomas is here too, do you?"

"Now, you're just going to have to go see for yourself. I can't do everything for you!"

Eddie said, "Mr. and Mrs. Tibbits, do you have any idea how hard it has been for me to say **"I"** all the time instead of **"we"**. You know I never would have left France without Thomas."

Henry said, "thank you Mr. Alec, bless you Mr. Alec." They both ran to Room 234, and yes, Thomas was there.

Willow got up and went over and hugged Eddie. Eddie was so glad to see her. She was such a big part of his life growing up. "It's so good to see you Willow. I know about the property thing and so much more. Alec has been keepin' me informed. I'm so glad you got to keep your land."

"That land thing ain't worth nothin' compared to seein' you here today. I would've traded all my land for this day. If you don't mind, I'm gonna' be your grandma from here on out. You need a grandma."

Willow really was Eddie's grandmother. Would he ever find out? Maybe someday a little birdie might tell him.

Alec said, "Eddie, I need to ask you a question."

"Of course, Alec, what is it?"

Alec looked at Sady. "Would you be ok with me marrying your mother?"

Eddie had a big smile on his face. "I would be honored if you would marry my mother."

Sady was just shocked. Alec actually got on his knee, pulled a beautiful ring out of his pocket and said, "Sady, will you marry me?"

"Of course I'll marry you Alec, but what about your job in Baltimore?"

"Sady, I quit my job right before I came back here. There was no way I was going to be away from you. I have a new family now and this is where I belong."

Sady said, "but Alec, you loved your job so much. You loved your work and helpin' other people."

"Sady, why can't I help other people right here in Harmony and in Boone?"

Sady said, "but how Alec?"

"After Willow's hearing, I was offered a job by the Town Council to be a prosecutor for the town of Harmony. I turned them down after what they were going to do to Willow. I found this little vacant office in Boone, right by the courthouse. I thought I'd put up a sign and anybody in Harmony or Boone who needs a lawyer, an honest lawyer, can knock on my door at any time. I figured being in a larger town, I would get more clients. And, Dewey, after you finish high school, we're going to work on getting you a job in the Sheriff's office in Boone as a deputy. How's that sound? And you're part of this family now Dewey, just like me. Oh, one more thing Dewey. There's a little dog at the dog pound in Boone whose name is Beebe. She's yours if you want her."

Dewey said, "I don't know what to say Mr. Alec. I want to thank all of you for lettin' me be part of your lives. I'm gonna' try to make all of you proud of me. And yeah, if you don't mind Miss Sady, I would like to have Beebe. I'll take care of her myself."

Sady said, "we're already proud of you Dewey and yes Beebe can be part of our family too. Now Alec, we got a lot of plannin' to do for this here weddin'."

"No, we don't Sady."

"What are you talkin' about Alec? You just can't have a weddin' just by clickin' your fingers."

"You're not getting away that easy Sady. I've got the license; all you have to do is sign it. There is a Chaplin and a chapel on the main floor and a magistrate in the office beside the chapel to approve our marriage license. It's 12 o'clock now. Everything has been set for 2 o'clock. We can eat our lunch that you and Willow packed then go see the magistrate. We've got everyone here, friends and family that we love. There are no excuses. So what do you say?"

"I say, I'm hungry, let's eat lunch, then take care of business afterwards."

Willow said, "that's my girl Sady. Don't you let this handsome man get away from you, or I'll marry him today if you don't. Right Alec?"

"You're right Willow. Instead of Sady and I watching that beautiful Carolina blue sky, it will be the two of us sitting on your porch looking up and admiring it."

"After you put it that way Willow, we better hurry this lunch up, because I ain't lettin' this man get away. No sir, I have a chance for love again. I have my family and my friends here with me. Before I met you Alec, I was feelin' like an old tree that had seen its last years and was ready to be chopped down for firewood. That old tree must have dropped a seedlin', and that seedlin' grew a new tree, with new branches that sprouted new leaves and a new life, my new life."

Made in the USA
Middletown, DE
20 February 2023

24621756R00130